DARLING DISCOVERED:

A TRUE STORY OF SUBMISSION

BY MRS. DARLING

Contents

To every person who has ever had to fight (*society, family, a partner, your own self*) to live your most authentic life.

Also to those who are still afraid to do so. I assure you, it is *so* worth it.

Author's Note

This is a work of creative non-fiction inspired by real life events, based on a husband and wife fighting daily to be their truest selves. The story is to be prefaced by saying that while the people are real, many events are real, and the evolution of the dynamic and self-discovery is very real, the time line has been adjusted to make for improved readability.

Also, in order to maintain anonymity in some instances the locales and identifying characteristics, and details such as physical features, occupations, and specific events have been changed. The characters names are entirely fictitious and any resemblance to actual persons, living or dead, is purely coincidental. Every effort has been made to recall memories of the happenings as they unfolded to make this memoir as accurate a depiction as possible.

Please, readers, remember to take ample time getting to know your partner before engaging in BDSM. Risk-Aware Consensual Kink (RACK). Learn it; live it.

One of the kindest things you could ever do for the Mister and his darling wife is to keep our secret sealed safe upon your lips. Now that you will know our tale, you never know when you will brush up against us in the grocery store, at yoga class. If you feel like you recognize us, please, dear reader, keep mum.

Discretion is key. Anonymity a must.

Much love from our home to yours.

Kind Regards,

Mrs. Darling

DARLING DISCOVERED:

A TRUE STORY OF SUBMISSION

Prologue

The clock strikes midnight in the home painted the color of seagulls. As the chimes begin to quiet, another noise fills the air around me, setting a chill down my spine. I move quickly to the front, flipping on the light and throwing open the door.

I see a man who was once somehow familiar but now is more of an enigma. The sight of him standing at the steps of the house this late quickens my pulse, with his dark hair wild and light eyes staring with intensity. Without the pretense of formalities he speaks words that make my heart leap in my throat:

"Darlin, I am about to do everything I can to destroy you. Tomorrow I want you walking in pain. I would suggest you fight with everything you have. Make no mistake, if I capture you, I will hurt you. You have a ten second lead. Go."

Wait. What?

Where can I run?

What does he want?

I'm in my nightgown!

What if he catches me?

All of these thoughts sprint through my brain in that single second until I hear him speak again.

"One."

Shit. Go.

I turn around and slam the front door in his face, locking it tight and sprinting towards the French doors that will lead out to the back side of the sleeping house. I kick off my loose slippers and the cold, wet grass hits my feet.

Run.

I hear him. Bursting out from around the side of the house and almost immediately closing the gap (thanks to his heavy black leather biker boots to my bare feet) my eyes begin to tear up. I have no idea what he will do if he catches me so I do my best to avoid it.

I am pretty successful despite his advantages. I know this yard surrounded by eight foot wooden privacy fence on all sides like the back of my hand. When I moved in recently I began planting flower and vegetable gardens and have spent countless hours in the early morning sun investigating every last inch of the new yard.

Being chased across the immense lawn, hiding behind trees and trying to sneak away, doing my best to reach the tool shed and hide, my whole body heats up, immune now to the cool and crisp air this Florida fall night has brought.

My blood is pumping. My heart is racing. The exercise in the middle of the night underneath the starlit sky feels exhilarating.

I can get away- is what I am thinking when the svelte man grabs the back of my nightgown in his fist and sends me crashing to the ground.

My ego is more bruised than my tailbone and now this has become a much harder challenge.

I will not let him take me. So we wrestle.

I do my very best to slip away, using my slick and now dirty silk nightie to try and maneuver across the ground. I use the force of my legs and try to push him off. He grabs my ankles and uses one hand to pin them both down and the other to grab my wrists. Twigs are scratching my flushed, tingling skin and I realize I am losing.

Out of animalistic fight or flight instinct I bring my mouth towards his muscular arms I manage to bite his right forearm. Hard. I may have even broken skin but right now all that concerns me is getting away. It catches him off guard.

The indignation on his face is obvious: nostrils flaring, mouth open in shock from my daring move. He moves on his knees to once again grab me and it's more callous this time. Painful. Just as he had assured. He shoves me back to the ground, with more force than before, and I hit the back of my head on the cold sod. He takes both hands and all of his weight and unceremoniously flips me over, shoving my mouth and face into the dirt.

I'm shocked and jumping out of my skin from the turmoil of emotions. The earth smells alive somehow, rich and murky and waiting to devour me too. He puts the entirety of his body down the length of mine pinning me.

I have the word I can say to stop this engraved on my lips but I don't want to speak it aloud. Not yet. Not now. This is what my day has been waiting for. This is what my *life* has been waiting for.

"Stop, please no please!" I beg, sounding muffled from the grass beneath me.

Immediately I am prompted to "Shut up. You know begging is pointless. If you want to stop, you know how."

Time stands still for a moment. Only our heaving chests move.

I realize that he'd never allow the neighbors to hear so I inhale deeply and start to scream. I barely get a peep out before a large hand clamps over my mouth, shutting out the noise, and he pinches my nose shut with his thumb and finger. I am, literally, breathless.

He whispers hot in my ear without offering me the grace of air in my lungs, "Do I need my knife out, darling?"

It stops all fight in me better than if he had doused me in ice water. The dominant man puts his knee in my back and reaches down with the other, throwing the bottom of my nightie up.

He just rips, just tears off my underwear, lifting the bottom half of me up from the sheer force.

The man lets go of my mouth and I gulp in the night air. He allows me the gift of three full breaths before he uses a hand to pull open my jaw and shove my torn panties into my gaping mouth.

"Better than the knife, right?" my captor asks, still pinning my body down tight, making me sink into the filth even further. I start to wonder if there are bugs on me and it sends me over the edge. This is where he has brought me to face my personal fears. Tempt my limits. Dare me to live just outside of the comfort zone.

The tears finally begin to spill over and I hear from behind me, "I asked you a question."

I do my very best to nod my head in agreement and hear him laugh a sadistic laugh. Keeping a knee in my back he pulls his leather belt out of the loops and both roughly and expertly wraps up my wrists, freeing himself in the process to proceed in successfully completing his mission.

I want him inside me so bad I can taste it as much as I can taste the faintest hint of laundry detergent from the destroyed panties in my mouth.

I am simply an animal caught in a trap. Any other thoughts are admonished. I am his meat, his reward, and I am about to be swallowed whole. Breathing through my nostrils only, my cries from the spanking of his bare hand across my chilled skin are muffled.

Hard as a rock with the excitement of capturing his prey he penetrates each of my holes with no regard for me. He succeeds as master of the chase.

Under the shining light of the late night stars, glowing bright but offering no assistance, I am entirely devoured by my husband.

Chapter One

The End of the Beginning

2 Years Earlier

234...235...236...

5,491...5,492...5,493...

9,138...9,139...9,140.

Nine thousand one hundred and forty.

I am staring at a twenty page packet that arrived via old-fashioned postman. I requested the report from my cellular provider on a whim (bullshit, Chloe, it was out of the inability to shake a feeling deep inside yourself) detailing my husband's phone records in four columned front and back pages laden in tiny black telephone numbers.

9,140. The number of text messages going both ways, sent and received over the past three months, between my seemingly so perfect Mr. Leo Donnovan's phone number and a strange one I don't recognize.

The shaking begins in my hands first, feeling like ice, turning the crumpling pages into a crude version of the paper fans I made by the dozens growing up in sunny South Florida. The shake spreads throughout my body and I set the pages onto the floral duvet covering the bed that I am sitting on in our master bedroom.

Ohmygodweretheyhere? Races through my brain faster than I can stop it from coming and I rise off the bed as quickly as my aching body can take me. I look at the bed like it is an accomplice in this tale of terror and walk the few steps through our Atlanta suburb Tudor home to the closest bathroom, where I promptly throw up my late afternoon snack.

I wash up in the sink and regretfully see myself in the mirror. A pale, average looking woman, face and body more plump than ever, feeling frailer than ever, hair shorter than ever, cut in a shoulder length dirty blonde bob with seven months of darker root growth. Not a stitch of makeup is on my blemished face. My ocean blue eyes even look like a duller version of what they were on my wedding day just a few months ago.

Newlywed (nearly dead?) and now this. Now with "9,140" burned into my vision.

I don't even recognize myself. Who am I? Who have I become? And importantly, maybe even mostly, who am I going to become in the next week or two?

I splash cold water on my face and brush my teeth and head back out moderately refreshed.

I grab the phone records and walk disjointedly downstairs, clutching the handrail in a death grip for support (emotional or physical, I am not quite certain) to get my smart phone that is charging on the kitchen counter.

Looking out the window over the sink I see spring just beginning to blossom. Green is just peeking through the brown, looking new and fresh, ready to give birth to a new year. Ironic. Here I am, perched on the edge of something new as well but I don't want this new. I feel hopelessly desperate to turn back time and bury my head in the sand.

I use my thumb to slide the phone awake and check what I have missed. Nothing. No missed calls. No missed text messages.

With a tremble that is almost painful I look at the pages and punch in the phone number my husband has corresponded with over three thousand times a month. Mental math gets me to an average of a hundred times a day.

One hundred messages a day for three months straight. I feel vomit rise up in my throat again.

Ring. Ri-

Voice mail.

Her voice gives no name but she sounds smooth and sultry, nothing like my voice that is always a little louder and harsher than most women in any given room.

I hang up. What message am I supposed to leave? "Hi, I think you are having an affair with my husband, can you please call me back to confirm?" The tears begin and go from zero to sixty instantly.

I am sobbing, hitching in my breath, doing everything I can in my power to tell myself that I can't get this upset right now, that it is dangerous. As the sun is sinking down in the kitchen window, neighbors entirely oblivious to my world falling apart just yards away, the loud pipes of Leo Donnovan's motorcycle are sounding louder with each teardrop that falls.

What do I say? What will he say?

Silence rings out around me as I do my best to calm myself, practicing my new breathing techniques, pulling deep in through the nose and slowly releasing out through the mouth. Repeat.

Mr. Leo T. Donnovan ("Leo" not short for anything fancy, just Leo. Just my Leo. The Mr. to my Mrs.) steps through the door looking like a picture torn from a business magazine: breathtakingly handsome in a trim suit, the tie undone at the end of the work day. Dark, neat goatee that is starting to show glimpses of silver makes him look more stately than old, and his tall, lean build matches his sharp facial features. Though I can't see them right now, his cool and piercing hazel eyes distinguish him from the typical "suits."

Of course I don't see those eyes.

His eyes are plastered towards the phone in his right hand, not looking up to see me standing in his peripheral vision just 3 feet away, waiting silently at the sink in the kitchen where I learned his favorite Mexican recipes.

I sniffle (accidentally? On purpose? Somehow both?) and he whips his head towards me. I watch his face transform from surprise to guilt to concern in the space of a single heartbeat.

"Chloe, what's wrong? Is everything ok?" he asks with concern.

With the unassuming hand of a professional magician he shuts down the smart phone and slides it into his dress slacks. *Now you see it, now you don't*, I think, and it makes me laugh out loud. I don't recognize the flat sound. It's as foreign to me as my mirrored image was upstairs.

Leo is looking at me with complete bafflement now.

"Chloe?"

I can't speak even though now is when I am supposed to be doing so. Since I don't know what to say I simply hand Leo the sheets I brought with me spelling out almost ten thousand accusations of deceit.

He takes them. And a look of absolute horror crosses over his face.

When his eyes meet mine we both see the truth reflected back.

It is in this exact moment I feel liquid running down my thighs. It isn't a gush or a burst like I had imagined over the past nine months. Just a trickle of steady fluid and try as I might I couldn't stop it from coming.

My water just broke.

***

Pain. White hot searing pain is all I feel over the next seventy-two hours.

The pain of childbirth, gripping my midsection in the worst kind of hurt I can ever imagine physically.

Emotionally? Pain just as equal.

I am with a man in the labor and delivery room who is now a complete and utter stranger to me. I don't want him there but I still can't imagine doing this without him.

A child is being brought into this world and handed to parents who are broken. 'Cause there is no going back from this. Right? I can't imagine how. The day my perfect little girl is born is the day my marriage dies.

I close my eyes and recall my mirrored image and what a stranger I looked like to myself. The feeling intensifies at the hospital. I don't recognize myself as a woman or wife, I don't recognize my husband, I don't recognize our relationship. It is as if somebody flipped a switch and everything that was black is now white.

Leo and I don't speak about anything other than bringing our child into the world the entire time at the hospital, neither of us bringing up the giant cheating elephant in the room.

What good would it do in this moment?

I wonder, in between contractions, if the pain inside is intensified because of how entirely uncharacteristic this is of the man I call my husband. Whenever I heard stories of marriage problems like this I always listened to it with a haughty notion of, "I guess that's why I made so sure to find myself such a good man before getting married."

Leo was perfect. Well, of course not, nobody is perfect, but I thought that Leo was perfect for me.

Is the pain now so great because of how far he has actually fallen from grace?

The fallen Mister Donnovan. What a fucking shame.

***

"Why two dozen?" I ask to a younger version of the man now helping me to "push!"

It is five years prior and I am in an office working, not in a hospital in the worst pain of my life.

Leo Donnovan, the thirty-ish year old bachelor who I have recently begun spending time with replied with a voice that sends excited chills through me even when on the phone: "One dozen for you to take home, one for you to keep there at your desk. So I can always be around."

I lean back in my office chair and begin twirling the phone cord through my antsy fingers.

There are two dozen just-blooming orange roses the color of fire sitting on my desk, scenting the entire front office.

"Cool, cool, I can do that. Thank you." I respond with nonchalance that I am entirely faking.

"Cool, cool," Leo says teasing, completely aware of my effervescent attitude.

My business cards still introduce me as "Chloe Larchmont," my mother's maiden name and mine as well. I had no idea I was currently falling in love but in hindsight I was a fool to have not seen it. Most of what I felt was lust.

I pull my compact from my purse and touch up my face. I am a sleeker, hipper version of the woman who years later would be married with child. My face is thinner; my hair is just past my shoulders and styled professionally in a lovely straight honey blonde, low lights and highlights painstakingly applied every six weeks. I am smaller than I will probably ever be again, spending my mornings at the gym running before work, eating tiny salads in my tiny bachelorette pad for dinner.

I like what I see but even then the mirror reflects a young woman with a secret in those blue eyes, a desire that remains unspoken.

I snap my compact shut with finality, mentally ordering myself to forget about that nonsense.

It scares me to wonder if Leo would be able to tell. Leo who can read me already.

A new set of twenty-four roses arrives every Monday without exception.

The blooms ensure that every moment of the day I am reminded of him. Red roses in a deep crimson and roses the color of raspberries and a rust color I've never seen before. Pink ones that looked like strawberry milk I used to drink as a kid and the color of my highlighter at my desk. The yellows, the oranges, the purples. The single rich-colored ones, the mixed ones that look like they were painted with a delicate watercolor brush somewhere in nature.

My favorite becomes the white roses. So pure. So simple. So very me. Those arrive on the special occasions.

I've neither asked nor have been told how he arranges for these deliveries or how much they cost.

In a day and age when romance is all but a forgotten notion, I let the gesture be a constant reminder that what Leo and I have is special. Different. Both able to be counted on and whimsical at the same time.

Until.

***

My body and mind are completely wrecked but I am leaving the hospital instead of heading to it.

Three days of pain have passed and now are days of confusion. I am lost. So lost.

My new daughter is perfect but she is a stranger to me. I feel like I should be more connected to her somehow.

Emily Jane Donnovan. She cries constantly and I spend my time that first week wondering if she is crying more than most newborns. I look at her face and my heart shatters, thinking of the sadness I brought her into the world amongst.

Leo takes paternity leave upon the arrival of our first child (he was always so upstanding) and despite still not speaking directly of the affair I can tell he has put a stop to the communications with the other woman.

The new father spends the next few weeks constantly available to me, helping through this transitory period. He wakes in the middle of the night, fetching the wailing hungry newborn, mixing bottles and feeding her hungry belly. He spends his days doing the work I will typically do: the errands and cooking and cleaning, heating up frozen casseroles I made just for this purpose while still heavily pregnant.

His phone has gone silent. No bleeps of texts or waiting voice mails. I wonder several times if I picked up his phone I could see the goodbye message he must've sent to the woman or if he erased any history of their communications. I never check.

What do I do these first few weeks?

I cry. A lot. I am furious. A lot. I question every decision I have made over the past few years. I reminisce on the good times. I do my very best to bond with my child.

I consider the choice ahead of me. Should I stay or go?

Remain with a cheater, a man I barely recognize right now but loved (still love?) so deeply a month ago? Or opt for single motherhood?

How do I leave Leo when I have already left my job? I have no money that is my own. No family nearby to help with Emily. How would I even begin to do that?

Does Leo want me to leave? Does he want out? Did he want to be caught? At some point I will have to figure it out. Until then, I just continue to pull the comforter of the guest bed where I have been sleeping back over my head, weep, and relive the good times over and over.

It may be pulling me deeper into a sickening depression but I can't help but wish for the simpler times of years ago.

***

Smack dab in the beginning of the white hot passion of Leo Donnovan and Chloe Larchmont's romance, I move away from Phoenix and the mister himself.

It is for business reasons. The job I took on as a means of income after college I begin to excel at and enjoy. When the company asks me to go help open their new office in Atlanta, a city I have never visited much less even considered, I jump at the opportunity.

When I tell him about the move he is as supportive as expected. He treats me to celebratory drinks and offers to help me pack. A teensy part of me hoped for him to ask me to stay but that was never "us" in the beginning.

I move to Atlanta and try as we might to end things (I mean, what is the point of maintaining a physical relationship if you can't be present physically, right?) Leo and I keep in contact. We can't break each other's pull.

We began by sending sexy texts and unclothed pictures back and forth. The roses continued across the miles.

More than anything: we talk. Both on the phone and texting.

We learn about the other's childhood. Each other's schooling. Favorite foods. Greatest fears. Bucket lists.

I fall in love with Leo Donnovan, the complete man. The moment I realize that I am in love I blurt it out over the phone connecting us. It is the middle of the night after a long work day and despite being exhausted and the several hour time difference pushing me closer to dawn, neither of us seems to want to end the conversation.

"I think I love you, Leo." I say with a tone of shock because shock is what I am feeling.

After a long pause I hear back from him, "Thank you, Chloe."

Thank you? *Thank you?* My heart is stammering out into the blackness of the still strange bedroom in the Deep South.

How could I have been so foolish?

I breeze past his response and end the call, hiding behind a brave mask but ready to cry myself to sleep.

Three months go by as if nothing happened and I never say "I love you" again. Leo doesn't mention it either.

But he does move to Atlanta.

He applied for and was granted a transfer within his company without discussing it with me. When he tells me about the move, he cites his reasoning as, "I've never lived outside Phoenix and it's time for a change."

He asks me if I'd consider having a roommate.

I say yes.

We move in together the following month and the fire for each other is greater than even before.

Still, though, no "I love you."

A year goes by and we are living happily together. I love this man. He is the sexiest balance of bad boy and good guy I have ever encountered: his back covered in tattoos, riding a motorcycle fast through the skinny streets of downtown Atlanta, a man's man who can change your oil and properly "change your oil," but at the same time with Boy Scout morals, incredibly brave and thoughtful and helpful. Trustworthy.

I am confident that Leo is in love with me, too. The man simply won't say it.

My birthday comes along in the hot Southern summer and my (lover? Boyfriend? Roommate?) Leo reserves a log cabin in the foothills of the Blue Ridge Mountains for us to celebrate.

The weekend is magical. We spend most of our time having passionate sexual encounters everywhere. In the hot tub, the shower, the couches, bent over the island in the kitchen. In between the sex we talk and laugh, tease each other, muse over which local restaurant to try next, be the friends we have become.

I can feel it coming. He is going to tell me he loves me on my birthday.

The day comes along and I wait for it every moment. Leo gifts me a lovely ruby bracelet (my birthstone) and he places it on me with gentle care. Still. No "I love you."

I fall asleep that night facing away from him, my silent tears falling onto the pillowcase in the mountain cabin rental.

I will never forget waking up that next morning, the day after my birthday, to seeing Leo awake, propped up on his elbow, and staring at me.

He reaches over and moves my sleep-mussed hair out of my face, our eyes meeting.

He speaks quietly in the room filled up with birds chirping, picking each word with grave seriousness.

"Chloe." Silent thoughtfulness rings out.

"I know what you were expecting me to say yesterday. I'm sorry I disappointed you, darlin. It pained me to not say it then, to not say it a year ago when you told me first. But I wanted to say I love you when I meant it, when I could tell it to you honestly. So I know it hurt. But I hope it will mean something more this way, knowing that my word will always be truth to you, that I will always speak in honesty. So Chloe... I love you."

The tears well up in my eyes at the sound it makes coming from his throat. I say back what I mean the most in the moment:

"Thank you, Leo."

***

It takes me three weeks to climb out of the fog of depression. I climb out with a plan. I dunno if it's a good one but anything is better than living in this darkness. There are three weeks left until Leo should return to work and I am alone with Emily.

I want to spend that time in the sunshine, to let the salt air go to work healing me.

I want to go home.

I have no way of knowing that once I push away the guest bedding and rise up to search out my husband and make this demand things will never be the same for Chloe Donnovan again.

Chapter Two

A Handshake

"**M**ove me home Leo," I blurt out while I bounce the fussy newborn baby gently.

Leo is putting clean onesies and burp cloths away and I can tell as he looks in my red rimmed eyes that he thinks he has misunderstood my demand.

"We are home Chloe," Leo replies gently.

No, I'm not, I think sadly. I continue swaying the now wailing girl in my arms, trying to find that speed of "gentle" that apparently every mother alive has been gifted but me. Seriously. Our daughter never stops crying. Like mother, like daughter, I guess.

The first pangs of mommy guilt hurt. I can't help but feel like maybe our girl who was brought into the world on the worst day of my life is suffering by default because of my overwhelming grief. I try my best to not sob now along with my daughter in the nursery that Leo and I painted yellow together, reflecting on the day we painted.

Him pulling out that damn smart phone of his and texting, me ignoring his actions while dying inside to ask, "Who are you talking to constantly?"

But no. I wanted to be the cool wife. The one who didn't nag or yell. Besides, I trusted him. I trusted Leo with my whole heart. I was wrong. Sighing, I repeat my request.

"Take me home Leo. Please. I want to be with my family right now." By "family" I mean my mother and he knows that without my saying so.

My mother, Victoria Larchmont, is the only one of my kin left who is still on that beachy stretch of Gulf Coast I grew up on. Mom is an inspiration of a woman who has a permanent love only in her child (and now grandchild) and in the heat of the Florida sun. Determined to never marry again after divorcing my father early on, she enjoys her fifties doing exactly what she wants. She works, and drinks, and tans. She dates, she attends church on Sunday, she calls me at least twice a day.

Standing at just over five foot tall and with jet black hair she is a lovely woman; an ideal inspiration for mothering. Which if the past couple of weeks have been any indication, I desperately need. My mom is my very best friend and she has no idea that her little girl is dying inside.

I switch from bouncing to swaying. No dice. The newborn shrieks continue.

"Chloe. I thought it would be best to not involve our family in our affairs," Leo suggests cautiously, like I am a ticking bomb.

I hand him the hysterical infant that is not hungry, or dirty, or cold, or hot, just miserable, and I spew out, "This isn't our affairs, Leo, this is your affair. You figure it out."

I go to the bathroom, determined not to let him see me cry yet again and take the hottest shower I can manage until the water turns icy. When I come out of the bathroom I am dry, slathered in lotion, dressed, hair styled, doing anything I could do to postpone myself joining the two heart-breakers outside this room. As I bravely step out, Leo is waiting in the hallway.

"Ok," he whispers, with a peaceful baby sound asleep, sucking on a tiny pink butterflied pacifier relaxed on his broad shoulder. "Let's go to Florida."

He leans forward hesitantly and for the first time since that Godforsaken day, I allow him to kiss me in his usual place smack dab in the middle of my forehead. I smile weakly, if only for an instant.

***

Ten days later and I am watching the sunset on the water of the Southern Gulf Coast of Florida, just as my husband promised.

Looking out of place in his dress slacks and bare feet (stripped of wingtip shoes and dress socks) Mr. Donnovan puts his arm around my still lumpy from pregnancy waist and leads me to where the dry sand meets the wet.

We plant our bottoms on the Gulf of Mexico. Grandma Larchmont is at her designer-decorated condo inland cooing over time alone with her only grandchild. Surprising Leo, I reach into the paper grocery bag I brought and pull out a six pack of beer. I haven't drunk a drop of alcohol since the day I held a pregnancy test.

Silence hangs between us as we behave in a pattern we have for years: swapping a single cold lager between us, the can sweating fiercely in the Florida "spring," versus having our own can. It always seemed intimate and personal, as if we wanted to share everything possible with the other.

Leo, a man so full of giving. Yet.

At some point we need to talk about what happened.

Handing the drink between us, the quiet roar of the waves converting the absence of talking into healing instead of hurting, we relax. For the first time since, well, maybe since a year ago finding out over a hot Fourth of July weekend about our unexpected and unplanned pregnancy, we are able to just be. Just Leo and Chloe. Like old times.

Without knowing the weight of the moment, the very first of a thousand conversations that will change our path forever takes place. Maybe it comes about because of the isolation of the two of us, surrounded by nature and nothingness. Maybe it is the desperation from each of our aching hearts to not let what existed between us be lost forever. Maybe it's the alcohol.

Leo breaks the ice.

"Darlin, the interview went great. I really think they're gonna offer me the job. Are you sure this is what you want?"

I drink and think. After a minute, watching a gaggle of spring breakers near us pack it in for the day, surely headed to get cleaned up and head to the next available party spot, he continues.

"I understand if you want to leave. That kills me to say, but I never want you to feel stuck. I love you so much Chloe. I'm so fucking sorry. I will do anything to keep us together. Please. I'm so sorry."

I continue to watch the sun setting full and pink on the gentle waves. I feel the need to make a choice. The choice.

I just feel so unequipped to know where I am supposed to go from here. Cracking open the next can of brew, I wonder about how other women deal with infidelity, if my giving him an opportunity to make things right makes me incredibly strong or terribly weak.

I realize that I don't really care about other women's choices. They don't have to walk my path. I do. I want to believe in something other than anger.

"Do you really love me at all? How can that still be true?" I ask him, bottom lip trembling.

His thumb reaches over to brush my cheek, detouring that first tear.

"Please, ahh God, my wife, please know. I love you more than I love life. It was a horrible mistake that would never happen again. I beg you. Give me this one chance to show you the kind of man I am meant to be for you."

I look with awe at the horizon: in the same sky, the moon perched and the sun dwindled at the same time, ready to make today yesterday so tomorrow can start with a fresh slate.

Draining the second beer, getting a buzz for the first time in a year, I turn to face my husband. His eyes are icy right now and I can see that he is desperately afraid. I don't see that often.

I speak with my heart:

"Ok, mister. Here's how it's gotta be. No more lying and no more secrets. No hidden life. You'll never contact that woman again. Ever. I'm gonna be checking. We'll move to Florida. Sell our old stuff. Erase Atlanta. New bed. New house. New job. New memories. And marriage counseling. I mean that. In one year, three hundred and sixty five days from today, we'll come back here to this piece of sand. Then and only then will I decide if I have any interest in staying married or not. Not a day sooner. This is the only way it can happen. Are you interested, Mr. Donnovan?"

No answer from him other than how he makes every business deal in his life. Across the sand his right arm stretches and we shake on it.

It's a deal.

Only time will tell if this is a successful proposition or not.

We call to check on Emily and watch the sky turn indigo and the stars pop out, competing with the beauty of the ocean. The six pack is finished in peaceful silence. At some point I get up and instead of continuing to sit next to Leo, I go in front of him and scoot back into his seated embrace. He holds me, wrapping me tight, his goatee scratching the top of my head, and we sit that way as long as we can stand it.

Together, we rise and hold hands, brushing off and walking first to the recycle bin to dump the cans and then to the car, to the beginning of our new lives. Our new marriage. Temporary though it may be.

***

I often wonder what drove me to giving my new and broken marriage another shot. I see myself there on the beach, a woman who was deeply scarred, betrayed by the person that I trusted in the most, and reflect on why I didn't throw it all away.

I think every person going into a serious relationship has said at one point or another that "cheating is a deal breaker." I have never heard somebody say, "Cheating is ok once or twice, but that third time, no way, nuh-uh."

It never happens that way. It is an ending to the relationship in theory; a hard limit. It turns out, though, that when actually faced with infidelity, things aren't always so black and white. You can't just pick up and walk out of a relationship that easy.

That person has become ingrained in you in ways that you don't even recognize. If I had packed up our child and walked out, yes, I would have changed our relationship status. But I would still continue to rock out to old school rap and picture Leo next to me singing along, the ghost of him still present. I would still cook things with too much cheese and fold my socks the way he taught me he liked best. I would watch the same television shows but would never forget lying in bed and my husband stealing my ice cream from a bowl perched on my pregnant belly while we watched that show together.

Over the years, Leo and I had combined laundry, borrowed toothbrushes, exchanged social security numbers, traded childhood memories in the dark of the night, and miracle of all miracles, created an entire human being.

To extract him from my life feels like using a dull butter knife to extract my appendix: painful and raw and horrifically unnecessary.

I want to say that I realized my emotions were too unprocessed to make a rational decision. That I was able to think and say, "Ok, Chloe, right now you are upset, and hormonal, but in six months how will you feel if you throw the whole relationship away?"

That I realized Leo could pay me any lip service in the heat of his indiscretion being discovered, promising me the moon and stars that don't belong to him to give away, and only time would tell if he could redeem himself.

I was firmly perched on a balancing scale between not forgiving right away and not committing to stay right away. I didn't dare hope he could make me feel like I could move past this, and I didn't dare throw away all of his positive light that made me fall in love with him in the first place.

Sometimes I feel like I was being a martyr for my daughter, like I wanted to give her a fighting chance at growing up in a two parent home. I had committed to become Mrs. Leo Donnovan for all of my days and I meant it. I didn't want to make Emily the reason for staying and I never want her to learn of this, but I certainly didn't want to throw away the chances of seeing her grow up with her father in the home. Or the chance of having natural siblings. To end our marriage was to end her family structure the way I had always hoped for and that seemed selfish and rash. The thought of making Leo a weekend dad and starting the hunt to find a new partner made me ill.

I've thought the main reason for my temporarily staying married was love.

Love. Sigh. How schoolgirl foolish does that sound? But by God. I love Leo Donnovan through it all. From the moment he first kissed me with those wide and naturally pink lips, when I first felt his facial hair scratch my smooth chin, feeling the warmth building inside of me, the very want of Leo Donnovan.

Ah, the lust. I fell in lust as hard as I fell in love. When we first met, Leo intimidated me with his eyes that read through my facade, his certain demeanor, his confidence in life. Leo was a man so sure of himself so young. His certainty of self followed him in the bedroom.

I felt a passion with him that seemed as natural as breathing. My body yielded under his every touch. I often felt under a spell. Even at first. It increased in intensity with every passing day.

I guess the reason I decide to give Leo a year to make things right is quite simple to explain: some relationships are worth fighting to save.

Chapter Three

Moving On

T he job offer from Florida comes in the day after our conversation on the beach and the wheels are put in motion.

Despite my meager hope that my marriage can be salvaged I spend much of my time angry as a viper, embarrassed that I wasn't enough for him, and feeling betrayed. Oh so betrayed. I just move through the motions each day and am glad each evening that Leo is doing as he promised.

It takes only two weeks and we are loading up a U-Haul, packing up the crib we had so recently put together, sweating in the sun that was promising summer, stopping only to fax employment agreements and eat take out.

We use the internet to rent a home on the beach for the next year until I decide our fate. I could possibly be leaving my husband by the time that lease is up. One year it is. Signed and sealed.

Leo drives the moving van south, erasing the bad memories with each mile, and I feel the sun enveloping my spirit. I'd be lying to myself if I denied that I am actually optimistic. This feels right.

I never envisioned our family on the beach. He, the desert child, raised amongst red rock and Indian reservations. Me who left the Gulf as soon as I could for college in the dry, hot air of Phoenix.

The more I thought of us making a home on the beach, the more it seemed suited for us. I daydream down the I-75, picturing Leo with a smidgen of tan on his typically pale skin, playing with Emily on the beach building castles. I dream of the sun and the sand and the salt creating new, happy memories.

We arrive in the smallish moving van (as promised, we sold much of our old home and rented a house with furniture included, sans crib) in front of our new little rental home that is in standard Key West style: bright to the point of obscene, colorful in a way that tempts any frown to undo itself, small, so much smaller than what we were used to but smack dab on the Gulf of Mexico.

The beach house is perched upon beams, protecting it from potential flooding and hurricanes and allowing for parking below. It is peculiar and nothing like I have ever lived in and somehow exactly what I need.

That first night in Florida I set out to the beach once Emily falls asleep laying curled next to Leo in the tiny master bedroom. They are both exhausted from the travel but I am wide awake, practically jittering with extra energy.

I exit out the creaky back kitchen door and carefully make my way down the rickety staircase that leads to the sand. It feels warm still and I walk out to put my feet in the water. I feel like I often did as a child growing up here. Alone in the world, tiny in the presence of the great sea. Lost but somehow also watched over.

I know in my gut that I am missing something in my life. Something I have vowed to keep secret forever. Something I could never share with my husband. The fear of discovery makes me tremble.

Maybe that is the truest reason for offering Leo a second chance. He had a secret and I have a secret too. It is just that mine has yet to be discovered.

I step back from the water that is flowing slowly and consistently, reflecting the moon on the tip of each tiny wave.

Halfway back to the completely unfamiliar home I stop. I lose my strength. Dropping to my knees in the sand I allow myself to fall into the earth.

I lay there, exhausted now not from a travel day but from the weight of my hidden desires and close my eyes to the world.

***

I see the me of a decade ago: a senior that tastes the freedom college will bring strutting through the halls of high school both hoping to be noticeable and praying to be invisible.

Chloe Larchmont, hippest of the geeks. Never involved in sports, never led any committee, never having seen the Friday night lights. What I did enjoy on my daily walk through the misery of secondary education were the boys.

It didn't matter if I am watching them cut streams through the water during swim practice, or in study hall nose deep in a textbook, or ditching lunch to meet me out behind the cafeteria for a smoke and a pseudo-deep philosophical discussion. I watch them and I want them.

The jocks with bulging muscles, the college bound gents who would taste of coffee, even the grungy boys who played video games instead of devoting time to anything remotely important all had begun to play a role in my sexual experience.

I am still a virgin at 18 but have been honing my skills of pleasuring my own body for some time. There is something so wrong about touching my nakedness while laying in my childhood bed, getting off while the stuffed animals of years past look at me from the corner across the room.

It feels wrong and I like that it does. I incorporate thoughts of the young men of my days into my nightly grope sessions.

I create fantasies in my head, mostly involving pretty minor league stuff: kissing, touching above clothes, hands going down pants. It increases the excitement of the mundane life that is high school. I picture the fantasy the following day again, turning fifth period English into a daydream about how Mike's (or Josh's or Kyle's) thumb would feel sliding over my nipple guarded by my sturdy white cotton bra, picturing in detail how the mounds would harden to peaks slowly, steadily, and I could visualize down to the light goose bumps that would arrive with the touch.

I'd shiver myself back to reality and look forward that evening when I could touch myself again and pretend it was him. Any him.

A particularly ordinary midweek day eventually courses my entire sexuality like a light breeze drifts the unassuming tide. Walking through the hallway between classes a folded sheet of paper slides onto my books.

I look up and see nobody in front of me directly, just streams of passerby teens. I spin around and see Zach, a friend of mine, glancing back towards me as he continues in the opposite direction. The smirk on his face and his long hair gives him a rebel charm that is quite attractive. He gives a brief nod in the direction of my books and heads towards his next class. I step to the side of the hall so I don't cause a traffic jam and open the letter.

I see a story. The title reads *The Sex Slave*.

So I can guess it's about sex but I have no idea what a "slave" would have to do with it. We watched *Roots* in history class last year but what in God's name could that possibly have to do with a sexy writing?

I feel a curious tingle in between my legs and seeing as how I am standing in an almost empty hallway at school I know I must:

1. Put the story away as fast as possible and get to class.

2. Get home after school and read this. Urgently.

Equally nervous to either leave it in my locker or tote it with me everywhere, I choose to keep it close. I make it through the day that moves at a snail's pace, the story that will surely be this evening's entertainment burning a hole in my folder.

My brain keeps flitting to the title. I say it in my head, repeating it over and over. Once, in the bathroom, I even say it aloud just under my breath. *The Sex Slave*. It heats me up all over yet I have no idea why.

Sprinting to my car to avoid well-meaning chatter about graduation and gossip I rush home, bring my backpack into the sugar sweet bedroom of childhood, and dig out *The Sex Slave*. I kick off my loafers and pull off my uncomfortably starched school shirt and fall backwards onto the coverlet. Finally I can satisfy my curiosity.

The Sex Slave

A woman woke up in a groggy, drugged state. She ached all over, body sore and head throbbing. Opening her eyes for the first time, she startled at the unfamiliar stone ceiling above her. Becoming increasingly scared, the woman went to sit up and *clang* chains heavy around her arms and legs tied her to the cold hard concrete she was stretched out upon, naked. Wild eyed, she screamed.

"Help! Please!" she begged. Looking around while thrashing, she realized with dread that she was even further prisoner. Not only was she strapped nude to a strange floor and spread open wide, she was in a jail cell.

Three solid walls and a set of padlocked steel bars was the only thing that she saw. Screaming for help, she finally stilled at the sound of heavy footsteps coming in her direction. Fear mixed with relief and she began to cry. Looking up at the sound of keys, she saw a sight on the other side of the bars that confused her as much as every other moment since awaking. There was a gargantuan bald man that she didn't recognize, muscles bulging, standing at practically seven feet tall, staring at her with the keys in one hand and a rope in another. He was clad in only leather pants.

"Who are you? Where am I? Let me go!" she shouted to the stranger and he stood silently staring.

This worked the woman up even more and her throat became hoarse from the crying and yelling and fear. At long last he moved slowly towards the lock and entered the cell. Instead of releasing the woman, he stood directly over her and said in a deep voice, "Whore, you are in no position to make demands. Last night you signed yourself over to become an owned sex slave. You will be trained as a sex slave and in time you will feel grateful for what I am about to do to you. Call me only Master. Or else."

Reaching down, without any further discussion or explanation, he plunged three fingers into her pussy. Shoving them incessantly in and out of her, the woman's screams and cries could be heard echoing against the bare cinderblock walls. As her brain feverishly reached out to the black spot that was the previous day of her life, her body betrayed her by accepting all that this strange goliath, this Master, was giving. Cum ran out of her in puddles, and he put his other hand down to her throat and pushed hard, blocking her air intake. Somehow this made her cum even more-

Oh. Holy. Shit. My mind is reeling with questions and nobody to answer them. Is there really some prison where ordinary women are brought to act as a "sex slave?" No way, this is made up. Did Zach read this? Of course Zach read this. Did Zach want me to read this? Of course Zach wanted me to read this. But as my friend crosses my mind, I find I can't lend him more than a passing thought. I still see the jail cell and a giant Master with three fingers inside of a woman.

Three fingers. I can't even imagine what three fingers would feel like. Is that even possible? I reach down and remove my shorts. I brush my hand across the cotton panties that are the only undergarments deemed acceptable by my Mom and I'm shocked to find the crotch of my underwear damp.

I am completely turned on. It must be the strangeness of the story. But my God that woman was being raped. Wasn't she?

I continue reading about the sex slave, about how she had voluntarily offered herself up to being taken and trained to service men and women sexually. I picture her journey, reading about being shackled, kneeling on cold stone in front of people who regarded her as only a series of holes to be used, being shaved in entirety, being stretched open and explored for their fun, the Masters and Mistresses fun. I am more turned on than I have ever been.

It is something in the slave's bareness, both in body and purpose. This woman, nary even a woman anymore, just a sexual object, didn't worry about a job or taxes or the news or the date on a calendar. She is rebuilt to provide sexual pleasure. I push my underwear to the side and lay a finger on my clit. I am shocked at the slick wetness that is there.

My whole mound swells with excitement and I move my pelvis up to reach that fingertip. Left hand clutches the story and my right hand moves through the folds of a body that seems perched between a teen's and a grown woman's.

I keep coming back to the beginning of the sex slave's path in my mind's eye. Three fingers. I set the pages to the side and use my now free hand to hold open my underwear, giving freer access to my entire womanhood.

I close my eyes, breath speeding, shutting out the Molly Muffin stuffed doll that has been my only bed mate. I become that sex slave, feeling the damp concrete underneath my bound, nude body. Nipples clench up under my bra (a bra that's still really one sad step from a training bra) into tight nubs. It's painful in the intensity. I conjure the slave's fear and confusion rippling through my body and rub my crotch with my whole hand, still not able to get enough fullness.

Chest heaving and *ohmyGodamImoaningoutloud* I envision what I have been waiting for since first reading it: a Master staring over me, wanting to take me whether I agree or not, preparing to invade me.

I lose the fear I have been holding onto and for the first time ever I clumsily shove a finger deep inside my hole. I cry out, in pleasure and pain and surprise and embarrassment and I begin to move it in and out, my middle finger touching the inside of my body that is somehow soft and rough at the same time, the heel of my palm landing soundly on my clitoris each time I move, picturing him, the Master, finger fucking me.

I can't help myself and add another finger. Feeling myself stretching, tearing, accepting what I have never accepted. The hint of pain sends me over the edge and I orgasm in a way I never knew possible. My whole body convulses to the point that my teeth are chattering, my two fingers still plunging but now filling with hot wetness like somebody dumped a fresh cup of warm tea in my palm (*oh God did I pee?*) and the muscles surrounding those two fingers are clenching and releasing repeatedly.

An unfamiliar moan deep and rich leaves my throat and continues to fill the empty room.

Once my hips bucking and breath heaving begin to subside I open my eyes. Everything looks the same but somehow duller. Younger. I let go of my stretched and soaked panties and remove my two fingers. There they are, pruned from the wetness like they used to be after a long bubble bath dedicated to playing mermaids at sea but this time covered with my adulthood and blood. The end of my innocence. There is no turning back thanks to *The Sex Slave* and I feel both grief and freedom.

Moving slowly I go to the adjacent bathroom I look at my young self in the mirror, stomach lightly cramping, insides still twitching. Will people look at me and know?

I certainly will, looking older now, seeing my adult self. I clean the mess: washing my hands and rinsing the underwear, running them under icy water until I am convinced the blood can never be removed. I toss them in the trash along with the possibility that life will ever be the same.

I run the bath and undo any evidence of my afternoon extracurricular. My blanket and clothes go into the wash and I stash the story between the pages of my chemistry book that also holds homework I won't be able to focus on later.

I finally sink into the hot tub, scalding my skin that seems somehow too tight now, turning my breasts to a deep pink. I close my eyes and relax my new body into the soft scent of the bubbles.

Behind the lids of my eyes floats in a face. The face of the Master.

***

I open my eyes to the moonlit beach on my first night back in Florida, located only ten miles from my childhood home but seeming like a lifetime away.

This haunts me. The desire to be owned by another person, to feel what life would be like under another person's control.

I have spent so much effort becoming something else, anything else. In college and working I'd been a ruthless, powerful, assertive woman.

But when Leo and I were dating I would secretly be thrilled at the chance to pleasure him in every possible way, including serving his dinner first, tending to the household tasks even though we both worked all day, and doting on him. I loved taking care of him. But when others were around, I became hardened and demand what I called "equality." Because no smart, independent woman could ever be in service to a man, right?

I felt torn in two, dividing myself between who I thought I should be and who I really wanted to be. Societal pressure lays heavy on me, raised to think that no good could ever come from submitting to my partner. But under the gaze of stars, still yearning and firmly in my thirties, I am sick of it. Tired of living a life I don't want, of denying my true persona. Trying to be the "strong" woman that society dictates I should be; hiding that I want to give up control.

If I really want that, and a man wants to give it to me, then so what? Who else has to live my life? Why do I have to justify my actions to anybody but myself and Mr. Leo Donnovan? Why can't I be considered equally strong in having enough conviction to be me? Wholly, truthfully, entirely, imperfectly me?

I want to scream out my frustration but instead stay silent, paralyzed from the constant worry of confiding this in somebody again. My breath catches in sadness at the thought of Patrick Johnson, the handsome Catholic boy who I dated throughout college. I tried so hard to ignore my desires and fit in. I really did. But once I bravely told Pat about *The Sex Slave*.

We were sitting in his dorm room, college sophomores at ASU, sharing a hijacked bottle of Boone's Farm that made Pat nervous. He was convinced that his RA would somehow know and kick down the door with campus police, arresting us for underage drinking and ruin his chance at become the CPA that he always dreamt of becoming. After finishing the bottle and tiring of listening to him talk about accounting, I blurt out my secret.

Eyes narrowing behind his glasses that used to make him seem so intellectual, he verbally ridiculed me. Asked how I dare talk of such "whorish ideas" and demanded to know if I had ever been sexually assaulted. When I insisted that no, I hadn't, that I had a wonderful upbringing, I was called a liar. Pat told me that if I wanted to become some kind of "slut," enjoying porn and talking of things "like that," I should leave and never contact him again.

Ashamed and humiliated, I stuttered out an apology and never brought it up again. Not to Pat. Not to anybody. I tried my best to convince myself that I didn't care about some silly erotic story I read years prior. But I could never shake the feeling that I needed more out of my sexual future, something different.

I became an expert at secretly masturbating while lying in bed once Pat was asleep. Rubbing my clit so lightly and delicately, circling, regulating my breathing to resemble sleep cycles, getting off to vision of the Master ordering me to do his bidding.

I broke up with Pat Johnson two years later when I knew he was going to propose. We were readying to graduate and both of our families expected marriage to be the next step. I saw the ring hidden in his apartment closet while putting away laundry and after putting the ring back I sought out Pat and ended things. He was shocked and I felt like a terrible person but I had wasted years with a man I had no chemistry with and I refused to live like that forever. Maybe it took all that time to get the guts to be OK with being alone. Maybe I never got the word "slut" in Patrick's voice out of my head.

I threw myself into my career. Paying back student loans by working in the first decent paying job I could nab I put my nose to the grindstone and worked. Saved. Waited. I dated frequently and casually, keeping my secret desires locked away.

Until the day I was sitting at the front desk of a medical office and the door blew open, bringing Leo Donnovan into my vision. Life would never be the same. Leo was the first man to ever make me forget. The sexual trysts were so intoxicating I didn't need more. Just him.

The fantasy never left though. It only became a sleeping dragon waiting to be awoken.

***

I lift myself out of the sand. I drag myself up the stairs towards my family. I convince myself to bury it all.

Life goes on.

Chapter Four

Salt Water Heals

I sit in the nondescript waiting room feeling equally nondescript. I look around the marriage counselor's office and create stories about the other couples waiting: who cheated on who, who spent the family savings at the local casino, which is unhappy with their in-laws.

I move my eyes around until I find myself staring at my husband looking deceivingly relaxed in his casual attire. "Deceivingly" because none of us are relaxed. It is the day of our first counseling appointment and I'd rather be anywhere else in the world right now.

My mister is holding Emily in his flexed arms and I blame the warmth in my chest on postpartum hormones. His hazel eyes are seeking mine out, trying to get any connection. He is doing everything right. I just need to work through this pain.

Our names get called by a woman who just entered the waiting room and I head towards the first shot at fixing my broken marriage. Leo, Emily, and I move together into the neatly decorated office of our new marriage counselor, Ruth DeLuca. My eyes sting with salty tears before she can even introduce herself.

***

Thirty minutes in and I am hysterical. I knew therapy would be hard but not like this. The only sound in the room is my hiccupping out my sadness and the building getting pounded with an afternoon downpour. In Florida it rains daily in the late spring and summer. In a few hours it will be as humid as a steam room and all around hot, miserable weather. I wish for that moment in three hours. It means I won't be here.

Emily sleeps oblivious in her infant car seat thankfully, so I am under the careful consideration of Ms. DeLuca, licensed mental health counselor, and my husband who looks devastated, turned white and unblinking, knee bouncing in an anxious way I have never seen before.

Leo has come clean. We haven't truly discussed the affair before coming into this appointment. It seems impossible but the days turned into weeks and despite my anger and sense of despair, I was almost more afraid of hearing the truth. Not knowing what happened was hard. Knowing is agony.

The other woman was a coworker of his. I instantly recognize her name. I know this woman, have met her, even dined with her at an impromptu lunch break when I surprised Leo at work. The woman knew he was married. Knew he had a child on the way. Knew and didn't care. They had a four month long emotional affair.

I wonder if I would have preferred a sexual indiscretion like a one night stand. Somehow knowing that he was talking to her about us, sharing intimate details of each other's lives, seems worse. Like promised, I've checked his accounts, and like promised Leo never contacted her again. It is truly over.

"Why? What did I not do for you? I gave you everything. Just… why?" My tears hit my lips, tasting like the salt air on the Gulf where I walked Emily yesterday.

Knee still bouncing, my miserable husband stares at the floor and I hear him say, "Nothing," quietly.

"What?" I demand, voice rising to a higher level, moving from mournful to irate.

He looks up at me and I see I am not the only one in the room with tears; it shocks me to see Leo this way.

"Nothing Chloe. There was nothing you didn't give me. Nothing you didn't provide for me. Don't ever for a second think you play some blame in this. You are incredible." Leo's voice simultaneously speeds up and chokes up.

"You gave me exactly what I wanted in life and I fucked it up. I should have talked to you instead, shared my concerns with you. I was scared and didn't want to scare you while pregnant. But that's no excuse. I should have trusted your strength. I fucked up. I fucked up so insanely I don't even know how to begin to apologize. If it takes until my last breath I will spend every moment gaining your trust back. I can't lose you. I can't. It took me so long to find you."

Time stretches out. I'm tired. Tired of crying. Tired of depression. Tired of a broken heart. Tired of anger and confusion and sadness.

I gulp down whatever is left of my pride and feeling like a complete let-down to womankind, I become the calm in the midst of his storm.

"OK mister. OK. I do wanna work towards forgiveness. I want to trust again. It ain't gonna be easy and it ain't gonna be fast. But let's do this."

He looks at me, hazel eyes the dullest hue of raw cement, and we embrace under Ruth DeLuca's watchful gaze. It feels good. It feels like a start.

***

Leo Donnovan screwed up. It's now up to both of us to repair the relationship. Ruth advises us, "Build a new foundation together. This is a fresh start for you both. It's time to start trusting again. To start proving that you are worthy of trust again. Ask each other, 'What did I do to push you away?' and 'How can we be more connected in the future?' Find a new hobby, an interest to pursue together, something as fresh as this new time in your relationship. Bond. Consider being intimate."

I stare at the woman through puffy eyes and actually see her for the first time. Ruth DeLuca is an olive skinned Italian woman with tinges of grey at the temple. With a slender build and masculine jaw line that contradicts her feminine aura, she sits with her knees tucked under her in a leather armchair that seems to swallow her whole. I realize that I like her.

After a silent drive home I need to be alone. I ask Leo upon arriving at the beach house, "Can you give Emily her bottle? I was hoping to go for a run."

I feel a spark as he brushes up against me, gently taking the baby from my arms. His touch feels realer somehow than before the appointment. Trust rebuilding? A hobby? My mind is churning and I need to escape, to run away from my thoughts like I have been doing for years.

Leo responds, "Sure."

As I turn to leave he grabs my wrist, stopping me in my tracks. I face him and for the first time since "the mistake," he kisses me firmly on my lips.

After an instant of cringe I force myself to kiss him back. It's a good kiss. Maybe even a great kiss. One that's full of hope and I'll be damned if I didn't feel a twinge of sexual excitement for the first time since that awful day in Atlanta.

Hating to pull away but needing to gather myself I break away and go to the tiny master bedroom. I pull out my non-maternity running shorts for the first time, looking rumpled and old, and am surprised when they fit.

I go to the bathroom and pause in the mirror. "Mom" ponytail and swollen eyes. Rounder than I used to be before pregnancy, softer somehow. I undress and eyeball the stretch marks that no amount of oil prevented despite serious effort. Settling for thinking I look better than feared, I make a mental note to shave my legs later. Maybe tonight will be the night that I touch legs with my husband under the covers. A small gesture but surely a welcome one by us both.

I miss our intimacy. As I lace my old running shoes I realize how desperately horny I am. How long has it been? Four, five months?

I sneak out the front door and hit the pavement still drying from the rain. I find my body pushing hard to reach a jogging pace close to what I used to be able to keep up with and I eventually fall somewhere near acceptable.

I run, feeling the steamy salt air in my nostrils, hitting my runner's groove. Thinking still about my absence of sexuality, I feel desire spread through my body, creating a heaviness in my loins that only plunging a finger (or Leo's sizable cock) into my hole can solve.

Leo. I fell so passionately in lust with him I convinced myself I could live a life without divulging *The Sex Slave* fantasy. Wild sex and old fear kept the desire for "more" at bay. But as of today we are supposed to have no secrets. Neither of us.

I am terrified to expose this to him. What if he judges me? What if he thinks less of me? Worst of all, what if I really am just a slut?

Ice chills my spine and I slow my pace that had turned into sprinting. I make a split second decision. If Leo wants me to live with his secret, he's going to at least hear me out. If he shuns me? Well then... fuck him. It's time to renew our relationship. We need a fresh start and full disclosure.

I turn around and slowly walk back towards our new home. The whole way there my brain turns over every possible outcome, queries every response that could come out of his mouth, and I prepare for admonishing.

Heading up the front stairs to the beach shack, I walk in and find Leo at the computer desk tucked into the living room shuffling through some bills and tossing junk mail into a recycling pile.

"Where's Emily?" I ask, almost visibly shaking with nerves by this point.

Turning towards me, "Napping. You ok?"

I don't dare hesitate and it comes out of my mouth in a blur: "What do you know about BDSM?"

The instant the words fall on his ears and he can process what his darling wife has just spoken aloud, he grins. A wide, genuine smile that lights up the entire room. I exhale deeply and suddenly become enthusiastic as hell about a fresh start with Mr. Donnovan.

Chapter Five

Firsts and Gifts

T ime really does work to heal old wounds.

When something harrowing happens, that first day you feel sliced apart and the devastating pain is all you can notice. The heartache is all that fills your soul. The next day, still, constant hurt.

Sure enough though a month later you can go several hours without being reminded of the root of the damage. When that realization hits you, you wonder, *Well, when did this get a little easier?* As if the healing salve of time soothed you when you slept in the night. You may never forget but you create a new normal, one that allows you to still function and at some point, function happily.

I sway my hips in the compact beach house kitchen a week after sharing my darkest secret, quietly humming an old reggae tune. Working in a joyful mood that matches the sunny paint that peels from the extreme humidity I wash my pots and pans from dinner the night before, a seafood dish that was mouthwatering. That's one nod for beach living. My cooking has never been better. I think back ruefully at the thrown together meals at the end of a long workday. I forgot how much I love cooking and baking and being in the kitchen.

The thought of being a dutiful, old-fashioned homemaker brings a peacefulness inside that is quite unexpected. There is something comforting in being this woman, in relishing a slower pace, in being available to tend to our home and raise our daughter. I feel calm in my heart only disturbed by the fear that it will one day disappear.

I can still feel the lingering of Leo's deep kiss as he left for work and I look forward to his return at the end of the day for the first time in as long as I can remember. Scrub, dry, quietly put the dish away. Scrub, dry, quietly put the dish away. Thank goodness for dear Emily napping easier. A visit to the pediatrician helped us get her colic under control and thanks to the static hum of a white noise machine she is one happy and well rested little baby now. I continue the housework in silence as I tidy the home being filled up with honest communication.

***

The mister is thriving at his new job: he is attentive and dedicated, a fast learner who redefines what it is to listen to a client. His transition to a career selling real estate suits him. He prefers working with more down to earth people and it doesn't get more relaxed than selling new houses in paradise to new retirees.

Leo has been in professional sales since turning eighteen and graduating high school, snubbing a nose at student loans and instead going to work to make a success of himself without debt.

This switch to real estate sales is like releasing a fish grown too big for the channel into the ocean. There have been eyebrows raised at his selling houses in a supposed "recession market," but true to form he has been successful from day one.

I get a text in the pocket of my kitchen apron and attempt to dry my hands on the damp kitchen rag before turning the vibrating gadget off. Pulling it out, I read the message from Leo:

How is the information I requested coming? I want to talk soon. Tonight?

A smile turns up the corner of my lips and I blush. A grown woman, a mother for goodness sake, blushing in a beach-worn kitchen shanty over a text from my husband.

Who am I? I wonder silently and before allowing myself to think too much of the hard-edged woman I once was, I pull myself into the present and start planning out who I want to be instead.

I text him back, simply:

Tonight.

I tiptoe-run to the desk in the adjacent room, untying my apron and tossing it across the white wicker loveseat in the corner where I throw open my laptop. I grab the spiral notebook that has become a journal and review for tonight, completing this first assignment that has ever been given to me by my mister, stopping only to text my mom about taking Emily after work. Grandma Larchmont agrees to take her overnight for the first time and my nervousness begins.

***

Last week after bravely spewing out the question of my lifetime to Leo he sat me down and listened to me ramble. I told him of the smut story I read in high school, of the negative reaction I had gotten from my ex. I blurted out that this is the fantasy I masturbate to at night when everybody is sleeping and I lay awake, mind spinning.

My husband is really great about this kind of stuff and always has been. He's an expert listener. He never gets distracted, never invalidates your feelings, or tries to "fix" the problem like so many men try to do. He just listens. Now, when it counts more than ever before, he doesn't let me down.

After all I had to say was out, after I had purged my secret fantasy upon him, Leo asked, as calmly as can be:

"Is this something you want to explore in real life? With us? With me?"

The words sent a tingle throughout my entire body. In that moment I felt dizzy and sick, hopeful and terrified. This was my chance. This was my opportunity. Leo awaited my answer with patience. I had to make a decision.

I could continue on course: an average married woman living a typical life, with great sex and mediocre communication. Or I could push my chips all in. I could risk it all, risk that comfortable life for one that I wasn't even sure I wanted, that I didn't even know much about.

I know I will never stop wondering "what if."

I fidget, feeling the heat of Leo's gaze upon me. Mr. Leo Donnovan, so calm, so strong in his composure. I decide to go all in.

"Yes. I want to try this... stuff. With us. With you."

"Define stuff," he replies back instantly, hazel eyes smiling along with his wide, familiar lips.

"I don't know I guess," I speak my thoughts, "this BDSM stuff. I don't know exactly. I need to find out about it, like the specifics."

"Well, let's do this then. You hop on the internet in your free time. Write some notes about 'this stuff.' What interests you. What doesn't. What you have questions about. What turns you on. Come back to me sometime soon and we'll go over what you researched. I have things to learn about too. I'll work on this for you. For us. Then, we can see what evolves. Fair enough?" Leo concluded.

I felt excited simply by his ordering me to do something. I like having a job to do for him. It seems less like burden and more like an important, purposeful task. I agreed and ran off to shower, feeling like a lucky Daniel escaping a lion's den.

***

On the night of my assignment being due Leo makes great time getting home and surprises me with a night off kitchen duties, citing reservations at a popular restaurant along the shore.

"Sounds great. Let me grab my bag and we can head out!" I head across the room to peck his stubbly cheek and move to gather my things.

Leo glances me over and with his lips curling up lightly at the corners; he grabs my hand and leads me directly to our bedroom.

Without speaking he gently nudges me to sit at the edge of the bed and walks away towards the bathroom, leaving me utterly confused.

"Leo? You need a minute?" I ask.

"Come here, Chloe," he shouts from the bathroom.

On the back of the bathroom door is a pale pink tailored sundress that I haven't worn since before I was pregnant. I had honestly forgotten about the dress in my current obsession with wearing what I considered "still acceptable" maternity shorts. My curling iron is plugged in and I hear the barely-there tick of it heating, noticing with embarrassment a layer of dust on the barrel. My makeup bag is sitting unopened. Perched in front of it is a new bottle of perfume I have never smelled before.

Ralph Lauren Romance, I read, and touch the tiny black gift bow stuck to the top. I look at Leo who is waiting on my reaction poker faced. I feel so considered. He thought of me when I hadn't. Maybe it's time I start caring about myself again. I turn to him and I kiss him open mouthed, tasting the only man I have ever truly loved. He tastes like home.

"I'll be on the beach," he murmurs when we break away, his thumb gently caressing my cheek and he leaves me there with my gift.

I look in the mirror and really see myself. I see a smiling ghost of the pulled together woman I once was. I peel off the fraying old shorts and, horror of horrors, the faded black maternity tee I am wearing that I see now makes me look about five months pregnant still only to realize that my undergarments are just as pathetic. I wrap up in a towel to sneak to my dresser for some sexier underwear and realize how ridiculous that is.

I want to become my husband's ultimate sexual goddess but I am scared to be nude in my own bedroom with the shades pulled down. I turn and march back to the bathroom and unabashedly hang the towel back on the rack.

Faking the confidence I hope to one day have, I strut naked to my dresser and pull out the push up bra that makes my breasts look fantastic in that particular dress. When I go to grab equally fabulous panties, my hand hovers above my underwear drawer and I make a decision to go without.

What would Leo think? What would it feel like walking down the beach in a short sundress, ocean breeze blowing up my skirt, caressing my bare mound that I shakily shaved after receiving Leo's text in the kitchen earlier? Would anybody be able to see through the material? All of this makes my pussy dampen a little just from the thought and I decide that makes it the right choice. I am going commando.

I toss the bra over the curtain rod and get to work. I brush my teeth and go the extra step of flossing and rinsing. Face next. It has been so long I have to completely remove the liquid eyeliner twice before getting it right.

In the end I stand back and realize how much more appealing I look: face clear and tan, my royal blue eyes glowing near the golden eye shadow, lips glossed over. I run my curling iron through my strands that are getting longer by the day creating soft waves once brushed.

I do the best I can to ignore my root color. I'll have to fix that soon.

I reapply deodorant and unwrap the gifted perfume. My husband has never gifted me a scent. The thought of him in a random Florida department store opening sample after sample until deciding makes my heart swell up. I feel like this is his first step in making me into the kind of wife (and dare I hope whore) of his dreams.

I want to be that. Both of those things. I want to be his cared for wife. I want to be my husband's own personal slut. Can't I be both?

I squirt the scent onto my breasts and get dressed, anxious to let the night begin.

I pause for a glance at the end result and am shocked by the transformation. I am seeing myself as Leo sees me. I am seeing myself as a woman instead of a mother. I vow to no longer allow myself to live as a frumpy new mom. Tomorrow I will go through every inch of this beach house and gather up every shlumpy sweat pant, every stained and pilling tee, every maternity garment, and free myself of the temptation.

I look in the mirror and take a mental picture. I want to feel like this, look like this, every day. And as much as I want to look this way for Leo it is so much more for me. This is the woman I want to be. This is the mother I want to show my daughter.

But that's for tomorrow. Tonight I see myself no longer as the lost woman that I used to be but instead as a preview of the woman I am becoming. I flip off the light switch and go outside, thrilled to share with Mr. Donnovan the real gift he left for me inside that bathroom. It meant so much more than perfume. The gift of caring about myself again.

I can't help but wonder, though, if he had planned that all along.

***

I walk through the back door onto the lofted porch sending evening shadows onto the sand. Leo is there on the beach, looking handsome in an ivory linen button down, khaki slacks and brown leather sandals. I take him in and when I meet his face, I see he is taking me in as well. Eyes smoldering, using his hand to shade the setting sunlight glaring off the white beach, he doesn't take his eyes off my face while I head to him. He holds a hand out, and I take it.

Alone for the night for the first time in months, we walk silently down the beach towards the pier where the restaurants line the water but I can't tell if he is enjoying the quiet or hiding himself away again.

"Are you OK Leo?" I ask steadily, the sky a now rich amethyst and orange that I have only seen in Florida over the water.

He turns to me and takes me in his arms gruffly, then turns my world upside down by dipping my head into what can only be described as a movie star kiss. Instead of kissing me though he just looks in my eyes now reflecting the first of the evening's stars and answers my question.

"Am I OK? Look at you. You are absolutely breathtaking tonight. Do you know how much?"

I feel the blood rushing to my head, curls already undoing themselves in the humidity of the night, feeling lightheaded. I realize he is awaiting my response and give one with hesitation, "Yes?"

"Good. Do you also know I can almost see your pussy and the slit of your ass through your dress, along with other gentlemen on the beach?" he asks seriously.

"Yes?" I answer again and though I try to stand up, hyper aware now of my position and the absence of my undergarments, he holds me there.

This is the first time ever being restrained by his masculine strength. It's honestly a little alarming. And arousing. God, I thought I looked different in the mirror earlier. Where had my old husband gone?

"Are you mad?" I ask timidly and he breathes the words "hell no" before crushing down on my lips.

Angry still or not, betrayed still or not, undecided if this would continue to be my husband or not, this is still the man I've had such passion with for years. Sometimes the body betrays all rational thinking. Sometimes all you are is *want*.

Breaking the steamy public kiss and regaining our composure he props me back upright and I fall into a walking pace beside him, holding his hand with my left and my right hand subconsciously brushing against my lip where his taste still lingers. My lips feel ablaze and full from the intensity.

We arrive and Leo leaves me sitting in the small waiting area while he speaks with the hostess. He comes back and leads me by the elbow through the busy dining room full of tourists and leads me to a two-top on the outside patio. The hostess hands us heavy menus and when the server arrives for our drink order, Leo speaks for me.

"She'll have a vodka martini, lemon twist, stirred, and I'll have a draft beer, whatever local."

I raise an eyebrow to him while the waitress finishes jotting her notes and we are left alone.

"OK. What's up? I have so many questions for you." I demand.

"I thought you were doing an assignment for me?" He laughs. "You first."

"What exactly do you want to know?"

I have yet to get any input from Leo regarding my secret fantasy and I hate feeling in the dark. He leans forward in his wooden chair, cloth napkin draped against his thigh neatly (I wish for my hand there instead) and instructs, "I'll answer your questions, but you go first. I asked you to gather information on what you called 'BDSM stuff' and to tell me specifically about what intrigues you."

Lowering his voice to continue, "I wanna hear you talk about 'this stuff' here in public, sipping vodka, with nothing between your cunt and the chair but a stitch of fabric. I like that very much Chloe. Excellent choice."

The word "cunt" slices the air between us simultaneously jarring me and turning me on. Even sexier is my pleasing him. I am glowing with the positive feedback.

"Ok, I'm ready." I sigh, leaning forward even closer so nobody else could hear.

"I started by looking up the term 'BDSM' itself. I really don't have much experience with it, except for what I already told you, and, um, I guess from porn, which I haven't really told you."

I look at Leo and his ever-changing hazel eyes concentrating on me, and it's his turn to raise an eyebrow. How did we ever made it this far, years of dating and engagement, hundreds of sexual encounters, and neither of us really know the other?

Leo surely reads my fidgeting hands and uncomfortable squirming but I plow on as best as I can, feeling braver with every word spoken.

I tell of my internet and book research I've been doing, pausing for our server to drop our drinks and take our dinner orders. Leo orders for both of us again and it is the second time in our relationship to have ever done it. Twice he ordered exactly what I would have chosen on my own. Maybe we do know some things.

I tick off the basics: "Bondage. Discipline. Dominance. Submission. Sadism. Masochism. That's 'BDSM.' It covers a wide range of things. Bondage includes things, like, that bond people to other people or things or themselves. Like restraints, handcuffs, rope, that kind of stuff. Discipline is when somebody punishes or, um, disciplines somebody else. Dominance is when somebody dominates another person, and obviously too, submission is when somebody submits to what another person says. Sadism is taking pleasure in bringing somebody pain. Masochism is taking pleasure in pain."

Leo jumps in and asks, "Of those six what is it that you are interested in?"

Before I have the self-control to hesitate I spit out, "Everything."

***

To save face from him thinking I am a total freak (though I kinda feel like one) I continue the awkward explanation.

"So I think, I don't know for sure, but I think it's the middle two that are the biggest for me. Dominance and submission. It's like, I spend all this time in life so in control and collected. I'm expected to be so great at everything I do, from being a wife to a mom to a career woman to a homemaker and it's the way life has always been, ya know? I'm the one making sure that the electric bill is on time and I'm the one who packs the diaper bag so nothing is forgotten and I remind you of garbage day and I always feel like the weight of the world is on my shoulders. And shit, Leo, I just want to give that control up for a bit. I'm not complaining and I like my life, except of course recent 'mistakes,' but I want to shut my mind off from decisions. So there. Dominance and submission."

Mr. Donnovan is staring at me, trying to process all that his innocent wife is saying, and his silence prompts me on.

"The others too but I think it all revolves around those two things. I want to be tied up, but that's about giving up control. I may want the whole discipline thing, but that is the hardest one for me to wrap my mind around. I dunno. And sadism and masochism, well, those scare me because I don't really know about pain. I do know that I am a lot... um... 'rougher' on myself than you are. My body is probably tougher than you know and can take a lot more hurt than you think. But again, those things are linked to dominance and submission too. I want you to take what you want, do what turns you on. And that's it, I'm done talking. What does turn you on Leo? Does any of this? What do you know about this stuff? Have you done this before?"

Phew. Sitting back I watch Leo who is watching only me. Our super perky college-girl-by-day, waitress-by-night comes by to deliver our entrées and still Leo just focuses on my face. We break from conversation to eat, taking turns feeding each other sample bites like old times. I drain my martini and Leo waves over for another. I'm feeling quite tipsy already and decide to throw caution to the wind, knowing Emily is in good hands for the night.

I'm having a good time and it has been entirely too long since that happened. The sea bass I am eating is so light and flaky in my mouth and for a while I am distracted by how wonderful it is to eat a meal without attending to a baby.

Once the plates have been cleared Leo orders a slice of key lime pie to go and decides to share his side of things. I listen with breath held, entirely entranced, waiting for the joke to be on me, waiting for my husbands' disapproval. What I get is this:

"Chlo, I grew up with a father who was an absolute asshole to my mother. He controlled her in every way and she hated it. Said she felt more like a kid of his than an equal. This freaks me out. I have a big challenge to be able to get to a place where dominating you doesn't make me feel like a dick, and like it'll make you want to run out of the door with our family. That's what I am trying to prevent.

"I want to make you happy. Nobody deserves that more than you, darlin. I need to learn about this lifestyle you're seeking and I've already begun to research on my own. I've watched bondage porn for years, and some other kinkier stuff than what we watch together. I've had significantly rougher experiences with my ex. I've just always been hesitant to do that with you. I'm a little scared to open this door and walk through it. With you. I don't want to hurt you, I can't do that again."

I brave up and ask, "Well, I don't want you to hurt me either but mister, can ya please spank me?"

Wide smile spreading, he tears away from my face and raises a hand, hollering across the room to any server who will listen, "Check please!"

***

"I'm only gonna to ask you once Chloe. I know you are... hesitant... about being together. This is your shot to take more time. I won't be mad; I want you comfortable and willing. Tell me to wait longer and I will. But say the word and I am going to fuck you tonight. Not make love to you but plow into you. It has been entirely too long for me and I have never wanted somebody as badly as I do right now. Do you need more time to consider?"

Leo gives this option back in the dimly lit master bedroom, light shining in from the ajar bathroom door. All I can hear is his voice and the sounds of the waves. I'm apprehensive. Will the spanking hurt? Will sex after childbirth hurt? Will my heart hurt later?

He's sitting on the bed, holding both of my delicate hands in his large but smooth ones while I stand facing him. Damn him, he is incredibly composed and calm while I simply shake. This is it. The moment I have been waiting for. Still swooning from the two drinks and Leo's unabashed conversation, the first true revelation of personal emotional information I can recall from him ever, I nod my head yes.

"No my wife. I want to hear it. I want to hear you say what it is that you want." His right hand begins rubbing my smooth thigh, tracing a line from the bottom of my short dress up to about an inch below where my sex begins.

I start to tingle, and building up the courage to start speaking my desires when they have gone unspoken for so long, I tell him what is easiest, what he just told me: "I want you to fuck me."

Just saying it makes me hot all over.

"Oh, well that's a start," he says smiling and stands to kiss my forehead. The act comforts me.

"If that's true, begin by asking me to do so. I know how badly you need this too. I hear you at night touching yourself and it takes every bit of strength for me to not help you. I want to hear you tell me you're ready. Beg for it, Chloe."

Jumbled emotions overwhelm me: the contradiction in my husband and I, shifting between being virtual strangers as we uncover these new desires and the couple who knows each other so well. My emotions are as bare as my crotch. I can practically taste my want.

"Please, Leo," I whisper into the semi-darkness, "please fuck me."

Leo moves his hand onto my mound and cups me, thumb up against my clit and the rest of his hand reaching back, middle finger across my crack, my cunt feeling hot in his grasp, and he moves his other hand around my back, pulling my side against him in a tight embrace.

Straight into my ear: "Again."

My nipples stiffen inside my bra as I plead, "Please fuck me Leo. Fuck me hard."

His hand under me goes slick and I start to move my hips but am reprimanded.

"Stop moving. I want you to beg."

I whimper at having to control my body to his will; this is new for us and it's harder than I expected. I sound whiny in my own head and try not to as I request, "Please fuck me. Please, please *please*. Fuck me. Destroy me. Take me. Please."

I am completely released and gasp at the unexpected cold air on my hot body. Leo steps back and tells me to undress and I slip off my clothes feeling like a slide under a microscope. Looking to him, he spins me to face the end of the bed, our brand new bedding the color of sea foam facing me like a great abyss, and he instructs me to bend over. I fold forward at the waist, feeling stark and vulnerable, and plant my hands at the end of the bed.

Mr. Donnovan takes his foot and uses it to kick apart my feet without saying a word. He stretches my legs out further than I feel comfortable. Ass open. Pussy open. I am trying to get in some way comfortable when his hand lands down for the first time ever.

Smack.

I don't know how to react or what to feel. I'm embarrassed by how much it turns me on, this fantasy come to life. I'm embarrassed to be spread to these limits. I'm embarrassed to be out of control for the first time.

His hands rub all over my bare skin and it restores me some. He silently strokes my middle back and butt cheeks, moving in a rhythm that soothes my hot backside, and I begin to relax in this position as best as I can.

"You OK?" he asks lightly, continuing the gentle caress.

"Yeah, I think so." I reply.

"Good," and he asks, "Are you ready for more?"

I manage a weak, "Uh-huh."

Leo whispers close to me, "I need you to be honest with me in this. Communicate. You told me at dinner I underestimate how much pain you can take. I need to learn that about your body. But I am not a mind reader. So. I am going to spank you again and I need you to respond each time, telling me how it feels. Can you be honest with me?"

I verbally affirm my understanding and consent and our very first kinky experience gets going. Leo's hand plants down and it is gentle, more of a love pat, less than what he did moments ago.

I tell him, "Harder."

I feel his hand leave my bottom, swing backwards, and it comes down again.

"Harder" leaves my lips instantly.

His left hand is on my lower back and I can tell this time he puts effort into it. *Swat!*

The spanking has enough force to sway my body forward, bringing me onto my toes for a second.

"Ahhh!" is my first response and on the heels of that comes, "Harder."

His hand moves in small circles on my warm butt and he increases the pressure of the hand on my back, holding me more in place.

I can hear the air move as his arm swoops up and back down. Hard. Painfully.

Smaaaackk!

Strange things happen when you are spanked that solidly. It is felt in more of your body than your backside. It registers in my chest first, strangely, and inside near my heart clenches up and the wind is knocked out of me. My breath is caught up in a strange whistling sound and only then I recognize the sting, the absolute smart that is blunt force turning from a prick to a tingle to a burn, spreading through my entire ass cheek.

It takes a moment to recognize the soft circles of his smooth palm again and blinking back tears in the corner of my eyes, I tell him the truth.

"That. Right there."

He doesn't disappoint.

He swings back and lands again on the other cheek using the same force as before and I feel it in my throat instantly, swallowing the pain down as he continues.

I feel my control over the situation disappear and as I am drained of the power, I allow the pain in and feel the pleasure that follows.

My body like a rag doll, he devours me for the rest of the evening, late night turning into dawn. By the time he does as I begged and fucks me, my pussy is wetter than it has ever been without orgasming and I am fortunate for that.

He presses his rock solid staff into my folds for the first time since I gave birth and I am tight, so tight. Tighter than when my fingers entered my virgin self when reading *The Sex Slave* half a lifetime ago. Upon entry I cry out in pain.

"Oh my fucking God Chloe" comes out of his gruff bedroom voice and I know it's taking him every bit of control to not start pounding away.

Tears well in my eyes again as he gives my body time to adjust to his presence and we spend the evening re-acquainting our bodies to each other.

I am overcome, and in the end tears of relief and pleasure fall, wetting my cheeks the same way my sheets are wet, releasing the pleasure and gratitude of this unexpected gift I have been so willingly given.

***

How did two seemingly "vanilla" people happen to click in the way that we did?

Once a person starts becoming familiar with the kink community they learn how vast and varied it really is. "BDSM" encompasses so much, too much to consider listing. Adults who enjoy everything from diapering each other to foot fetishes to shibari rope enthusiasts.

What are the odds that Leo and I are so compatible? That when I came to him and professed my secret fantasy it would be so in line with his desires?

We personally never compromised, never did things we didn't want to do in order to please the other. That first night I thought I was the luckiest girl in the world to have found that one kinky man whose interests were so in line with mine and not only found him, but found him and married him before even knowing each of our real desires.

In reality, the odds that we happened to pair up so well in the kinkier version of ourselves were high.

Our foundation didn't begin that night. The start of our dynamic wasn't at a seafood dinner when I outlined my limited knowledge of "BDSM" and it wasn't with that first land of his bare hand on my bare behind. It began even before we met.

Leo Donnovan was a Dominant well before he knew what to call himself. It is his natural personality. Simply the way he was built. He was always referred to as "the little adult" growing up because he was so responsible, serious, independent in his decision making, and hyper aware of his surroundings.

Leo is the man that when you meet him, you instantly want to be his friend and if you've met him once, he'd leave the house at midnight to help you stranded on the side of the road. "The mistake" in Atlanta was so out of character for him and in hindsight it was almost a relief to find a chink in his armor.

Then little old me. Sweet, secretly submissive Chloe, who learned somewhere between adolescence and adulthood to hide every bit of my instinctual nature, mistaking my softness for feebleness, my desire to serve my partner as anti-feminism, my wanting to please a man for being spineless and weak willed.

The reality is these natural dominant and submissive personalities are likely what drew us together in the first place. I reeled under his dominant personality in the beginning and he warmed to my docile self once I let my guard down a little bit.

Societal pressures and teachings combined with being raised in homes emphasizing the opposite of these old fashioned ways prevented us from truly being ourselves. We were both in hiding, both denying who we were, who we wanted to be. When we found each other we gripped each other like two people lost at sea.

Fuck you society. Fuck you for raising a girl to be one specific way and a boy to be another specific way. From the moment that first spanking landed, Leo and Chloe Donnovan said no more. Not us. Not ever again.

Chapter Six

On the Road

Leo and I have a history of taking road trips together. We unplug, put everything else aside, and enjoy being in good company. It's my birthday weekend in the heat of July and we are on our way to Orlando to celebrate with our little family, Grandma Larchmont included.

I watch the miles pass sitting in true Chloe Donnovan road trip style: barefoot, shaven legs crossed underneath me, hand holding Leo's, blaring hip hop tunes both of current day and days long ago, throwing in some heavy metal and old time rock and roll for variety. All while belting every tune in a terribly off-key voice.

I am the passenger. I am always the passenger since meeting the mister; he prefers to drive no matter the length of the trip. Shocker. The man likes to be in control.

He sings along equally off-key and we couldn't care less about how foolish we look to the cars passing by. My mom is driving in her own vehicle with Emily tucked in behind her so the two of us are alone in Leo's car.

I love my birthday. I enter those days of summer mentally preparing to bid adieu to last year's happenings and welcome with open arms the future.

It's been four months since discovering my husband's affair. Three months into the year I've demanded to decide to remain married or not. One blissful month living with BDSM as a part of my life.

The emotional indiscretion still rips at my heart and the decision to stay or go weighs heavy on my mind. But the intermingling of marriage counseling, of being distanced in both miles and time from Atlanta and what happened there, the salt water and fresh air of Florida, and the newfound sexual play with Leo all help to heal.

Leo is trying so hard. I can tell with each passing day just how sorry he is for his mistake and each day my fears of it happening again wane a little bit. He does love me. He doesn't want anybody else.

Every day is an improvement for us, each activity in trust-building assigned by Ms. DeLuca brings us one step closer to coming home to "us" again.

I am living in the very new and exciting time that is the beginning of a Dominant/submissive relationship. I don't even really know that this is what is taking place but every day, both in and out of the bedroom, Leo is a little bit more in control and I give up a little bit of it. Each time I relinquish being in charge of something a bit of pressure fades. We are both learning at a speedy clip. Outside of work and Emily, this is how we dedicate our time together.

Reading, researching, talking. More than ever before. Fucking. Better than ever before. Repeat. There is still so much more to learn.

BDSM has its own vernacular. For every single word we search out the definition of, three more appear that we need to define. We start using phrases like "power exchange" and "munch."

Texts go from me to Leo while he is working saying things like:

What have you learned about the difference between a "Top" and a "Dominant?"

One day while at the playground I hear the familiar notification and Leo's text reads:

I can't wait to see your tan body tied up in rope. Soon darling.

I look forward to Leo's arrival each evening. By day we research. By night we play.

Books galore, as fast as we can take them in. It seems like the brown delivery van is at our door daily, dropping off a veritable library of BDSM books. We read fictional series of Dominants and submissives giving each other exactly what they desire, non-fiction about actually living in Power Exchange, and even seemingly non-related books that pop up in the suggested reading bar of the online store. Books about control, about good housekeeping, about owning your assertive side, about etiquette.

We read at nap time, lunch time, break time, on the toilet. Handing books across the dinner table where we eat in mostly silence, nose in the black and white text of a world that is so foreign to us but feels like a mirage somehow, a blurry eyed fulfillment of the needs of two parched individuals.

We note-take in the books, the mister using his black inked fancy pen I gifted him several Christmases ago and I use a plain old blue ballpoint, as cheap as they come, because the likelihood to lose something nicer after tucking it into my bun and forgetting it there is high. We scrawl question marks and exclamation points and underline sentences that describe us; ask each other questions in the margin. I read his notes. He reads mine. We talk some more.

Each night Leo and I tiptoe away from Emily's room, closing the door and grabbing the monitor, and like horny teenagers sprint to the haven that is our master suite.

Things have begun to change in our sexual dynamic. Instead of our old way of getting naked (him undressing himself and me undressing myself), now Leo comes to me and strips me bare. Sometimes it's slow. Dreadfully, deliciously slow. He'd stand me in front of the bed, his serious eyes piercing mine that radiate desire and raise my arms above my head while directing me to "Stay." His fingertips run down my arms sending tingles along with it while his stare takes me in. Unbuttoning my blouse. Taking the time to kiss each inch of skin he exposes.

Other times he strips me down fast and rough, as raw as it gets. The second we hit the bedroom he'll grab a handful of my lengthening hair and shove me against the bed or a nearby wall. He just rips whatever I am wearing off, giving no care to buttons popping or the sound of splitting my panties apart at the seams. This rough manner is typically accompanied by his teeth biting down on my skin as if he wants to eat me whole.

Either way though it's his choice in how I am baring my body. The first time I move to help him unbutton the top of a blouse while he is at the bottom he immediately swats my hand away. Hard. Following is a look demanding that I stop moving.

I am learning that Dominance and submission is akin to dancing. There's a leader and a follower. In order to learn submission, you have to learn to follow. Sometimes this is as natural as breathing. Sometimes it takes practice. I am learning to follow Leo Donnovan's lead and I love every minute of it.

***

Smiling on the Northbound I-75 drive I look out the window and see my mother's peppy coupe in the side mirror.

I turn down the radio to call and check in.

"Ma, how's it going? She sounds quiet." I ask with concern as soon as I hear her pick up.

Grandma Larchmont assures, "Oh she's fine honey. I can see her in the little mirror Leo set up. She's playing, cooing, simply adorable. Hopefully until we get to the park. I am going to get off the phone, let me go drive. I'll see you in an hour or so."

I think my mom has suspicions about Leo and me struggling. As the closest female friend I will probably ever have, it's hard to not go to her and spill everything.

Two things keep our secrets at bay. First, DeLuca's advice. Our marriage counselor had advised us that as long as we are unsure about whether we are staying together or not to hold off on telling those close to us. That if I did decide to stay together, I may one day forgive my husband but there is no guarantee that anybody else would understand the reasoning. That we live in a society of people tossing things away when they become broken and that my mom or his family may never understand the hard work we are putting in to fix us.

Secondly, my mom and I never talk personally like that. We are just so different. She is logical, independent, put together. I have always been emotional, incapable of a poker face, wearing my heart on my sleeve. I hide myself near her, the over-dramatics in my personality, the need to feel when others simply think.

She's been offering up her physical help in exchange for her emotional support. Help cooking meals, dropping off groceries, watching Emily (who is quickly replacing me as Victoria's new best friend) so Leo and I can be alone.

I know she thinks something is going on with us and she's right. But I won't bring it up and neither will she, so she grandparents instead of parents. When she offered to take Emily on the drive up to the amusement park full of dinosaurs and wizards and stay with her in the evenings so Leo and I could go out, we jumped at the chance.

The thought of a weekend alone-ish to focus on BDSM and our changing relationship dynamic seemed like the best birthday gift possible. I look out of the car window and wave good-bye to Mom and Emily as Leo steps on the gas and starts gaining distance through the light Florida traffic in the sweltering early morning sun.

Smiling, putting my smart phone down, I turn up the radio and sing.

Speeding up a bit with mom's sensible import fading away behind us, Leo reaches across his sports car that he uses to escort clients around during the work week and clasps my hand in his. It feels like a dozen past shared experiences. I smile and sing and relax, loving the road underneath us, feeling the miles move us through life.

"Take off your shorts," Leo instructs clear as a bell, voice rising over the music.

My ponytailed head whips to him incredulously. With that one sentence, it becomes like no other drive we have ever taken.

***

Leo raises an eyebrow and asks, "Do I need to tell you a second time?"

I laughingly object to this. "Leo, we're driving. No." Silence but for the purr of the engine.

"You can't be serious." I brush him off, crossing my legs.

He grips my hand, tiny in his, harder.

"Off. *Now.*" He demands.

I look to him dressed in comfortable driving clothes and bright white walking shoes as he prepares to wait in the long lines of the latest rides. He isn't joking around about this "request." This is the point in our old marriage he would have given up; conceded to my denying his request. But things are becoming different now. In me. In him. In us.

Bravely I test him.

"Or what, Mr. Donnovan?" I chide.

He sighs half-heartedly and I can't quite tell if he is getting annoyed or giving up. In the cool car I hear him ask: "Are you ready to dip your big toe into the pool that is discipline, my darling?"

My heart speeds up at the uncomfortable predicament. I can't take my shorts off. Can I? No. Goodness no. I'm on a public road, in broad daylight, in a car that anybody can peer into. Wait. That almost makes me want to do it more. What is that called? Voyeurism?

I reach for my phone and search, feeling the tension build in the air while I still avoid Leo's instruction. No, voyeurism is getting off on watching or spying on others. What I am feeling is exhibitionism. Exposing myself in public.

I am completely turned on by the idea and at the same time terrified. What if a cop sees me? That's illegal right? Can I go to jail for that? What if a trucker sees me? What if Leo sees me (as foolish as this is, I am still building back confidence in my new post-pregnancy body and there is no hiding here) and horror of horrors, what if my mom sees me?

I feel like a nervous teen in high school again trying to meet up with a current beau and find a place to grind on each other in a curious frenzy. I don't think I have fooled around in a car since high school. I'm an adult. I thought I was past this. But then why is my whole lower half starting to heat with excitement seeping in?

The alternative? Discipline? I am having a bit of a "what the fuck" moment with that. Do I believe him? I dunno. What would that entail? I dunno again. I am enticed to explore this too.

This is how I feel so much of the time now. Overwhelmed by the options available to me. Kid in a candy store syndrome. I want to sample everything and there just aren't enough hours in the day to do it.

I am in a live version of a Choose Your Own Adventure story I used to read as a kid.

Pick a path:

1. Either safe word (standard yellow and red that the BDSM books and sites preach: yellow meaning slow or caution, red meaning stop). I can't at this very moment imagine having to "red" anything Leo would ever do to me.

2. Take my shorts off.

3. Learn about discipline.

I brave up and make my choice, shaking away Leo's right hand that is clutching my left, and proceed to unbutton, unzip, and push off my khaki shorts that I picked for comfort. Here I am. Pink lace-trimmed cotton boy shorts against the cool leather seats.

"Good choice." Leo praises, running his palm up and down my thighs that are clenched together at the knees. "How do you feel?"

I sit on my hands to avoid flipping open the vanity mirror and seeing how I look, afraid to see the roundness that is new to my body. I force myself to focus on how I feel instead of how I look. I feel sexy. Horny. I say so to my husband.

"Good. Now lean the seat back and spread your legs."

Instantly my eyes glaze over with tears that I do my best to blink back.

"I can't babe. Please." I tell him, quivering.

"You can darling. You can, and you will. I'm here. I'm in control now. Do you think I will do anything to put either of us at risk?" he asks.

"No," I spew shortly, sniffling back the fears and shame that has wrapped up my sexuality for the past fifteen years.

"Do you trust me?" he inquires.

I flinch at the question and am brought back to the mistake in Atlanta.

Pissy sounding, "I used to."

Undeterred, he more gently asks, "Do you want to trust me again?"

I sniffle, nodding my head in affirmation.

Leo encourages, "Chloe, this is the first step. I'll protect you. I'll keep you safe. I'll never have you doubt your trust in me again. Just... start here. Start slow. It's simple and I'm here with you. Put your seat back. Spread your legs. Will you do that for us? For you?"

I take a moment to collect myself and slowly send the whir of the electric passenger seat down, feeling more nervous at every moved millimeter. I see a ceiling that I have never paid attention to (*huh, dove grey*) and look to the right where I see the perfect summer sky. I look to the left and see an upside down view of my husband. Already scruffy from going the morning without shaving, excited to toss aside work for a few days, and hazel eyes reflecting the blue sky.

His view goes between me and the road. I clench up every time I see a semi-truck breeze past us but each time is a little easier going. Starting to enjoy doing something risqué, I slowly bring my knees apart, feeling so exposed to the world.

Each inch makes me a little more aroused.

"So fucking sexy Chlo," he exhales, running his hand again over my thigh in a consistent pattern, up and down, the same pressure, the same place, from my knee that is pressed deep into his center console, to about an inch below my pussy that I am dying for him to touch. But he has other plans.

"Move your panties over and touch yourself. Tell me how you feel."

I am ready to submit to his instructions. Ready to trust again. I take my left hand and staring at the ceiling, I use it to move my underwear to the side of my thigh, really exposing myself now.

"Touch yourself." Leo demands.

I move my finger into my folds and shiver from the chill of my air-conditioned hands against my hot, slick spot.

"Wow." I breathe out, and shudder visibly at being watched touching myself for the first time ever.

"Well?" comes the inquisition from Leo still rubbing my thigh up and down. I continue rubbing my clit, circling, relishing the wetness Leo's command has created.

"Good," I exhale, "I feel so good... so... smooth. I mean, like, slick."

I hear Leo's voice behind my now closed eyes.

"Nicely done my love. Now listen. I want to try something that I have been learning about and I think you are ready to start training your body. I want you to start controlling your orgasms. Do you think you can do that? I don't want you to come until I tell you that you can. Do you understand?"

I am working myself up and each roar of a vehicle passing by makes me a little closer to the edge. I rub in tight, light circles, masturbating in the way I have only done privately. If I pause to think about my fear of being caught, my body cools off and doubt seeps in so I push away the thoughts, keeping my mind in check.

I tell him in my most convincing tone, "Uh-huh..."

I feel his hand come off my thigh and grab my wet one into his, stopping me and forcing me to look up and acknowledge him. With a stern voice, he says, "From now on you have a choice in response. 'Yes, Sir' or 'Yes, Mister' are your only options."

I stare at him wide eyed and feel a bubble of laughter in my throat as I try to decide if he is being serious or not. His hand drops mine and he lifts his and smacks my inner thigh, hard, stinging it and instantly turning it red.

"Yes, Sir." I blurt out and wait, stunned.

"Yes Sir, what?" he asks for clarification.

I stutter over my words, "Um... yes... Sir... I will ask to come?"

As I speak the word "Sir" out loud for the first times in my life to a sexual partner it comes close to undoing Leo's experiment because it almost makes me come right then from the sound of it leaving my lips.

The feeling is cut short by another swat and sting on my thigh.

He corrects, "Wrong answer. If I'm talking, I expect you to listen. I said don't come until I tell you to do so. You don't ask me. Not today, that is for another time. Today, wait for me to tell you when I am ready to see you come. I want to read your body. Understand?"

The quick learner I am responds, "Yes, Sir."

I lay back, free to return to my pussy and all of what has transpired races through my mind. Being told what to do. The pleasure masquerading as pain. How good that sting felt. I want to come but swallow the urge down, slowing my rubbing despite wanting to get off and then speeding up again once back under control.

When he finally gives the order, "Come," I am more than ready and it takes me all of fifteen seconds to pace back up and orgasm. It rips through my body, from head to toe, shaking, convulsing, tingling.

My moan empties into the car and feel my boy shorts dampen through surely wetting down to the new smelling leather beneath my bottom. My eyes stay closed in hopes that I can shield myself from the interior scene of the car; hide from my out-in-the-open sexuality.

Leo pats my thigh, "Good job Chloe, I'm proud of you, that was such a good job."

I cover my eyes with my left hand, bringing my weak knees together and laughter seeps out. I'm positively giddy. After a peek at Leo through my fingers I see him focusing on driving but chuckling along with me.

Who the fuck are we right now? I wonder silently. It makes me giggle harder, and he glances at me, starting to laugh out loud as if reading my mind. He shrugs his shoulders as I lean my seat up, undoing what we have done, and we casually go back to singing the all but forgotten radio tunes. One moment, the old us. One moment, something entirely new.

***

So much of the formation of a power exchange dynamic takes place during the non-sexy moments. These types of relationships aren't always crafted in the heat of the night or while masturbating in a luxury car streaming towards a family fun park.

The important learning, the times when structure is built, often happens in the light of day. Sober. Spoken in plainness and honesty.

During my birthday weekend spent walking through an amusement park after finding a gas station to clean up and switch into dry underwear my mind drifts to an old Bible parable, something about building a house on rock instead of sand so it can withstand any storm.

A successful dynamic, hell, a successful relationship of any kind, is built on rock. The basic core values- trust, honesty, respect- are the rocks that can withstand anything. They need to be crafted through constant, open communication. Talking may not be the sexiest thing we do but Leo and I do more of it during this year than in all of our previous years combined.

Debating. Questioning. Discussing. Learning. We both said and heard things that hurt us. Things that built us up. Things that we didn't know about each other. But if there was one thing we learned from both our marriage counselor extraordinaire as well as from the mountains of BDSM reading we do, it is that talking is necessary to make things first better and then great. So talk we do.

Chapter Seven

New Words. Old Fears.

Walking through the land of animatronic dinosaurs, melting in the hot sun along with tourists chattering in foreign languages while fanning themselves with the park map, I stop at a shaded snack bar table and sit. I pull Emily out of her infant stroller and get to work adjusting the sweaty baby. Prim and proper Grandma sits next to me with a sigh, glad for a break, and pulls out a bottle of water that is likely reduced to lukewarm in the half-hour since purchase.

Leo, absolutely drenched in sweat underneath the cap touting his favorite football team, bends over and gives me a hot (temperature hot, not in any way sexy hot) kiss before heading to the restroom.

My mom tells me to give her "my girl" and after an internal eye roll at her corny phrase I hand Emily over to her grandmother for a dose of doting. I stand to stretch, pulling my short sleeves up, shocked at how golden my skin is.

I ask Grandma Larchmont, "Ma, I'm gonna grab Leo and hit up that water ride. Ok?"

She answers in her now becoming typical way, in baby talk, to Emily:

"Tat's ohhhhkay! Huh Emmie? Huh wittle baby? Are you hun-gee? You want a bah-bah?"

Smiling at my girls I pull out the mini cooler with bottles and after setting them up I feel a hand slide across my sticky back. Hairs stand up all over and I am surprised at the magnitude Leo has over me right now. Every touch, or word, or day seems of vital importance. I grab his hand and lead him, heading into the long line to wait for a ride to plunge us into a cooler existence.

I fall into one of my favorite hobbies: people watching. I see older folks standing in silence. Younger folks face down in their smart phones. Pre-adolescent girls in matching cheerleading camp tees and requisite matching ribbons practicing their arm moves and giggling together. And everywhere, families.

Groupings of all kinds, with younger children and older children and lots of children. Moms busy cleaning up dirt smudged faces with a stray napkin and water bottle. Dads holding toddlers, doing their best to keep them entertained in the claustrophobic line. Siblings trading inside jokes that each family seems to own in surplus.

It hits me that as of right now I don't know if Emily will ever have a natural sibling. Less than a year from now Leo and I may be quits. He had an affair. It may have been the death of us. I begin to cry and am glad for my dark sunglasses.

We shuffle forward and stop and the mister catches a glimpse of a stray sniffle.

"What's goin' on?" he asks in a kind tone close to me.

In my old life, in our old marriage, I would have replied with the predictable "nothing" and moved on. But.

Talking. Communicating. Honesty. These are gonna be instrumental if I expect the same from him.

I huff out, "It's just hard still, you know? It's still hard. Every day."

We shuffle with the moving ride line.

Leo responds simply, "I know. I'm sorry."

I have heard "I am sorry" more times than I can count. It helps though even if just a little bit each time. I do my best to clear my head and move forward with my day, pushing the hurt as deep back as I can manage.

My mind reflects on the exhilarating car ride and that breaks a sunny smile across my face. I tiptoe closer to my husband's ear and whisper, "What did you think about earlier?"

An equally sunny grin breaks out on his face. "What did *you* think of this morning?" annoyingly answering my question with a question.

I insist, "No way. Nu-uh. I'm asking you. You know what I thought of it."

Shuffle, shuffle. I can see Leo processing the question. Each moment brings more concern that he was somehow displeased with the naughty drive.

He pulls me close, my back against his front and his arms crossed over my chest and he lines up to speak directly in my ear.

He shuffles me along in the line, nearing closer to the giant waterfall that spills over willing passengers and at long last Mr. Donnovan begins to share his thoughts.

"I've never seen anybody as sexy as you today. You looked so hot all stretched out, trembling. But it's hard Chloe. It's an adjustment," he sighs and continues in a pained tone.

"When I was raised up, my parents taught me how to be the best man possible. I was raised up to be a nice guy. To put women on a pedestal. To allow them freedom... and... and... 'options.' So it's really difficult to move towards the opposite. I don't want to be a shitty husband."

I pull him away and spin to face him, to reassure him, "But Leo, I am asking you to do those things. I want you to take control of me. I like doing what you want. When you are being pleased, it pleases me too. You're not shitty at all-"

"Stop Chloe. Stop. I know this, I can tell. I'm learning to read you in a way I never knew possible. I watch you now. I really see you now. But listen up darlin and here is the hard truth of it. The control thing, that's an adjustment. That's getting easier. But I have heard the same thing since, God, I was probably five years old over and over and over again by everybody in my life: Men. Don't. Hit. Women.

"A real man never lays their hand on a female. Ever. Now here I am and we have opened up this Pandora's Box and I stand dealing with the fact that I liked slapping your leg. I liked spanking you the other night. The sound of it, the sting on my palm, reprimanding you, hearing the squeals that came from your mouth. Seeing your shock. It turned me on. It was so fucking hot and all I can think of is when we can do more. What kind of monster does that make me Chloe? Huh? What does that say about your husband?"

I can practically feel his heart beating across the foot of air between us. I am shocked at hearing this confession. So much emotion from him; so much of the once silent storm now swirling inside of my mister.

I had no idea of this struggle. Had never even stopped to consider the toll this may carry for him. I stare at his dark sunglasses through my dark sunglasses and now I am glad for his eyes being hidden too. I don't think I want to see the pain he is feeling right now; the internal struggle.

I shuffle walking backwards towards the front of the line and take his stubbly cheeks in my hand.

I move closer and say, "Thank you, Leo, for giving me this chance, for letting me explore. I don't know how I can ever say thank you."

He grabs my wrists, holding me tight, and tells me how.

"Stay with me Chloe. Stay married to me. Please."

It's the first time he has made the request since our agreement to give it a year. It chills me all over and I don't know how to respond. I am too scared to say anything. The fear that he would dishonor our marriage again is too horrible, but the thought of not waking up to him in the morning rips my heart in two.

Instead of responding, I let go of his face. We untangle and I turn to face the jungle boat ride. We move the rest of the time not touching, our silence amongst the surrounding chatter and carnival music and screams of joy suffocating us. Finally it's our turn and we are led onto the boat with a dozen others.

At the highest peak I look over the edge into the watery abyss and realize my stomach is already in my throat even before the fall.

Nothing is as scary to me right now as the thought of forgiving. I take Leo's hand next to me and we plunge together. I'm glad he is there with me, along for this ride.

***

Late that night I close the door to Mom's hotel room, waving good-bye.

Grandma is lounging in her nightgown with a glass of wine and a puzzle book, a conservative news show playing quietly in the background. In her room is my sweet little girl, sound asleep. I am free.

When we checked into the hotel, all of us dirty and worn out from the long day of travel and excitement, Mom said that she was going to go relax and get clean so to meet her in an hour. Emily and I set off to track down some dinner for us three Donnovans and Leo toted the suitcases (and diaper bag, and overnight case, and his backpack surely containing work stuff, and the stroller) in from the car.

While I was waiting for room service, I gave Emily a bath and got her into her bedtime routine. Each time I heard Leo's card click the hotel room open, I felt his presence pull at me.

It may be because we spent so much time after his mistake emotionally distant but I feel like I can't get enough of him in my life. I want more. More of his time, of his essence, of his manhood. Damn it. More of his dominance.

I feel him more than hear him as he crosses the room and comes to the bathroom. The mister peaks around the edge of the door, seeing me kneeling in front of the tub, a scratchy hotel towel under my knees washing the baby, and he asks, "Hey girls! Dinner?"

I tell him I ordered food and that it should be delivered soon and he disappears. All of ten seconds later I see him out of the corner of my eye as he pops back around and in a hushed tone adds, "I like you on your knees."

With a wink he is gone, leaving me this time with my jaw dropped.

Leo and I work together to get Emily dry and dressed and then eat perched on the end of the hotel bed together.

Now our babe is fast asleep under Grandma's care and we are left as husband and wife.

Leo is waiting in the hall and as I wave my way out he grabs my hand and we race down the hall together eager to begin our evening, to celebrate my birthday; quite possibly the last one with us together. But that is a care for another day. Today? I just want to be filled up.

We hit our hotel room, still holding hands and doing more giggling than talking, and I realize I feel disgusting. I'm still wearing the same shirt and shorts that I put on after feeding Emily in the dawn, before packing, before the X-rated drive, before the hot day at the park.

I turn to Leo and see him in the same situation, dirt on what once was a crisp white tee but his hazel eyes still glowing with passion.

I ask him, "Heya, mister. You wanna go shower with me?"

He responds with a "Fuck yeah Chlo" and his wide lips nibble on mine before I can pull away.

**

I turn the shower on and set up the bathroom while Leo strips in the bedroom.

After lining up our mini travel bottles, I toss in Leo's shower poof he prefers over a washrag. It's a small detail but I am glad I remembered it when packing. Something like that I never would have paid attention to a year ago, deeming my husband quite fit to pack what he wants for himself.

While this is still true, a big part of me enjoys taking care of him. I don't know if this is a homemaker thing or a submissive thing or just a "me" thing. I don't care. I like doing special services for him. So be it.

As the steam of the shower starts to fill the bathroom, I get inspired to try something new. Leo enters and stands before me in the nude; I am overcome by my want of him. As always now, I feel saddened by his mistake in Atlanta but I can't help but wonder in awe at it catapulting us into a new lifestyle together. If he hadn't had his affair, would we be communicating the way we are now? Would I be having my deepest fantasies fulfilled?

While I am confident I will never be happy for his indiscretion, are we coming to a point in our relationship where we are now better, happier, healthier, after the affair?

I offer him a hand and a smile and we hop in the hot shower.

Leo and I shower together often and it usually looks like this: taking turns in the cold air and under the heated water, taking turns shampooing, rinsing, soaping. It is a bit of a dance, moving in circles, wet naked skin brushing up against wet naked skin when passing.

In an effort to learn about my husband in new ways I ask him, "I'd like to clean you. Can you teach me how you like to shower? Like, what order you do stuff in? I've never really paid attention."

I wait for his laughter or eyebrow raise to the foolishness of this request but he surprises me by simply saying, "Sure, I'd like that," and gives me a wet kiss on the forehead.

Under the water he teaches me. You can learn a lot about a person by the way they shower. The speed; the particularities. I give Leo a hug to start and eagerly become a student of my husband.

Hair first, taking much more time than even I do with much more hair. He asks me to use my nails and scratch. I do, and ask him if he prefers scratching in lines, like this, or circles, like this.

He answers, "Lines."

A light moan escapes his lips as I take my time giving him a scalp massage. The scent of his minty shampoo fills my nose and I feel a peace settle in my being.

I stand back, ass hitting the cold shower wall as I ask him to rinse and he does. I continue the massage with the conditioner. Before I rinse my hands, he tells me to run the conditioner through his goatee and I do.

I learn his pattern; tab it in my memory to be able to recall for future opportunities to shower together. Next comes warming the poof in the water before applying the soap. Weird.

Lather, and a very specific order: chest, arms, back. Underarms. Groin. Legs, butt. Feet.

I go to wash the bottom of his feet and it brings me, determined to do as thorough of a job as possible, to my knees in front of him.

Soap bubbles covering the both of us, I go down to my right knee first and then my left.

It's not an unfamiliar position per se, because I have certainly provided "sexual services" to him like this. But this is different somehow. I gently lift his first foot and use the loofah to clean it, running my finger in between his toes. Setting it gently down, I repeat it again on the other side. Finishing this act of service to him, for the first time since I landed on my knees, I look up to his face.

He's staring at me, watching me with concentration. When our eyes meet, several feet apart instead of several inches apart, an energy flows between us. A connection ignites; a spark flares.

Before my brain can interpret what is leaving my throat I hear my voice say clear as a bell: "Thank you, Sir."

I have come home.

***

Leo grabs a handful of the wet hair dangling behind me at the base of my neck and pulls me to my feet in a twisting, slippery way. The soap bubbles run down each of us like ten thousand tiny fingers sliding over every inch of skin as he looks deep into my eyes, giving my submission nowhere to hide.

I hear him growl into the space between us, "Say it again."

"Thank you. *Sir.*" I repeat with conviction, certain of this place in my life.

As much as it turns me on to say this, I see the words arouse him equally, his shaft growing stiff in front of me and I repeat with volume, "Thank you Sir. Thank you my Sir."

I hear a primal, guttural sound come from my normally composed and calculated husband as he uses my still-clasped hair to spin me to the back of the tile and mount into me. He cracks me open without hesitation or warning and I pause only for a moment to adjust to his size before I return in kind, bringing my hips to meet his, pounding. His hand slaps my ass painfully, sending droplets everywhere and he orders me, "No. Don't move."

I follow his bidding. I let go of control, close my eyes, and feel him ride in and out of me without controlling the pace.

I feel my orgasm building and am reminded of his instructions earlier. Hoping to show him how quickly I am learning his desires, I moan in a breathy sob, "May I come Sir?"

He responds with a moaning, "Mmmm... no Chloe... wait for it."

I feel his cock slide entirely out and he moves his hand around to the front of me. He uses his entire palm to caress my outside folds, engorging my clit, allowing me to grind against him, creating the friction I have been seeking.

"Wait..." he reminds again, and I am surprised at how easily I am able to swallow my peak down and just ride the wave that is almost coming.

I keep myself perched between agony and ecstasy. When he finally utters, "Come now," I let go of the hold and feel the warm gush of female ejaculation fall from my crotch.

My knees shake and my insides clench and all the while Leo continues the friction, prolonging my orgasm much longer than ever before. I keep coming and he keeps rubbing. When he finally stops, I am relieved to find his solid grip holding up my weakened body.

My husband gently holds me from behind for a moment, his familiar arms allowing me to recover. The water continues to stream down at a steady pressure and I can focus on nothing but gaining my sea legs back. Once I do, he helps turn me around and brings me into a loving hug.

I feel like our old selves again. Simple old "Leo and Chloe." I open my eyes and I find myself blown away by the intense love I feel. Standing on my tippy toes, I reach up to his lips with mine, and kiss him with smiling gratitude. I can feel his arousal pressing against my stomach still, but for now, I want to make out with my husband.

We meet with wet lips that move slow and just live in the moment, taking in the heat created. I can feel his very breath of life flow into me. We proceed delicately, tenderly, as if it is our very first kiss instead of the billionth. Only it isn't. There are two versions of us standing in that shower, steam rising, arms circled in a sweetheart's embrace.

There is the old "us." The ones who met and felt a connection so deep it propelled us to a wedding chapel in a crazy Vegas moment. The ones who fell asleep on the phone with each other after talking for hours states away. The ones who sent and received roses by the dozens. The ones who were content just a year ago to continue on an entirely normal, vanilla path. The ones who have to face the facts that something was wrong enough, broken enough, that we have to be working through an affair. The ones who were searching for something else.

Then there is a set of virtual strangers kissing: a man and a woman forging new paths in uncharted territory, nervous of plowing forth with the changes but unable to think of stopping. The ones that say screw you to the thoughts of "normal" and "acceptable." The ones who had conversations in the witching hour about things like how "Risk Aware Consensual Kink" applies to our new selves. The ones who had a dirty little secret from the rest of the world; who hid things and day-dreamed about each other and wished for more time alone in the week. In the day. In every waking hour. Just... more. Two people finally being filled up.

I feel like Alice entering Wonderland as I stand there in the shower. Life doesn't make any kind of sense. Slavery is freedom. Repression's a gift. Pain is pleasure. I am touching tongues with my husband, tasting him, feeling him caress my mouth with his, increasing each other's emotional connection by the moment, his erection rock hard against me, and I feel myself shattering the mold.

I know what I want to do, what I need to do more than anything in the world. I break away from his mouth and slowly, deliberately, kneel back down in front of him where a short time ago I was washing his feet.

I sit my bottom back onto my heels and through the spray of the shower coming through his legs I look up to him and proclaim, "Use me as you will Sir. Please."

I wait. Time stands still as our eyes meet through my declaration. My dignified dark haired and light eyed husband stares back at me.

He pauses for a moment, taking in my drenched naked body being offered to him and instructs, "Open your mouth."

I do. He infiltrates me. This is no ordinary fellatio. He is ramming into the back of my throat without hesitation. I know he wants me to stay still as he did before when he was fucking me so I kneel steady and take in as much of him as I can tolerate.

I gag at some point and it makes my eyes water. This doesn't deter the mister, in fact, it only intensifies his hammering. I reach out with bulging eyes to hold a hand against the wall; his release is coming. His cheeks clench tight and his penis engorges and he is spasming, shooting his nut deep into the back of my throat, turning my insides to cream. He lets out a deep exclamation and I feel the weight of him coming down.

He scoops me off of my knees and lies down in the bottom of the bathtub first, pulling my soft, wet body on top of him.

We look at each other and smile, collapsing as much as we can into the too-small tub and relishing the still hot water reaching down to us. I love the taste of him upon my lips. I love the word "Sir" upon my lips.

***

We proceed in our typical bedtime routine after peeling ourselves out of the bathtub. Without talking, just relaxing in our satisfied bliss, we take turns getting dressed, using the bathroom, brushing teeth. I towel dry my hair in front of the mirror reflecting Leo in the other room pulling back the comforter and lying down.

He has always been so quiet in contrast to my bubbly demeanor but there are many times, like now, when I'm glad for it. I want to be alone with my thoughts. By the time I turn in and finally cuddle up next to the mister he is sound asleep.

This is no shock; he is blessed with the ability to fall asleep the instant he lays his head upon a pillow. I am not so fortunate. I lay there watching a black and white sitcom, doing my best to convince my body and mind to shut off, and that's when I hear it coming from the other nightstand.

Leo's phone. Receiving a message. My heart quickens and I am immediately brought back to the nightmare that was the time during his affair.

How he started to call me after work and say, "Hey Chloe, I am on my way home. I'm going to let you go and I'll see you soon."

It was such a contrast from his typical call: chatting with me the first chance he got at the end of the workday until the moment he walked into our old home, both of us locking eyes and saying "bye!" out loud into the room where we saw each other.

The middle of the night texts. The deleted messages in the morning. His hour long bathroom hang-outs.

"Are you OK babe?" I'd call from outside the bathroom door, and I feel like such a fool now, knowing what he was doing when I was pregnant and concerned about him. Why didn't I look harder, insist on a more legitimate explanation on certain happenings? I can't blame myself for what happened but I can't help but wonder if I could have prevented it in some way if I had a bit of a spine.

My heart pounds at a sickening pace in my chest and I move stealthily out of bed. I creep quietly over to his side and gently unplug the charging phone with trembling hands. *Ohpleaseohpleaseohpleaseohplease* is all I can think.

I sneak out to the balcony of this hotel room overlooking a sleeping amusement park and slide the glass open just a foot as quietly as possible, his phone feeling strange in my hand in comparison to my own. My body moistens all over from the extreme humidity hitting my air conditioned skin.

I plop into the lounge chair and with unsteady hands, slide Leo's smart phone open. No password, not anymore, not after Atlanta.

New message, the screen blares. 2:12 AM. I click open the message.

Buy one large pizza get one for one cent! Click here for details!

This gleams in the backlight, illuminating my jealous and insecure face. When will I feel like me again? Like my old self? Then it hits me. I can never be my old self again.

I've been changed forever. Part of it was getting married and a big part was my new life as a mother. Part of it was certainly Leo's affair. Now I am changing again, exploring this new world of kink.

I sit alone, dejected, snooping through his phone, reviewing his emails and deleted files and social networks and checking his browser history with a fine toothed comb. I reflect on who I want to become in my new life, as the new me. I come away with the certainty that Leo is not currently doing anything dishonest, and maybe even a new outlook on life.

I am ready to shed my old skin like a snake does in order to make room for new growth. I will let go of who I thought I was, the woman who was sarcastic, and demanding, who pitched a fit about Leo forgetting to take out the garbage, a woman who saw the negative in a situation.

I will reinvent myself, highlighting the goodness of these changes instead of wallowing in the struggles. I will be the hardest working and most grateful homemaker out there. I am lucky, after all, that I live in paradise, spending my days at the beach or pushing a stroller through open-aired malls while Leo Donnovan works all day to pay the bills. He's never for an instant made me feel like I do less than he because I don't go to work anymore.

I am going to embrace motherhood and relish every moment I have with my sweet Emily. She will help mold me too, teaching me patience and to stop and smell the roses, how to not sweat the small stuff. How to love unconditionally. How to be lighter and laugh more.

What about this Atlanta mess? What goodness can I possibly ever pull from living through that hell? Forgiveness? Maybe one day. To never put an imperfect human on a pedestal like I used to do with Leo? Yes. To trust my instincts. To make my voice heard. To stop living a lie.

Then there is this new thing that is really not a new thing at all to me. BDSM. Would I have ever worked up the nerve to approach Leo with these ideas had I not felt like I had nothing to lose? I dunno. Maybe. Maybe not.

I think back to reading *The Sex Slave* and to the images described in it. The woman being shaved bare entirely from below her eyebrows down, the training of a specific position to kneel in to offer her sex, the whippings. The feeling of a leather flogger being brought down upon her exposed spots.

Now thanks to some gumption and feeling like Leo fucked up so bad he would have no choice but to hear out this secret side of me, we are living it. The more I taste of it, the more I want of it. I want more sex. More pain. More kneeling. More "Yes Sirs." More control given up. More serving my husband and not being ashamed in it. Leo isn't just allowing this to happen he is thriving in it too.

This is coursing us. We are changing. We are finding a new normal.

Satisfied that I have entirely spied the mister's entire past four months of actions and correspondence, I return to the hotel bedroom and listen to Leo lightly snore as I have so many times before. I plug his phone back into the nightstand not making effort to conceal the fact that I have perused it while he was sleeping. He knows that I check in on him and offers access to everything of his without restriction. When working with Ruth, we discussed what things we would need to change in order to start moving forward and this was one of them. Full disclosure. Full access.

I lay down next to my hunk of a husband. It's clear as day that where we are heading is where we should be. He is a Dominant. There is no denying. I am a submissive. To the ever living core of my soul. I wrap an arm around him and he shifts, turning to face my direction, and he engulfs me in a sleep-filled embrace.

I close my eyes, relieved, telling myself that I can rest now. I'm satiated. I have a brand new, positive outlook on life. But try as I might, my brain ignores my orders and like a neon sign flashing bright repeats:

Fool me once, shame on you. Fool me twice...

Chapter Eight

Punishment in the Air

2 Months Later

I am running at a clip on a treadmill in a small Florida gym several months after the first time I laced up my running shoes and bravely ran to a new beginning. Months of marriage counseling every week. Months of brutal honesty. Months of learning how to undo thirty years of being told to be a certain way in order to be accepted and proper. Blissful, content months of the Donnovans spending every moment that is not dedicated to work or family diving headfirst into the world that is D/s.

Dominance and submission. The sound of the words is like a sigh of relief. This is becoming where I belong. I feel freer than I have ever felt. Since our weekend away in Orlando I've begun transforming into Leo's ideal sexual temptress. I walk a fine line in my playful bedroom demeanor.

There are times when I automatically do as he requests and bathe in the warmth of his positive affirmation like a cat sunning in a sunny mid-afternoon window. When he says to put my mouth around his cock or bend over, I do. I allow him to maneuver my body and we create a means of communication that's incredibly intuitive. He leads the dance I follow, noting just a split second after he makes a decision to change my direction and follow suit.

I feel important and worthy and tended to. I feel cherished and loved. When you submit to somebody and offer them the world the natural turn of events is that they are so fulfilled, they return the favor in kind and you are given everything you need.

It is called power exchange (PE, or total power exchange, TPE) and more than anything Leo and I have explored it is where we are focusing our learning and practice.

I give him his power by relinquishing mine. Without me, there is nobody to dominate. Without him, I have nobody to submit to. We exchange power in the bedroom and it is now seeping into our daily, non-sexual lives.

I balance my proper submissive attitude with times of appropriate smart-assedness. One of Leo's biggest concerns so far is that I will change too much, become too docile, become a doormat. The mister likes having a wife who is smart and poignant. Who can debate with the best of them and hold her own. I maintain these qualities. We continue our natural banter and fun.

As a submissive, as Leo's submissive, I begin to hold myself to higher standards than I ever did as his wife or girlfriend. I want to look my very best for him (and let's face it, for myself too) so I focus on healthy eating. On exercise. On making sure that at minimum when he arrives home to his wife and daughter after a long day in the real world, I am showered and shaven, wearing a touch of makeup and my hair decently styled. Each night I add a spritz of the perfume he gifted me not long ago between my breasts. Who says you can't smell sexy while sweeping sand out of the kitchen? Looking good and smelling good sometimes means feeling good and damn, I feel good.

We still learn so much every day and "things" have begun to infiltrate our small beach house master suite.

After a nervous trip to a hardware store, convinced that the elderly man cutting the nylon rope down in 10, 20, and 30 foot lengths had to know what we intended to use it for, we raced home to watch instructional videos on how to tie me up properly. Leo was a quick learner and after several tries can now hogtie me tightly. Or get my arms suspended above me, tied to a plant hook with the azalea basket removed on the lofted back porch of the beach house, leaving my heart hammering at the fear of being exposed. The exhibitionist in me is getting stronger.

While at the hardware store getting rope cut I also picked up duct tape, clothespins, and at the last minute asked for wooden paint stirrers. Once you start looking around with a more analytical eye, many ordinary things can be used for kinky purposes. I have now been spanked with the back of my hairbrush, the leather belt slid from Leo's suit pants at the end of the work day, even the television remote.

Our nightstand has become overflowing with lubricants and a new vibrator that is more intense than anything I have ever held against my body. We created a "tool box" out of an old suitcase. In it lie these new devices of pleasure and pain. There seems to be two distinguishable types of impact sensation: things that sting and things that feel like a "thud." I like the sting better. The bite. The sharp pain that causes me to lose my breath for a moment. *Shiver.*

I wonder about meeting other people in our local BDSM community. What would they be like? Would they judge us? What it would be like to stand in front of them nude in a local lifestyle club that I now know exist and be paddled by my husband?

Here I am at the gym like most days, running off what remains of the baby weight, glad to have an hour to myself every day. I've started learning yoga, focusing on relaxing and toning my body up.

Two miles down; one more to go. Knowing my baby is in safe arms at the tot-drop and feeling my running feet take over for my body, I am able to think about my upcoming first wedding anniversary.

Leo came to me about a week ago and brought it up, asking what I would like as a gift or to do as a celebration. I made a shitty joke, something about, "Well, better make it good, it may very well be our first and our last," and after watching his handsome face drop in sheer disappointment and pain, I made a commitment to him to let go of the remaining animosity from Atlanta.

I've become determined to make the anniversary exceptionally special because, though it may have pained him to hear, it may very well be true. I set up reservations at a local fine dining restaurant and have been hard at work putting together the perfect gift for Leo.

We decided to do traditional anniversary gifts, meaning the first year is to be a "paper" gift. I knew precisely what to give and have been secretly working on it since. I am wondering what to wear and daydreaming about what paper gift Leo may get me when my phone rings from the cup holder on the treadmill.

I see Leo's face and simultaneously lower the set speed and slide the button on the smart phone screen to answer.

"Hello!" I gulp into my phone, leaning forward with my head down and one hand on my hip, the other holding my phone up while I fight off the stitch in my side from stopping the sprint.

"Chloe."

I hear my husband's no-nonsense tone coming through the phone. The hair on the back of my neck stands up.

"What's wrong Leo?"

I can hear the wind blowing behind him through the phone and I can picture him pacing outside of his office building. He is readying to have a conversation that others cannot overhear.

He demands: "Have you been masturbating without me knowing?"

Even though we have not made things "formal" with a Dominant and submissive arrangement, my insides turn to ice. There is no choice but to answer honestly.

"Yeeeeah?"

He sounds curt as he says, "I thought you told me that you were going to come only at my will, at my hand. Darling, we *will* address this tonight. Have no doubt."

Click. I stare at my phone while slamming the big red "stop" button on the treadmill to run to the bathroom and release my bladder. I am a little in shock and maybe my masochistic side is curious, of all horrors. I am going to be punished.

***

Leo is the latest he has been since working for his new company. Dinner is long over, Emily asleep, and I sit alone turning over the issue in my mind. Leo and I haven't agreed to make things full-time yet but ever since that drive to Orlando we have worked under the arrangement that I ask for permission to orgasm every time we have a sexual encounter.

But masturbation... have we set that in stone yet? I rack my brain. Leo and I have discussed so much over the past few months it is honestly hard to keep track. What will my mister's punishing me feel like? Will he spank me? Scold me?

I burn some nervous energy taking a shower. I dry my hair straight (sigh, I still need to put a beauty day on the calendar, the color is so drab and my split ends are outta control) and put on a clean nightgown with nothing underneath. I hear Leo's car pull into the parking area underneath the house.

I meet him at the front door and watch him walk in. In his hands are his keys and an unfamiliar brown paper bag.

I look to him with a smile and cheerfully say, "Heya, mister! You hungry, Sir?"

I see the corner of his lip go up into a crooked half smile and he shakes his head. His tie is already removed, he's rolled up the sleeves of his navy blue and white pinstriped business shirt, and the first few buttons are undone from the top.

He sets the items down and begins to remove his wingtips and unbutton his shirt, "Not now Chloe. Meet me in the bedroom."

I turn and head there and sit on the end of the mattress. He follows shortly after in just his black suit pants. The brown bag holding I-don't-know-what comes with.

He sits next to me and kisses me on the forehead, whispering closely, "Get on your knees. I wanna talk."

I give him a dubious look. I've knelt to him many times now. I have continued to shower with him whenever possible, cleaning him first and then he gets out chatting while I shower myself. It's a nice little ritual we have. Of course I've knelt to him for sexual reasons too. But not once has he told me to kneel for conversation.

It feels different; I know this is a pivotal moment for us. This is power exchange. He gave me an order. I need to participate, or not and suffer the consequences.

My body moves, sliding my butt off and dropping to my knees. I smell my freshness mixed with his smell of outside world and it melts my heart. I look up to him.

I am entirely intimidated by this man. Not scared of him, God no, not afraid. But looking to him from this position of vulnerability, staring at his manly chest with the right smattering of dark hair there, I am blown away by his masculine energy, by how oversized he feels in front of me. He is tremendous.

Expecting to see anger, I am surprised to find him looking at me with a bemused expression. We do have the conversation I have thought about all day but it begins with another train of thought I've also focused on.

"Darling, are you excited for our first anniversary?" Leo asks.

"Uh... yeeees...?" I answer with hesitation.

"Me too," he says. "I've got the perfect paper gift for you. Just wait."

Before I can respond he plunges forward:

"I thought we said you were gonna ask permission to come. I went to look something up on your phone last night and saw the... ahem... 'site' you were on. Did you masturbate yesterday?"

I blush deeply. We've never talked much about self-love other than when I first described *The Sex Slave* to him and admitted to that fantasy while taking care of myself. We have just always assumed the other did it privately and that was that. I guess in our new lives secrets like this are secrets no longer. It will take some getting used to.

"Yes," I mumble.

"Do you think you should be punished for that?" Leo asks.

"What's in the bag?" I throw back at him. I mean, a girl needs to know what she's up against, right? A bright smile crosses his face before he can contain it.

"Never mind that. I asked you a question and I expect an honest answer. Answer me Chlo. Do you think you should be punished?" Leo states firmly, while keeping my chin up to meet his eyes. Locked stare, I feel something build inside me.

I am no spineless woman. I am strong. I enjoy serving him but I refuse to shut my mouth and be seen but not heard.

"No," I spew with certainty. "No, I don't feel like I should be punished. I mean, sure I have been asking permission. But it was never discussed about, you know, when I'm alone. I didn't know. If that is what you had expected you should've said that. Specifically speaking."

I watch his face register this speech I've subconsciously come up with over the course of the day. I finish, he pauses, and then bursts out in laughter.

Wait. Do Dominants laugh? Can we be silly and serious at the same time? I join in, tittering nervously.

Once calm he says, "Ok. You're right. Come here." His arms motion me into their embrace.

I hop off my knees, stretching out a little bit and curl up in his lap. I tuck my head into the crook of his neck and feel his hot breath in my ear.

"Technicality, my love. Let me say it clearly now. I want you to ask permission to come from now on even when you're alone. If you want to get off and I'm not here, call me. Text me. I want to know. Understand?"

I nod my head under his, affirming both my understanding and compliance. Again, he whispers in my ear.

"Now lay down over my lap. You better not have any underwear on."

***

I look to him. "Wha... what are you going to do?" I ask tensely.

He raises an eyebrow and asks back gently, "Do you really want to know?"

I don't want to know exactly; not knowing is part of the thrill. I answer by simply sliding across his lap and bending over it, feet above the floor and face in the air, hanging like a rag doll. Blood rushes to my head. Leo uses his strong hands to adjust me, perching me further forward. My ass is directly on his lap.

He lifts up my nightgown and rubs a hand over my bare behind. He reaches down and touches my clean gash. He slowly diddles my clit, moving in light circles. His growth beneath me hardens and the arousal gets me damp. He stops and goes back to rubbing my cheeks again.

I tense, expecting a spanking, and find myself tensed for no reason. Instead he asks me a question that sets my other cheeks on fire.

"So. Chloe. What did you masturbate to yesterday?"

I cannot imagine being more uncomfortable. I am bare-assed and have nowhere to hide. So vulnerable.

I stutter it out and even this is hard for me: "P-porn?"

Smack! The spanking comes down now that I am not expecting it. It wasn't too hard though and brings a pleasurable tingle across my bum.

"Ah, smart girl. Taking the easy way out. Try again, specifically speaking this time." Leo directs with a smile in his voice, rubbing circles on my exposed butt while I squirm.

Oh fuck. Did he see exactly what I watched? Why didn't I clear my history? Has he done this before? I can feel his anticipation and give what I can manage to mutter: "Anal."

Hard *swat*. This time it stings closer to pain.

"Ow!" leaves my lips and tears well in my eyes.

In hearing me say it his manhood twitches with excitement underneath me. A broad hand moves over my entire crack, fingertips down near my clit, palm stretching across my opening, and his thumb presses at my anus. My breath speeds up as Leo is introducing himself to an area that has been for the most part forbidden. Apparently not much longer. His thumb puts pressure down over that hole and makes me hold my breath in wait. Horrifically, in want.

"Tell me specifically, now. What did you type in? What did you get off to? What did you seek out?" Leo demands.

I hate it but tears spill over. How did we ever get to be married with child and still so damn embarrassed at having a conversation about sex? I am though; I'm mortified. I feel like the dirtiest whore in the world as I whisper into the dimly lit bedroom, "Anal slut."

Sniffle. He reaches with his other hand down to the back of my neck and pins me; I am almost in an exact "V" over his knees.

One hand holds me down and the other works at my exposed pussy, fingering me, warming me up, stretching me out, puffing up my clit. Leo leaves my other hole alone. I lose my shame in my sexuality and am overtaken by him. Using three fingers in and out of me, I begin to moan. He increases the speed and allows me to come.

I do, feeling the heat squirt out of me, creating a puddle between the two of us. The euphoria is calming me when his hand leaves my sex and grabs the brown bag.

I lift up to look at what he is getting and he holds me in place, saying only, "No."

I flop down and when he trusts I am not lifting up again I hear more shuffling in the bag. Leo moves his other hand off my back. I close my eyes and enjoy the post-orgasm glow. Until I feel something being inserted in my rear passage. Then I freak out.

Leo and I have tried this before. Drunken, late-night spontaneous attempts at anal sex and the searing pain immediately stopping us. We've given up hope. Certain that anal sex is off the table, I enjoy watching it and getting off to the idea. The unattainable aspect was so hot. Now the unattainable is supposed to become reality? Nope. Nuh-uh. I do my best to squirm off his lap; he does his best with one arm to pin me in place, shushing me.

"Shhh darlin, it's ok. It's just me, it's ok."

Partly because of his comfort and partly because of his being physically stronger than me I force myself to go back to the position. I breathe deep, heart speeding up, knowing I am in good hands. Tears well up again and I can't identify if they are tears of fear or of the sweet release of surrender. Probably a little bit of both.

He rubs his free hand over my back and moans quietly, "Good girl, Chloe. Good job. I'm proud of you. Listen up. If you want me to slow down, what do you say?"

"Yellow," I mutter, sounding defeated already.

"And to stop? I want to hear you say it out loud now, to know it's on your lips if you want it," Leo asks in a gentle tone, still caressing my back.

Sighing, sounding like the saddest word in the world leaving my lips: "Red."

"Are you saying red now?" he asks clearly.

There is my choice in this matter. I have already made it this far so I simply say, "No."

Smack! Stinging heat spreads across my butt cheeks and I stammer, "No, Sir."

Leo is done talking. One hand rubbing my smooth back and the other is holding something, a plug or a dildo or something.

There it is again, up against my other hole. It feels wrong, only in that all of my life nothing has been inserted there. It is a small point and Leo moves slowly. He inserts the object a half inch and pauses, allowing my body to adjust.

Then a half inch again. Pause. Push. Pause. I feel "it" increasing in diameter, stretching me out while filling me deeper. I feel invaded. Helpless. The word is there on my lips; I am glad Leo made me say it before starting.

I keep mum and he continues to stretch me out. There is fear there: of mess, of dirtiness, of failing. I do my best to get rid of the "what-ifs" and only feel. What I feel is the pain beginning. It is a stretching fire and I cry out.

I lay there and work through it while I am lubed up more and given a moment to adjust. I focus on anything else: my breathing, the light coming from the bathroom, the smell of my sex in the air. Anything to avoid the pain.

Until he moves again. This time slowly and continuously.

I am breathing deeply like in yoga. I am able to feign mind over body, pushing past the pain and accepting this. The increase in diameter increases the pain but also the pleasure and the desire for more.

It fills me up entirely and there is a release of the searing sensation and it is simply "up there." A small base is holding what I can now surmise is an anal plug (larger than I would have chosen if it had been me from the feel of it) and it feels... phenomenal. I am filled up in a new way and it has me grinding my hips against Leo's lap.

He uses his hands to pull me up into a standing position for the first time since we began and the plug shifts inside of me. It feels stimulating as it plays with my insides. The walls inside my vagina push together in a tighter way than normal. I look at Leo with a giant grin on my face; he is smiling wide too.

He says, "Go get me a wet towel for my hands."

My face shifts from happiness to horror.

"I can't walk!" I squeak.

***

Mr. Donnovan laughs at me and insists, "Sure you can. Towel. Now."

I give a pouting and sarcastic, "Yes, Sir. Your wish is my command."

I squeeze my butt cheeks together and tip toe awkwardly towards the connected bathroom. It feels awkward and sexy at the same time. He snorts behind me and once I arrive back, handing him a warm, soapy hand towel as ceremoniously as possible, he directs me, "Sit."

Hesitating, I slowly move my full buttocks towards the mattress in the empty spot next to him. The pressure increases and my nipples harden.

Leo leans forward and kisses my forehead, beard scratching my nose. I rub the spot while I watch him get up, cross the bedroom to the closet, and return with two clothespins.

Standing in front of me, where I sit with my new plug drilling me, Leo pinches my nipple tight, twists, pinches harder, twists painfully again, and clamps the teeth of the wooden pin across my areola. I inhale sharply and deeply, feeling an instant connection between the pain flaming across my chest and my hungry cunt. It is as if the two are meant to be experienced together.

He bends over and kisses the top of my head, murmuring, "Nice Chlo, very nice."

I flush with pride as he pulls my next breast out and repeats. Again, the pleasure flows to my genitals. I am aroused all over but feel empty where it counts. I reach to unzip my husband's pants and stop, realizing I am not in charge. My hands hesitate mid-air and I promptly lay them back in my lap.

I look up at Leo, feeling horny and naughty, and while I stare into his eyes I open my mouth. Wide. It's a gesture; an offering to him. He accepts.

I watch my husband as he slips his belt out of the belt loops, the sound of the sliding and slipping leather adding to my excitement. He unbuttons and unzips his slacks and in one swoop, his lower half is bare and his dick springs out, straight as an arrow and rock hard. Mouth still open as far as I can get it, the only thing I move is my eyebrows, asking him without speaking to take advantage of my oral skills.

He hesitates no more; I devour him.

As I slurp up his hardness, I begin to bounce up and down just the slightest and for the first time in my life I feel I am experiencing anal sex.

Before I can even begin to enjoy sucking on my husband, he pulls out of my throat and a moan of regret escapes my lips. He yanks me off the edge of the bed and flips me around doggy style. Without hesitation, he plunges into my cream.

"Ahhhh... fu-uu-uuck..." is all I can coherently moan.

The thin wall separating my two main holes is being stretched thin. Not only is Leo at a steady and swift pace pounding my pussy, he is keeping equal rhythm by pressing the back end of my plug harder into my rear. I have never been double penetrated and it only takes a minute of the fullness to start to beg:

"Puhh-lease Leo, may I come, puh-uh-uh-leeeease!"

"No, you better not. Not yet. Unnn-uuuhhhh." He hoarsely answers.

It takes every bit of focus I have to prevent my release. Breathing heavily, I continue being taken. Distract, distract, distract. Don't come. Stay focused for him. For Leo. Do as he commands and be rewarded. Go against him and be punished. It's becoming ingrained now.

Pound, pound, pound. I feel like I am being split in two from behind; my knees get wobbly from the intensity of the fucking. The intensity of his dominance.

I am not his wife right now; I am his anal slut, just like I had sought out. I build to my peak again and his hand reaches down to my bottom and the strange object there. He grasps the base in his fist and begins slowly pulling it out of me, the bulbous end stretching my hole.

Leo rips it out of me and plunges his cock there instead. I back up to him, taking his size with ease now.

"Come."

I do. I let go of the control I have been using to prevent my orgasm and it spills out of me now. Leo is coming too, holding himself as deep in as possible and filling me up. We are a sopping mess of mingling juices flowing down my leg. For what feels like an eternity, long after he finished squirting inside me, I feel the come roll out of me.

I have wetness covering every inch of my thighs, calves, and feet.

He finally breaks the bond and empties the man out of me. I collapse in a heap of submissive woman onto my knees at his feet, feeling wet floor underneath me and an aching emptiness inside of me.

There at his feet after accomplishing the impossible together: I would have done anything in the world for Leo Donnovan. His command would be mine. I keep that knowledge hidden in my heart, afraid of what it may mean to us. The feeling will haunt me for months to come. I'd risk about anything to keep this in my life. Maybe even risk forgiving.

Chapter Nine

Paper Anniversary

T he following weekend ushers in our anniversary. Leo has two days off and we putz around lazily the first morning. I set Emily in her walker and she scoots around the kitchen while I swap the tiny dishwasher from clean to dirty in between frying bacon. I flip on some tunes and sashay while keeping house. Leo is off... somewhere. Getting ready for the day perhaps?

I've begun to see my daily tasks as a thank you to my husband for providing for us financially and find new joy in doing chores with purpose. I fix Leo's eggs in his favorite style, making sure when I butter his toast not to get any on the crust because he hates his hands messy from eating, and when I squeeze a slice of lemon into his ice water I take the time to grab a spoon and fish out the seeds that fall into his glass. They're simple gestures and don't take much more time or effort but I feel like I am showing him respect.

"Happy anniversary, my love!"

I turn towards the door as Emily rolls over to her father. He is standing there freshly showered holding two dozen white roses. My favorite. I move to smell them (and him) and give him a kiss hello.

"Well thank ya mister, they're stunning. Happy anniversary to you too." I move to toss last week's pink roses that are wilting and replace them with the fresh ones.

"But you know you can just get me a dozen roses now. I don't work and there's really no need."

Leo picks up our girl and carries her over to me. He kisses me on the forehead, then meets my twinkling eyes with a serious stare and says:

"You work Chloe, you have the hardest job I can imagine. You're a wonderful mother to my daughter and no amount of flowers could show my thanks for taking such good care of her. Now. Where's my bacon?"

He winks and sits down with Em at the table. We small talk about life over breakfast: Leo's work and interesting clients, the satisfaction in his career that mirrors my newfound satisfaction in homemaking, the weather, our anniversary dinner later, my new mommy friends from a playgroup I've joined.

We laugh and ask questions and for just a moment we are the old us again, best friends, nothing so serious, playful, enjoying being each other's confidant first. I make a mental note to remember this unimportant moment and the lesson that lives here.

We don't always have to be "on." Living as Dominant and submissive isn't about living naked and on your knees and awaiting direction all the time. It's just two people, in a relationship, living the ebb and flow of daily life. It's life with the knowledge that the Dominant is in control of the decisions. Simple as that. Something seeming so big is actually quite basic. Regular life, only with power exchanged.

I move to clear the plates but Leo says he will instead; tells me to go pack up a diaper bag for the day.

I ask him where we are going and he smiles instead of answering. I roll my eyes as I leave the room with Emily to count out diapers and burp cloths and changes of clothing and pacifiers and toy keys.

When we meet at the door I blush and realize my all too common mistake: "Ahh shit Leo, look at me."

I realize that I am still in sweats with never-brushed hair from sleeping. I have gotten rid of all of my maternity stuff like I had promised myself but I have to be comfy sometimes, right? How could I have forgotten to change? Sigh. I can be so absent minded sometimes.

He looks me over, trying and failing not to laugh; he points to my head, saying, "Ponytail" and then to my lower half saying, "Yoga pants."

I dash off while Leo and Emily head out to cool down the car. Once we all gather again, we drive off the thin strip of land surrounded by water where our beach house sits and head into the actual city.

I relax and relish in the happiness that is Leo being in charge. No petty bickering like before: the constant, "Well, I don't care what we do, what do you want to do today?" and "I don't care either, whatever you want."

We pull into a local department store and I perk up. Oh my goodness. I hope we are going shopping. Are we going shopping? I love shopping. We walk inside and I smell the newness, smiling dreamily.

I push Emily absentmindedly in the stroller, following my husband as he walks straight to the... linens department register?

Ok what is he up to?

The sales lady picks up a phone and calls somebody. Leo walks back to his girls and I ask him, teasingly, "What the hell, Sir?"

"You'll see," is the only response I get back and he places a hand into the small of my back and leads me through the bright fluorescent light and smelling just sampled perfume.

I see a stylish young woman headed towards us at a brisk clip and like most mommies I push the stroller over to the side of the aisle to make room. The woman slows as she gets closer though and stops in front of us.

"Mr. Donnovan?" she asks, extending her arm to shake with Leo.

Leo does and confirms, "Mandy? Hi, I'm Leo and this is my wife, Chloe, and our daughter Emily."

This "Mandy" shakes my hand and gives the obligatory greeting to Emily; with a giant smile she says, "Follow me, Mr. and Mrs. Donnovan."

She walks away brusquely. I follow with an eyebrow raised, Leo giving a light laugh and a kiss on my forehead, saying with a grin, "Follow her, I guess."

Mandy is halfway through the store and I push the buggy quickly to catch up with the long legged woman in a snazzy peach suit. Reaching the women's section we slow down, walking into a small room just off of the fitting rooms. Mandy puts her bottom on the edge of a desk and says to Leo, "Ok sir, tell me a bit more of what you're looking for today. You said on the phone you're looking for a new wardrobe for your wife. Let's talk about what exactly she needs."

My jaw can do nothing but drop to the floor. I am flattered but uncomfortable; so thought of but ashamed it came to this. Tears well up as the woman (obviously now a personal shopper) and my husband talk about me in front of me.

"Mandy as you can see my wife is a stunning young new mother who needs a little... er... 'help.' She wears gym clothes everywhere and needs new casual wear. Show her clothes that are appropriate for her new body and her new job at home."

Leo pauses and glances at me as a big fat tear spills over my cheek. He's shocked and asks the woman to excuse us. I can finally cry. I cover my face in shame.

To his credit the mister doesn't miss a beat. My thoughtful husband reaches in the diaper bag to find her toy keys and hands them to Emily in the stroller, and then embraces me.

I tuck my messy head into the nook of his shoulder and hold tight. He whispers, "Darlin, this is supposed to be a good thing-"

"It is-" I sob and he shushes me quiet.

"I'm here with you. I want to help you be everything you can be, to be comfortable in your skin. Just trust me on this. Can you trust me?"

There is that question again. Can I trust Leo Donnovan?

I sigh out, "OK," with my bottom lip trembling.

I hurl my apology as fast as I can:

"Leo I am so sorry I have let myself go if that is why you sought out somebody else I am sorry I brought you to that and I understand that I have not been very sexy for some time now-"

His voice stops me with an edge as sharp as a knife, "Stop. Chloe. Don't you fucking dare, don't you ever blame what I did on yourself. Never again. This isn't about that. This is about me allowing you to become who you want to be. Find some clothes you enjoy, clothes that make you feel as sexy as I see you. That's it. Just clothes. This is supposed to be an enjoyable thing. Together. I'll be right here, Chloe, right by your side."

Once composed I look up to him and say, more sure this time, "Ok. Let's do this. I... I trust you."

He kisses me on the lips this time and I taste my tears.

Leo goes to find the personal shopper and I smile at Emily to lift my spirits. I hear Leo through the open door, "I like her in dresses or skirts, whichever she prefers. Cool colors, particularly purple, make her eyes stand out. She always wants to wear black. She gets one black dress, no more. I want her in color, bright, like her. She is a bit of a... I dunno... hippie. Flowy things. She needs undergarments, both nice and day to day things. Accessories, like shoes and whatever else. And tonight is our first anniversary. She needs a fancy dress. Let her surprise me. I'll be here with the baby and I want to see what she's trying on."

Leo walks back in the shoebox of an office looking like a modern day prince offering his hand delicately to mine. I kiss Emily good-bye and give him my hand to lead me, feeling more like a lady than my mussed hair and too big clothes should allow.

***

Mandy takes me through the store and we look at everything. I point out garments that I think are stylish; she suggests things that land in the fitting room regardless of my opinion. We get into a pretty good routine.

The personal shopper hands me bundles of clothes to try and I put each piece on and walk out for Leo to see. He sits on the couch in the waiting room with Emily who keeps him company while watching. Each new garment he'll advise on: shakes his head no, nods yes, or says things like, "I liked the other long grey skirt better" or "hem it a few inches" or just "wow." It does become fun (though exhausting) and at the end I really do have a brand new, beachy, bohemian chic wardrobe. Accessories included.

Garment bags in tow, I hug Mandy good-bye but Leo surprises me again by halting at the designer makeup counter. A made up woman loads me up with tips and tricks and more tubes and bottles and sticks and brushes and wands than I can probably use in my lifetime.

I am hungry and exhausted but joyous. Despite all of the newly purchased items hung in the back of our car, the elation comes from being with Leo; being under his direction all day. After a quick lunch together at a nearby diner he makes a last stop in front of a local beauty salon known for pampering the pickiest of tourists. Putting the car in park, he looks across at me and says, "I'll be back at six. I'll drop off Emily at your mother's, go home to shower and get ready, grab your gift. Just give them your name here; it's all paid for."

I look around the area and see a place that can help me with the gift I'm giving.

"Can you make it six thirty instead?" I ask.

He responds with a nod and a deep kiss. I get out, grab the new dress, shoes, and makeup for tonight, and wave my family good-bye until they're out of view. I go inside and give my name and the miracle workers do my hair and nails the way Leo must've instructed them when making the appointment. They even take my new make-up and do my face for me. When the chatty spa girls spin me around at the end of the appointment I barely recognize myself. Hair extensions bring my now thick hair just past my bra line and I am blonde. Like, blonde-blonde. White blonde. I look like a bombshell.

I go to the massage room to put on my new clothes. The dress is a rich purple, the color of royalty, in a light silk that makes me feel vivacious. It stops an inch above my knee and the front is a square neck, modestly placed. But the back. Oh boy, the back. The silk scoops down in an arc three quarters of the way to my bottom, showing off my tan skin from the past summer and adding a sexy surprise to an otherwise simple cocktail dress. I pair it with the chosen accessories and nude heels as directed by my personal shopper and I am ready.

I walk over to the office supply store I spotted earlier to finish up Leo's paper gift, beginning to get nervous about it now. I can't help but notice several double takes from men in the store. I have never had hair this long before and certainly never this blonde. I feel glamorous.

When Leo picks me up as guaranteed I watch him stare as I approach the door he is holding open for me. All he manages when I get close to him is:

"Oh-holy-shit."

Now that, ladies and gentlemen, is a compliment.

***

I spend the half hour ride trying not to crumple my purple dress and reminiscing. One year ago, I married my husband in Las Vegas, Nevada, filled up with impulse and hope. Our daughter was turning around inside my belly and halfway through our vows the mister choked up with emotion.

Oddly enough I am not thinking of our wedding but instead our first date long ago.

Phoenix, Arizona. I remember clearly a certain Mr. Leo Donnovan walking up to me at my desk that morning to exchange pleasantries. We had begun to notice each other about a month prior and it's getting friendlier with every interaction.

You know how it goes. Two people meet and a spark is created. Amongst a sea of strangers you have a connection with that one. Each time you glance around the room you check to see if they are looking your way. Sometimes they are and you smile, looking away as fast as possible.

When he approaches my desk I sense him before I look to him, smelling his sandalwood aftershave and confidence. I feel like I'm glowing.

Once I started noticing him and noticing him noticing me, I put more effort into my appearance before dragging myself into the office in hopes of crossing paths. I search my closet each day for something remarkable, actually blow dry my hair, daydream about the strange man in a suit on a motorcycle that sends electricity through me when our hands briefly touch.

So this day, our to-be-first-date day, I am dressed to impress. I can still close my eyes and picture us.

I am in a cyan cotton blouse, cuffed and collared in pressed white linen. Matching knee length white linen skirt and rope wedges complete the look. I felt like a cool breeze in the desert warmth.

Leo arrives at my desk with a day's worth of facial hair scruff, no suit coat or tie, and the sleeves of his starched dress shirt rolled up. He looks more haggard than usual. Tired somehow. I wonder (not for the first time) about his personal life. Does he have siblings? A roommate? A girlfriend? Where does he live? What does he smell like when he wakes up in the morning after a passionate night of lovemaking?

Oh the horror: I am daydreaming about a man in front of the man who has obviously asked me a question. Now he's waiting for an answer.

I have to say, "Excuse me, Mr. Donnovan, I'm sorry, could you repeat that?"

I force myself to pay attention instead of getting lost in his hazel eyes that look almost army greenish today. I expect him to correct me and insist I call him by his first name like most young professionals do, but nope. The man gives me a look that indicates he thinks I'm being quirky (which, of course, I actually am) and Leo repeats his question with a half grin, "Miss Larchmont, I came to ask you to dinner tonight. I've had a trying few days and would like some company and a hot meal."

I titter a little bit at his formality but when I realize he's entirely serious I flush and answer, "Sure. Where?"

He gave me the name of a pizza joint on Bell Road and his phone number, "In case you should find yourself in need of it."

When he walks away I dash to the ladies room to give a quiet little squeal of delight and spin in a quick circle of happy dance.

The hours tick by slowly as end of the day is approaching. I gather my things and take the time to freshen my appearance before heading to the restaurant, stomach fluttering and empty.

A curious thing happens. I walk to my small compact car and Leo is sitting in his silver sports car he drives sometimes in lieu of the bike he frequents just sitting and talking on his phone. He pays me no mind but as I start my car and pull out, he follows suit. I follow the directions to the restaurant and watch Leo in my rearview mirror behind me.

I change lanes, he changes lanes. I brake, he brakes. Once we get there he parks directly next to me, hops out, circles his car, and by the time I shut off the ignition and grab my purse, he has my driver's door open and a hand extended to help me out.

I grab it and find myself standing about two inches from this strange man, too mature for his age, and I can feel the pull between us like two magnets finally facing the right side of each other. I stand in his masculine presence and ask teasingly, "Were you following me, Mr. Donnovan?"

He smiles lightly, his wide, pink lips a stark contrast to his dark, trim goatee, "Yes, I was."

"Why?" I can't help but ask.

He cocks his head to the side like it is an awfully strange question and responds, "I wanted to be sure you arrived safely."

Raising an eyebrow, I step to the side as he closes my door and places his hand on my lower back to escort me inside the restaurant (igniting that spark again as we touch), pulling the heavy wooden door open for me.

Huh, I guess chivalry isn't dead, is all I can think.

***

We dine. Well, let's be honest. Leo eats. I talk. My single piece of pizza that I cut up into small pieces is mostly there at the end of the night but my vodka martini is drained.

Leo asks me really smart questions in a way that makes me feel interesting instead of pressured. He absorbs everything and I feel like the only person in the room. When it comes time to leave (he nabs the bill of course but after arriving with such courtesy I hadn't really expected him to allow me to pay) I look up and am surprised to see the dinner crowd emptied out and the dark night sky speckled with the stars instead of blazing sun. When had that happened?

I go to my car, unlocking it on the way with my fob. Leo gets there first and opens the door for me. When I turn to thank him for a nice night, I find myself just where I was earlier. A few inches from his face and this time, he lowers down to meet his lips to mine.

It's a closed mouth kiss, polite but connected, his incredibly soft lips on mine. It leaves me wanting more than a kiss ever has before. The still strange gentleman looks in my eyes and brushes my hair behind my ear. For the first time I hear my name upon his lips and it sounds angelic:

"Chloe. I'll leave first and if you're interested, follow behind me. You can visit my home, have a drink with me. I'd like that very much. If not, that's fine too and a good night to you darling."

I shiver at the directive. The ball is in my court. The good girl in me is screaming *goooo hoooome!* But my loins are begging with every cell to follow the curious Mr. Donnovan to his home.

I fold in my seat, he closes my door, and our cars both start next to each other. I flip my headlights on, illuminating his car as he pulls out and heads to the driveway to lead him onto Bell Road. He turns on his right blinker, showing me my choice, and I pull up behind him.

He waits until traffic clears and heads east. I react in fear. Fear of what? I still don't know. Fear of how badly I want this stranger.

Fear of being seen in a certain way for going back to his place the first night. Fear of being led; of what kind of woman I would be if I followed his lead.

I turn left and head westbound. I look in the rearview mirror and hope for his brake lights to flash. They don't. Of course they don't. Leo Donnovan isn't the type to second guess himself.

Crap. I think I made the wrong choice. I should have followed. What the hell am I doing? What am I so afraid of?

As soon as I get the chance I burst into the left turn lane and flip a U-turn. I speed down Bell Road, saying an apology to the god that controls traffic cops and street lights and look for that silver sports car containing a magnet I am helplessly drawn towards.

It's nowhere. He's gone. My stomach drops.

I pull into a gas station and park in the lights of the pumps, disappointed. I reach in my purse to grab my wallet, readying to head inside and grab a drink for the ride home and a post-it sticks to my hand. I pull it out and recognize my company logo on the top in blue print. Handwritten is Leo Donnovan's phone number.

I stare at it for only a moment knowing I will chicken out if I wait and grab my phone. Dialing, heart hammering, trying in the brief silence to plan what exactly I will say, I hear a ring once, twice, thre-

"Leo Donnovan" booms through, obviously not recognizing my number. I go speechless.

He asks quietly, "Chloe?"

Hearing him say my name breaks my silence.

"Leo?" I barely manage to squeak out.

"Are you OK?" Leo asks curiously.

"I... I... um... I think I... ah... *Ithinkturnedthewrongway*," I rush out in one breath.

"Where are you?" he demands.

"Um... at a gas station? On Bell Road? I tried to find you..." The words drift away; I'm shocked by the weight of them in my voice.

"Give me the name of the gas station. I'm coming for you." I hear him say over the increase in purr as his smooth engine revs higher.

Looking around I give him the information and sit there with the phone at my ear in silence, both of us still on the line but neither of us speaking.

Five minutes later I see his car pull into the lot and he pulls around the back in a half circle, leading him to the exit pointing back out to Bell Road and turns his signal on, directing east again. He breaks the silence between us with only two words: "Follow me."

This time, I do.

***

I look into the vanity mirror while riding to my anniversary dinner many years later. Many dates later. Many tears later. Taking one last look at this woman transformed I grab the legal sized manila envelope that contains my anniversary gift and accept the hand of

Mr. Leo Donnovan at the passenger door waiting to lead me inside the restaurant. He stands in front of me like on that first date, still a magnet, still with that pull. He presses in close to me and whispers:

"Mrs. Donnovan. I never thought I would see you look more beautiful than you did walking down the aisle on our wedding day. But damn Chloe. You may have just gotten yourself *beat*."

The double entendre rings out to both of us and the thought of myself being "beat" via a riding crop across my silk-draped backside makes me simultaneously blush and laugh. The mister puts his hand on my lower back and directs me inside, a wrapped box I hadn't noticed in his other hand.

He says casually, "I don't know what you have in that envelope lil darlin but I bet my gift is better. In fact, I'd put money on it."

Laughing, I teasingly remind him, "Right. I don't work anymore, remember? Sure, I'll bet you with your money against your money. But that doesn't even matter Sir because nothing in that box can compare to the gift contained in this envelope."

Leo declined to participate in my goading, instead pulling me close to him who is also dressed to the nines in a modern style black suit, white shirt, and golden tie, smelling fresh and clean and familiar. He kisses me gently and pulls back.

"You really do look beautiful, my wife. I love you."

When I say, "I love you too," I mean it.

We head inside to our very first and maybe only anniversary celebration.

***

God I wish I had a camera to record the look on Leo's face. No matter the destiny of our relationship, how old I become, or where life takes me, I will never forget Mr. Donnovan's reaction right now.

We're at a table that was an hour ago set in the most proper fashion for a multi-course fine dining experience. Now all that is left is the memory of sumptuous cuisine made by the top rated chef in town and the silver is set for coffee and dessert.

Leo looks at me over the paper envelope containing six sheets of printed paper stapled together. I have entirely shocked my husband.

"When did you have time to do this?" he wonders incredulously, eyes moving over the first page so fast I am wondering if he's even reading.

I fidget nervously. My heart is racing. My hands are shaking a bit. Maybe not my entire life but certainly the next six months are about to change drastically.

I answer in the calmest voice I can bear, "You know. I get stuff done."

He looks to me and sees me and stares as if I am a creature he's never encountered. Keep cool, Chloe. Keep it together. He looks back down and now he's really reading.

When the waiter in his serving tux arrives at the table to ask Leo a question Leo simply puts his hand in the air with pointer finger extended in a sign of "just a moment," not able to draw his eyes from the sheets.

The server stops mid-breath and looks at me strangely. I smile wide, afraid if I speak aloud at this exact moment I will heave up my dinner and shrug my shoulders to dismiss his service at the table.

He reads and flips between the pages for ten minutes before looking up. He seems shaken; unnerved. It is an uncommon look for him and it's endearing. It's nice to know he is as serious and possibly as nervous as I am.

He holds up the pages and asks with eyebrows up and his voice deep, "Are you sure this is what you want Chloe?"

I respond so much calmer than I feel, "Yes. Yes... Sir. I'm sure. I've spent a lot of time considering just that question."

Leo asks another question with the same severity, "And the date you have written at the end? Not exactly six months from today, is it?"

Shit. How did he notice that smallest of detail? I answer honestly because he'll expect it, because he deserves it, because brutal honesty is about to become the absolute norm. I say it as gently as I can.

"Leo, that date is the date we are supposed to meet on the beach. It's one year from... well... you know... when we are supposed to decide to make it work or not. The rest of that *(I wave my hands at the pages still in his hand)* won't matter if we aren't, ya know, together."

The server brings a decadent looking crème brûlée with berries and two cups of hot coffee and sets it in front of us. We sit in silence.

Leo considers the gift. Almost exactly six months. The entire remainder of our relationship possibly. Is this how he wants to spend it? Will he even sign? He stares at me, the woman who turned her car around and followed him home so many years ago. He pulls a pen from the inside of his pitch-black suit coat, flips to the last page, and signs and dates with the flourish of a man who spends all day signing contracts.

When he looks up, any trace of indecision is gone. My new Dominant is dark and solid, exuding confidence. Without moving his eyes from mine, he hands the papers across the table and I take them.

Leo demands, "Read it."

I answer quietly, "Sir, I wrote it-"

"Read. It. Again."

His growl makes my hands begin to visibly shake. I wonder if I really know what I am doing after all and with that doubt in my heart I put my head down and read.

24/7 Dominant/submissive Contract

I, Chloe Donnovan, with a free mind and open heart request of Leo Donnovan that he accept the submission of my will unto him. I ask that as my Dominant, Leo Donnovan takes me into his care and guidance and encourages growth together in love, trust, and mutual respect. It is my desire as a submissive to satisfy his needs and desires whenever possible, in hopes that I will be found pleasing to him. In order to do so, I offer him the use of my body, abilities, and purpose.

Further, I ask that as my Dominant, he will accept the responsibility of using my body for the fulfillment and enhancement of both of our sexual, spiritual, emotional, and intellectual needs. In order to achieve this, he has unrestricted use of my body any time, any place, and in front of anyone as he determines appropriate.

As a Dominant, Mr. Donnovan may bestow upon me any symbol of ownership, including a collar, as well as any other future marks or tokens he may wish to bestow upon me. Symbols of ownership are to be a visible reminder of status and will be worn with pride.

Section One: Code of Conduct

Duties of Servitude

-Above all, the primary duty of this submissive is to please.

-Personal Duties: Attend to the physical and emotional needs of Mr. Leo Donnovan, behave as his sexual plaything, offer physical comfort, act in obedience, remain honest and loyal, wait on the Dominant as desired.

-Household Duties: Cleaning and maintaining the home, laundry, shopping, all cooking and baking, running all errands as needed. Any task assigned should be considered permanent until further notice. Tasks may be added at any time.

General Behavior

-Attitude: As a submissive, I will show an attitude of respect at all times. Disrespect is a serious offense and will be punished.

-Respect includes: manner of speech, promptness, kneeling to serve (when able), proper answers, obedience, and wholehearted honesty.

-Respect and obedience are the two most valuable aspects of attitude that I will show at all times. Failure to do so will be punished.

Behavior in Private

-I shall address Mr. Donnovan as "Sir" or "Mister" at all available times. I will pay full attention to him when being spoken to.

-My Dominant is more important than any other activity I may be engaged in with the exclusion of immediate child care needs.

-I will sit, stand, walk, kneel, and lay where, when, and how he desires.

Behavior in Public

-I will address my Dominant by his given name or "Mister" at all times when there is not enough privacy to use the aforementioned "Sir."

-I will remain within eyesight of my husband unless permission is given to do otherwise.

-I will be courteous and prompt at all times.

-I will dress as Mr. Donnovan desires. I will do my best to always have a put together appearance in any social setting where I represent my husband.

-I will not argue or complain in public.

Training

-Training activities will include: domestic skills training, offering of self every evening on bended knee, proper answers, orgasm control, anal training to increase my ability to offer every hole as he wishes, learning to present myself as a submissive full of poise, grace, and beauty in public and private, learning protocols and rituals throughout this contract on an as-needed basis; any other training activities as Leo Donnovan deems fit.

Orgasm Control

-I am to achieve orgasm only by express permission of Mr. Leo Donnovan.

-I understand that a submissive's orgasms are controlled for proper training and reminding me that it is with my Dominant's good grace that sexual pleasure is brought, providing motivation, physical and sexual energy. Mr. Donnovan will allow me this reward when he desires.

Punishment

Punishment will be given for the following offenses:

-Cockiness/rudeness

-Disobedience

-Incorrectly addressing Mr. Donnovan

-Failing to properly serve

-Achieving orgasm without consent

-Any other punishable offense as dictated

Forms of Punishment

-Punishments can include: spanking, nipple pinching, cropping, hair pulling, withholding of orgasm, caning, any other punishment as he sees fit.

-Punishments are intended as full and complete penance for offenses. Punishments should always fit the crime, and would be executed with full understanding that once over, the issue is over.

Section Two: Limits of D/s Contract

Limits of submissive

-Hard: Bestiality, pedo play, branding, cutting, injections, scarification, permanent markings (excepting mutually agreed upon tattooing), any toilet play, animal play, catheter use, diaper use, gun play, permanently giving away to another Dominant, infantilism, prostitution, illegal activities.

-Soft: Humiliation, fisting, electricity, temporarily giving away to another Dominant, spitting, slapping.

Safety

Safe words for the duration of the contract will be the same in public and private settings. "Red" will indicate an immediate stop to all activities. "Yellow" will indicate an approach to the limits of play.

Section Three: Submissive's pledge

I will do my best to serve my Mister.

I will work hard to correct any insecurities or inhibitions that interfere with my capability to serve you.

I will grow as a person.

I will maintain honest and open communication.

I will reveal my thoughts, feelings, and desires without fear of judgment or embarrassment.

I will bring you any wants and perceived needs of mine.

I will be the very best mother and homemaker possible.

I will work to repair our marriage.

I will not hold past mistakes against you.

I will do what I can to try and trust again.

My surrender as a submissive is done with the knowledge that nothing asked of me will demean me as a person and in no way diminish my own responsibilities towards making the utmost use of my potential.

In recognition of my family obligations, I know nothing will be required of me that will in any way damage or harm my child or interfere with the performance of my duties as a mother and as a wife.

This I, Chloe Donnovan, do entreat with lucidity and the realization of what this means, both stated and implied, in the conviction that this offer will be understood in the spirit of faith, caring, esteem, devotion and the love in which it is given.

Should either of us find that our aspirations are not being well served by this agreement, find this commitment too burdensome, or for any other reason wish to cancel, either Mr. or Mrs. Donnovan may do so by verbal notification to the other in keeping with the consensual nature of this contract.

We both understand that cancellation means a cessation to the power exchange dynamic indicated and implied within this agreement, not a termination of the relationship as friends, lovers, and spouses.

Upon cancellation, each of us agrees to offer the other his or her reasons and to assess the new needs and situation openly.

This agreement shall serve as the basis for an extension of our relationship, committed to in the spirit of loving and consensual Dominance and submission with the intention of furthering self-awareness and exploration, promoting health and happiness, and improving both lives.

Section Four: Signatures

This contract is valid from this day of signing until this date _____, and at that it may be renewed or renegotiated if the Dominant and/or submissive is of that interest.

I offer my consent of submission to _____ under the terms state above on this, the _____ day of _____ in the year _____.

X_____

(Signature of submissive)

I offer My acceptance of submission by _____ under the terms stated above on this, the _____ day of _____ in the year _____.

X_____

(Signature of Dominant)

***

Black and white as I had typed it. I've spent countless hours scouring the internet, crafting each word with my intentions; reviewing, rewriting. Now at the bottom it's signed by my husband,

Leo T. Donnovan, followed by his handwriting today's date. Our wedding anniversary.

I keep my head facing the pages, nervous to look up yet, and for the first time that day I really think back to the day we married. We signed a contract that day too. A marriage contract and within months it had been broken.

Leo had been under such immense pressure. A new transfer and work position in Atlanta. Atlanta itself, a city so different from what he was accustomed to. He left behind the only home he ever knew; the desert mountains. Left his friends behind. His family behind. He moved in with me right away and it became so serious so fast; he'd never loved anybody enough to live with them. We bought a house together. Gotten pregnant years before expecting it to happen. I went from pregnant girlfriend to pregnant bride to pregnant stay-at-home mother, saddling him with financial stress and obligation and burden.

Leo Donnovan cracked under the pressure; a rock turning to dust. The man made the abominable mistake of seeking out another person to help sweep up the rubble.

Would this arrangement, this D/s contract and the added responsibility it would add be the death of "us" for good? Could he handle it? I don't really know.

What I do know is that if Leo and Chloe Donnovan are destined to meet with a divorce attorney in six months and negotiate things like co-parenting and child support payments I want this beforehand. I want to submit to him. I want to try and trust again. I want to go out with a bang.

Putting on a brave face I glance across the table to my husband who is staring at me with the intensity that he had stared at the contract. Damn is he menacing. I put out a hand as steady as I can and gesture for his pen. Making no indication that he's giving it to me I lay my extended arm back into my lap covered in new silk. He leans forward and speaks seriously.

"Chloe. Darling. Before you sign. I'd like to add a few things here to this offer of yours. I'd like you to look at me in the eyes and tell me you understand what I'm saying to you."

Without hesitation I lean forward and match his fixed gaze and with the same severity, "I understand. Sir."

"Good. I am going to push you to your limits. Both your physical and mental. Do you understand?" he asks, pausing for reply.

"Yes Sir, I understand." I repeat.

He furthers, "I am finding myself to be quite a sadist. I want to get you alone and make you writhe in pleasure and in pain."

Shiver. I don't know if I am a masochist. Yet I know I can submit to him and I will give him all of my body to experiment and learn. I expected this going in but it's quite different to hear it leaving his lips.

"I understand Sir."

Leo continues, "I will hold you to incredibly high standards. And if you break these standards, I will punish you. Have no doubt."

"I understand, Sir." I rush out. I mean, I am going to try to do my best, what could I possibly be punished over?

"And finally," he says with his eyebrows deepening, "you trust me again for the duration. Not 'try' to. Trust every day, every moment, every decision. If you can't trust in me entirely, I want nothing to do with this. There is no room for negotiation in this matter."

My eyes tear up. Damn it. I mean, I know he's right but the words are salt in a wound. Staring at him, seeing his sorrow reflecting mine, I seal my fate:

"I understand, Sir."

Without breaking my sight, he hands me his pen and smiles, instantly lightening the mood at the table, "Wait until you see the collar I've picked out for you, darlin."

With that, I sign. I am a submissive.

***

Leo looks up and motions across the room for service while taking the contract and putting it away. I relax for the first time in several weeks with my big secret now unveiled and the decision made. The air feels different somehow. Calmer. I am completely free of decisions. I cannot possibly understand the entire consequence of this new way of living but I let go of the concern and look forward to it all. Starting with dessert.

We apologize to the waiter who brings us fresh cups of coffee. Smiling ear to ear still, Leo hands me a spoon and we dig into the brûlée. I can't imagine how life could be sweeter. That is until I spy the not-so-neatly wrapped box sitting on the table.

I've forgotten all about Leo's gift to me in the nerves surrounding mine. I give him a sly look and point at the box with my spoon, blueberry and all.

"Hey, Sir, whatcha got in the box?" I ask with a curious grin.

His smile goes from a beam of light to a more solemn look. He must be realizing that I trumped his gift. I mean, what could he possibly have in that box that could compare with giving him a signed and sealed full-time submissive?

He hands the gift over to me and I take it, setting my silverware down to accept.

I give the package (lighter than I had expected) a shake and feel a minor shift inside. It's been obviously wrapped by him which is strange because he hates doing that task and typically will find a coworker to ask politely for assistance.

I pull off the wrapping and find a thin, simple box that hinges like a holiday clothes box only smaller, about a quarter of the size. I lift open the lid and see white tissue paper covering whatever the gift is. I make the obvious "Oh Leo, you got me tissue paper, thank you!" joke and not getting so much as a hardy-har from him, I lift up the paper to see inside.

This time, it's my face with jaw-dropped shock. I can't breathe.

Leo has to verbally remind me and he does so barely above a whisper, "Breathe, darling."

I'm frozen solid. It is paper, that's for sure. I don't even know what to do with it. Touch it? Take it out? Cover it back up?

I look to Leo and stutter, "H-h-h-how much?"

Quietly he answers, "Twenty thousand."

I lose my breath again. There are two stacks of bills. Hundreds. I can't move to touch them.

"Breathe Chloe." Leo reminds gently again.

With my breath comes the only other question I can process in the moment: "Why?"

Leo explains.

"Chloe, this is your money. It is your freedom; your get out of jail free card. I know you've struggled giving up your job to stay home and all that comes with it. I don't ever want you to feel stuck with me. Not now, not six months from now, not ten years from now. I want you to be with me and- look at me Chloe- stay married to me, because you want that not because you feel like you can't leave for financial reasons. For any reason. Hide it. Invest it. Keep it however, wherever, you want, just save it. As your husband and now as your Dominant, I want you to know that I'll do my very best to keep you. But you can leave. That is your choice. It should buy you-"

"I love you. I love you so much Leo." I interrupt him, throat choking up, blown away by the gift he has just given me. I didn't even know that it was something I needed or wanted until I had it.

"I love you too," he whispers back. "Still wanna make that bet from earlier? You have the money now."

It turns my almost-tears to relieved laughter and I sniffle up and finally put my body back in motion. I fold the gift back together, the power of that much cash sitting in my lap a lovely contradiction to the power I have just given away.

I look up at my striking husband feeling like I have lived through as many emotional swings as courses we have eaten. I give a satisfied sigh and ask Mr. Donnovan, my husband of exactly one year, "Sir, can you take me home please? I want to kneel to you."

Reaching across the table to take my hand: "I thought you'd never ask my love."

***

We sit quietly on the way home listening to low tunes, Leo's thumb drawing circles around the back of my hand he holds tight. The box of cash and the envelope containing our contract are sitting at my bare feet, stripped of the new heels. Cute shoes, certainly. Practical? Not so much.

Upon arrival at the beach house I gather my bag and shoes and "gifts" while Leo comes around to open the door for me yet again.

I step out with arms filled up and Leo pushes me up against the car, the glass window slick on my bare back. We kiss sensually before backing away and his directing me to, "Go ahead."

I walk ahead of him and as we climb the stairs I call out teasingly behind me, "Like the view back there?"

On the tiny wooden porch he answers with a look of consideration. "Yes actually. I like you walking in front of me. I like to see you, what you are doing. Catch you if you fall. Keep doing that. Walk in front of me whenever you can."

I look at him like he's nuts, wondering if this is something he has always wanted or if it's now occurring to him, but it doesn't matter. I do as he says now.

I continue the lighthearted conversation as he gathers his keys out and ask as a joke more than anything, "Should I walk on the left or right, Sir?"

I glide into the opened door as gracefully as I can in a cocktail dress and arms full of stuff, hearing him reply from behind me. "Left. Walk in front, on the left."

Now I laugh hard; I can't help it. At the absurdity of him actually having a preference. At the realization that it is a simple request I can easily accommodate.

Leo helps me unload and hands me my money box, instructing me to go hide it somewhere and meet him back in the living room. I go to our bedroom and do some quick searching for the right place to keep such a serious lump of cash. I know Leo is doing great at his job, selling about a half dozen homes every single month but wow. I wonder if he sold some of his stocks.

It's an incredible relief knowing that I have my own money. I think briefly to that awful day when I discovered his affair and how that being one of the first things I processed: how can I leave when I'm pregnant with no job or income? Never again. He really did give me freedom back moments after I gave it up.

I put the box in my underwear drawer (so obvious I know but I can move it somewhere safer tomorrow) and I brush my teeth, refresh my perfume, and return to my waiting Dominant.

Leo is in the living room, suit coat off, tie off, top of his collar unbuttoned and sleeves rolled up. He looks more like the everyday him, comfortable but still classy. He is leaned up against the back of the loveseat in the center of the room and in his hands is a strip of black leather.

I cross to see what can only be a collar. It's different than the ones we have seen in research. Feminine and strong. Patent leather, black and shiny as a pool of fresh oil, trimmed in a thin strip of black lace across the top and bottom. The shape is different too. The bottom center dips down into a "V" bringing the collar an additional inch lower on the wearer's throat. I will learn in the next few weeks of becoming Leo's submissive that it is called a "posture collar," and it does insist on great posture. In the center lies a silver Celtic heart, with a metal "O" the size of a dime hanging off of it. I consider the possibility of a leash being attached, wondering if that is Leo's intention, and shiver.

If I were a collar, I would be this one. It is me personified. A little bit tough, a little bit frilly. Needing reminding to stand straight because I am worthy of being noticed but hesitant to do so. Wearing my heart where everybody can see it. Delicate. Sexy.

"How did you know?" I ask Leo, confused. When he told me at the restaurant to wait until I saw the collar he'd picked out I assumed it was a thing to come. Not tonight. Had he figured out what I was gifting?

Mr. Donnovan smiles and says, "I didn't. Well, not about tonight. You really surprised me Chloe and that doesn't happen often. But I knew it was coming. I saw the want in your eyes. I saw your pleasure when serving me in the bedroom or out. I will never take advantage of you again darlin. I will continue to earn the trust you gave me tonight. We will have some fun together. Are you ready for a little fun in our lives?"

I think of the work we have done the past months. I run my fingers over the collar for the first time and warm all over at its craftsmanship. It feels like the future.

Smiling at Leo I affirm, "Hell yeah Mister. Let's have some fun together."

With a charming smile back he directs, "Good. Get naked."

I answer in the becoming familiar, "Yes, Sir!" and pull off the soft silk dress, letting it fall into a pool at my feet. I stand naked, bare except my earrings and wedding band. Nothing to cover the flaws. Nothing to hide behind. He is looking at me with the same tenderness and love as he watched me walk down the aisle a year ago.

"Kneel."

I do. I go to one knee first and then the other, knees spread hip width apart and shoulders straight and back, never once leaving his eyes. I know with certainty that this is where I belong; what I have been seeking out since an ordinary school day a decade and a half ago. My body belongs to him. My service to him. My heart, for now, to him.

The air-conditioning and vulnerability of my position is chilling my skin, bringing my nipples to a stiff peak. The air circulates from the vents and I can feel it swirling around my exposed womanhood.

Leo bends at the waist and places the dark as night collar upon my neck, clasping it tight. He plants a kiss on my forehead and steps back to see his wife.

The collar is snug and the dip causes me to lean back a bit, to both straighten my shoulders and drop them away from my ears at the same time, even adjust my spine. The soft backing of the patent leather clenches me and it feels soft and solid like Leo.

I suddenly wish for his hand around my neck, tightening. I am a collared submissive. I am becoming the woman of my fantasies. I am still, simply, me.

Chapter Ten

What Goes Up Must Come Down

The Schedule

6 am - Wake up

6:30 am - Coffee/Bottle

7 am - Breakfast/Leo's Lunch

8 am - Morning Chores*

9 am - Morning Outing*

10 am - Nap

12 pm - Afternoon Outing*

2 pm - Gym

3:30 pm - Afternoon nap

5 pm - Dinner prep

6 pm - Dinner

6:45 pm - Bath time (Leo) Clean kitchen (Chloe)

7:15 pm - Emily bedtime

Monday - Laundry, Linens and Library day

Tuesday - Meal planning and grocery shopping

Wednesday - Play date and pay bills

Thursday/Friday (Leo off)

Saturday - Grandma's morning with Emily/Deep clean

Sunday - Playground and journaling time

It takes about a month living 24/7 as Dominant and submissive to come up with a precise schedule in the household that works for us. It's handwritten and posted on the slightly dented white laminate beach house fridge, and I, Chloe Donnovan, go to look at the note about a half dozen times a day for direction. The schedule creates a motion in my day; a nudge from my Sir even when he's out of the house.

I condense my duties as a wife, my duties as a mother, and my duties as a homemaker into a routine that once we all adjusted it'd be hard to try and veer away.

Don't get me wrong, life happens. I get a flat tire on the van, I take Emily to the pediatrician about a cough, that kind of stuff. But with a firm plan in place I am able to accomplish more than I ever thought I would be able. What the new expectations are in the home boils down to this: Leo is in charge of earning money and the financial well-being of the home. I am in charge of virtually everything else.

I am Leo's cook, his maid, his personal shopper, his errand runner, his secretary, his everything home related. I love every minute of it.

This structure is actually freeing. We can now eliminate a lot of discussions and disagreements that we used to face.

Before power exchange, a common conversation sounded like this:

Person 1: What sounds good for dinner babe?

Person 2: I dunno. Anything. What sounds good to you?

Person 1: I really don't care. That's why I asked you. Chinese?

Person 2: Meh. I had Golden Dragon for lunch today.

Person 1: (sigh) Well if you would have said that, we could have gotten somewhere.

Person 2: (eye roll, and sarcastically) Sooooorry. Let's order a pizza. What do you want on it?

Person 1: I don't care. You pick.

Person 2: (sigh) Well, you know I like pepperoni, but you don't, so why even ask me if...

This happened day in and day out. About everything.

Who is taking the trash out this week? Who's cooking dinner? Who is cleaning from cooking dinner? Who is getting up in the middle of the night when a baby cries? Who is responsible for paying the bills? Who is stopping to grab dry cleaning? It was exhausting. In hindsight, it was a major reason for the break of Chloe and Leo Donnovan's old marriage.

The constant bickering. The never-ending negotiation. The physical and mental drain that comes with complicating everyday tasks; the fallacy of assigning a husband or wife as the "good one" based on accomplishing these secondary tasks.

Since signing the D/s contract we've lived with the burden off of our shoulders. The tasks are assigned. The negotiating is over. For six months or so, the fallen Mr. Donnovan and his darling submissive wife can stop the back-and-forth balancing of scales and instead spend their free time having fun. Enjoying each other.

Here is the above conversation in our D/s household:

Chloe: What sounds good for dinner tonight Sir?

Leo: Chinese. That place down the road we like. What's the name again?

Chloe: Panda Palace?

Leo: Yup. Get cashew chicken, noodles instead of rice, and those little donut things for dessert. Have it here at six fifteen.

Chloe: Consider it done! Did I show you this adorable picture of Em I took at the splash pad yesterday...

Ahhh. So much better. So much easier. Distinct lines. Leo works and makes the decisions. I do everything else.

Now that I have a specific list to do every day, targets to cross off and goals to reach, I am thoroughly enjoying my job that is staying home and caring for my family. After quitting my career I honestly began to see myself as less than those people working in an outside job. I now see that I'm an equal. As we continue our growth in the world of BDSM from the comfort of our home we come across a phrase that will help shape the next half year: 1950's household.

That is who we are outside of the bedroom. June and Ward Cleaver. We are the upper-middle class American dream family, as unassuming as it gets. In front of others we look normal, talk normal, act normal. Discretion is our key. Anonymity is a must.

When the doors close and we come together alone? We are anything but "normal."

***

Leo Donnovan circles me in the entryway of the compact two bedroom beach house as if he is a predator circling his prey. I feel cornered. My eyes stay at the floor. I kneel still as a statue under his pacing view long enough that my knees begin to ache on the tile.

At long last he directs, "Stand."

I do so as gracefully as a woman who spends her days in flip flops being a homemaker can manage in tall stilettos and weak knees. I still can't bear to meet his eyes. I feel his heated body smelling like outside and man come closer to me and the hair on the back of my neck stands up.

Directly in my ear, "You look fucking fantastic. I am gonna wreck you, you pretty little thing. You're gonna wake up tomorrow and ache on the inside."

He slips his tie off his neck and creates a blindfold over my eyes. Glad to be relieved of the headiness of his animalistic presence, I tilt my head up to what would be eye level. He pushes me from behind into the direction of the bedroom; into the den of the lion. Standing steady he strips me of everything except my wedding band and the dark-as-night posture collar. No more frills. I am humbled.

The mister's strong and guiding hands lay me on my back across the bed, still blind, and I hear him go over to his opened toolbox. Aching from my hummingbird-fast heart beat and listening to the sound of the waves, I push all of my available senses and seek him out. Leo, silent, returns and ties me spread eagle to the bed using the nylon rope from the hardware store. My arms and legs are stretched to capacity and tied tight. There is no struggle capable; no avoiding whatever there is to come.

The feeling of fear is roiling in me. My stomach lurching to the point of almost sickness. He puts his hands under my lower half and lifts my bottom, shoving a folded towel under me. He pauses to brush my heated and damp crotch and I instinctual go to throw my legs together like a steel trap.

But of course not. He knew (he always knows) that this would be my reaction so there I lay tied, ankles spread to the full width of the bed. Unable to move my legs a single inch I moan in frustration mixed with arousal and try to relax for what will come. He will give me what I need. Lately he always gives me what I need.

I feel Leo's presence over me. The makeshift blindfold is removed and there he is. My Mister. My husband. My lover. My Dominant.

He knows my body, my soul, my history, my longings. He watches with that half smile as I struggle against my bindings (something about not being able to move really makes a person want to move).

Sir leans down to put his wide lips on mine. His tongue pries open my mouth, somehow moving that shaky feeling from my stomach to my groin. I feel tingly like I always do upon his taste.

Leo gently pulls away and looks into my eyes, "Shhh... darlin... calm yourself."

With those four words I am empowered, shedding the skin of the world and becoming the newer, truer me: the submissive. I let go of my pulls against the rope, fully trusting in Mr. Leo Donnovan. Full trust. This is what I have been seeking.

I stare at his light eyes and muster the voice to say aloud my intention.

"Yes, Sir. Please use me how you will."

Running his fingertips up and down my soft body, drawing a trail of heat with each stroke, he says, "Tonight you will give all of yourself to me, darlin."

Huh? All of me? Leo has conquered all of me, hasn't he? We are smack dab in the middle of anal training. It was just a few nights ago that he pounded my asshole so hard I felt like I was going to faint from the intensity. He has fucked my mouth and my pussy for years now. As my Dominant, he now owns my days and my nights, controls my clothing and my collar. Every orgasm is his. What else could I possibly give him?

I watch nervously as he walks to his tools and pulls out a stingy leather flogger. A gasp escapes my lips at the first strike on my inner thigh.

Swat! My other thigh is stung. He moves around the bed striking up and down my body; I start to mentally fog over. My body becomes numb and accepting while my mind becoming that of a woman submitted.

As I feel less like a person and more of captured prey, I hear my instructions for the night. He announces it into the dimly lit bedroom, still stinging my arms and tits and stomach along the way, working every angle of my bound body:

"Chloe, you have control of your orgasms tonight and feel free to come whenever you want. But know that each time you do I will continue to stretch you open, inserting one more finger into your hole. Finger fucking you until I crack your body open and you will feel my whole fist inside of you. You have control of your orgasms tonight. But I have control of when you can stop."

***

He is pushing my limits. And not just any limit. This limit. Of all the soft limits in our contract how did he know this was both the most terrifying and the most provocative act imaginable to me? I feel my cunt get wet and am instantly afraid that he will judge me for wanting such an act.

I'm so comfortable serving him now. Yet I'm still afraid to be his whore. Why does it bother me to be thought of as a slut? Tears of humiliation well up in my eyes. Raising an eyebrow, as simply stated as possible, I hear my husband say, "This will happen."

And so it begins. My first orgasm rips through me before he even gets a single finger entered. Skin still singing from the lash of the flogger, his soft thumb circling my clit pushes me over the edge and also begins the fulfillment of a fantasy never spoken aloud.

As soon as my clitoral orgasm rips through me, his middle finger plants deep and strokes my g-spot, finger fucking me in a "come hither" motion until I come for the second time. I shout out my gratitude to him as he makes good on his promise, instantly adding a second finger and maintaining speed.

I am helpless to do anything but get back to that point again; ass clenching, stomach tightening, drowning for breath and feeling that earthquake rip through my stretched out body. As a woman who has had orgasms severely restricted for months now I find myself in quite the predicament. I'm so relieved and excited to have the rights to orgasm whenever I want, yet here I lay, terrified to do so.

There is no way he can put his whole fist inside of me. Impossible.

I feel three fingers start to pry open my tight hole and he feels me clench uncomfortably. He takes his left hand and pins my stomach to the bed, keeping my hips from squirming, and he waits like that until my body submits to accept his increasing presence.

Leo meets my eyes and whispers, "Good girl," and in that instant nothing else exists in the world.

He starts moving around in my wetness again, stretching, bringing me back to my brink. As I squirt my drenching female orgasm for the fourth time he takes advantage and adds another digit and there I lay, spread eagle and exposed, four fingers full sounding like a hungry animal: howling and sweating and coming. He lets go of my stomach and I can now buck my hips up to accept him, greedily wanting more; ready to give him all of me just as he had predicted.

In this moment something bizarre happens. I leave myself. I am there, being devoured yet I am not "there." My mind detaches itself from my body and the two exist apart now, one not able to control the other. My body is limp meat; I couldn't prevent myself from having an orgasm again if I tried. A guttural low growl is coming from deep in my throat and I am unable to stop it or change it or reduce it.

Mentally I am hovering outside of myself in a darkness unresponsive. The only thing I can do is feel want. Need. Desire. The pry of his entire fist enters inside of me. A rush of tears run over my cheeks as he makes good on his promise, gaping my slash open and splitting me in two with his whole self.

I cry and come. I come and cry. Every time he moves in and out of me he brings with a gush like has never been seen before in our bed. I hover over the oh-so thin tightrope between absolute pain and absolute pleasure. I hear nothing but the blood rushing in my brain. I feel nothing but his complete dominance over my body. I see nothing but his face, my Mister, who knows me so well.

I continue to uncontrollably orgasm while waiting for his choice on when I will stop and I become Leo Donnovan's perfect, beautiful whore. Gone are any thoughts of humiliation or shame. Only existing is the connection of he and I, Dominant and submissive, power exchanged, fulfilling our needs.

***

His hand brushes my cheek and the first thing I consciously notice is the crust of dried tears on my face. Coming through a haze I cannot tell if I have been asleep or passed out or what exactly. I feel drugged and hung-over and everything aches.

I move to a fetal position and only give a passing thought to my wrists and ankles being free now. I couldn't care less how or when that happened. I remember snippets of being fisted, of being fucked, of teeth clashing in hard kisses and my begging for more.

I hear my voice in my head remembering, "More Sir, pleeeeeease more uhh-ahhhh-more-more-more!" *Cringe.*

Curled up on top of sheets soaked straight through the towel I cover my eyes with one hand and grasp my destroyed vagina with the other and in the darkness I sob and shiver uncontrollably.

Leo consoles me: asking how he can help, enveloping my nakedness with a soft blanket, rubbing me lightly. I don't give a shit about him in the moment. I just need to live in the blackness of my overwhelming reality of being treated like I just was. And I begged for it, I fucking begged for it. I got exactly what I wanted so why the tears? What is wrong with me?

In enters that question, the fear that has hounded me all along since BDSM entered our lives and bedroom: What is wrong with me to want this?

It causes me to lose any grasp on control I have left. I feel sick and helpless. Leo gets off the bed and I slip back into unknowingness.

Five minutes later? Thirty minutes later? I feel Leo lifting me up in his arms and I move my hands to hold him around his neck, feeling like a needy child. He carries me into the bathroom and I slam my eyes shut, not ready for what I see in the mirror. I am already struggling to cope with the all-over stickiness that is his come lingering with mine and the discomfort of my loins and the smell of sex everywhere.

He kisses me lightly on my forehead and lowers me into an almost too hot bath. I hiss inward at the sting and then relish in the comfort as the warmth engulfs my tortured body. I feel like I have been hit by a truck. Or, I think as a smile curls onto my lip, mauled by a lion. I guess that is exactly what happened. Leo presses a cup to those smiling lips and the cool fresh water fills me back up after I have been so emptied out.

My husband pays me back the favor I have given to him many times recently. He bathes me; cleans my stinging skin more gently than I would have assumed possible. I let him tend to me because I am too helpless to do much else and once clean he lets me soak while I hear him changing our sheets to the spare set that I laundered earlier today.

Eventually I'm helped out and wrapped in a fresh towel. The scent of him and our laundry soap helps me smile again as he tucks me into bed, damp and naked, hair soaking, between the crisp sheets.

After feeling a kiss at my temple I barely register the sound of Leo running a shower for himself in the dead of night before I drift off to a dreamless sleep.

***

I awake; the sun is wrong. Fumbling for my phone I let out a gasp of pain. Every inch of me throbs. I fight through the soreness while hearing Leo talk to Emily through the closed bedroom door. I finally get to my phone and see the time. Holy crap. Ten fifteen.

I start to call for Leo but stop to evaluate my body first. I limp into the bathroom and look at myself in the mirror. My hair is a monstrosity of gigantic proportions only achieved by sleeping on wet, untended to extensions.

I grab one of the dozen bands strewn around the beach house and throw my coif into a big sloppy bun atop my head. My body is riddled with tiny bruises all over: by my armpits, my inner and outer thighs, calves, breasts. How am I gonna wear a bathing suit like this? Sighing, I move to the toilet to relieve my bladder.

I am unable to contain the scream of pain that comes. I don't feel cut or torn, it isn't a stinging pain, but I feel swollen and shut and as predicted, destroyed. I hear a gentle knock at the bathroom door and am glad I closed it in the first place.

"Chlo, you ok?" I hear Leo through the thin door dividing us.

Meagerly, "Hey Sir, I'm fine. I'll be out in a minute."

Leo says no more but I can sense him still standing there wanting to check on me, to fix me, to help his wife and encourage me to talk to him. He eventually leaves giving me the privacy I seek. I clean myself up, stifling my groan when wiping, and wash my hands. I brush my teeth and splash the cold water on my face a few times. Looking at myself clearer, into my familiar ocean blue eyes, I see myself for who I am today.

An attractive, kind, smart woman who decided to sign her body over to another human being (a sadist) for training and use. I am conflicted for the first time since bringing this into our lives. Is this who I am? Is this normal? Is there something wrong with me? To want this? To enjoy this? I fight back the prickle of tears and go to the bedroom, dressing in sweat clothes, not bothering with a bra or underwear that would surely press into my soreness.

Taking several deep breaths before opening the door to the rest of the house I plaster on a smile and join my family in the real world ready for the day off to recoup and reflect.

***

"Subspace. Subdrop." Leo says to me a day and a half later.

The words carry a tinge of familiarity but I can't put my finger on exactly what they mean. I've probably come across them in books and research but they don't have a meaning to me. Yet.

"Huh?" I ask, looking across the bed where I am propped up under covers and reading a piece of carefree chick lit that doesn't make mention of Dominants or power exchange or anything BDSM related.

I have continued serving as Leo's submissive but the three of us Donnovans have been homebodies; the mister has been overly gentle and helpful.

I've been thinking about the decision I'll make soon. Once the winter holidays are over our D/s contract and the one year lease on our marriage will be up. What am I going to do? I am utterly clueless.

Over the past two days I have withdrawn inside of myself. I feel too exposed. Too vulnerable. Too... I dunno. Too attached I guess. I'm frightened. Of myself. Of Leo. Of our lifestyle. Of ending our marriage. Of staying in our marriage. Of how good it felt to be devoured the other night. That shit scared me. Bad.

I tab the corner of my library book to save my place and look to Leo. He's sitting shirtless, looking innocent and charming in just his red plaid boxers. He could never hurt me.

Then I remember the ache in my heart that day in Atlanta. Sure he could hurt me. He has in the past. He passes me the tablet from his hands; I browse through the couple of web pages he has opened.

Sure enough here it is in more places than I could ever have the time to look over. What I experienced the other night is sometimes referred to as "subspace." It's the result of a body becoming so overwhelmed with adrenalin and an endorphin rush that it reaches a heightened space of consciousness. Many describe it as a feeling of floating, or a trance, or an inability to typically function.

Afterwards, it's possible to experience "subdrop" and apparently that's what I am living now. After those hyper-intense feelings flood out of you and your body adjusts to the real world again it can lead to temporary depression or a crash of sorts.

As I read on, I am in some way relieved to know that this is a normal reaction to BDSM play. I realize there is still so much I don't know about what we are doing and while we are each doing things as responsibly as possible, we need advice. Help. Camaraderie.

"Leo?" I ask not moving my attention from the page I am skimming and hearing him say, "Hmmm?" I continue.

"I wanna meet others. Other people who do this. I think we need help or advice or whatever. I want other submissives I can talk to about this stuff. Whatcha think?" I ask, turning my gaze to him across from me.

When his eyes meet mine, as always, I feel him reading my soul through the gaze.

Unwavering I hold his stare and after a minute he replies gently, "Sure darlin. I'll set up a profile on that social networking site we keep coming across in our research. Sound good?"

I give a faint smile and tell him sure and hand his tablet back. I turn away from him and lay down straight under the covers as more tears begin to fall. Mr. Donnovan makes no move to make me stop or explain the crying; only acknowledging me with a light hand on my hip. I fall asleep like that, with a still aching crotch, reading lamp still on, silent teardrops amassing on my pillow and my husband letting me know he is right there if I need him.

***

A week later and I feel like a new woman. I take several days to work out of the funk of subdrop and emerge as happy and horny and excited to serve as before. Eventually I pull out the yellow sticky note Leo left on my library book with a website, log-in, and password written in his fast handwriting that I'd recognize anywhere. Ready to return to the world of D/s I log in during Emily's nap.

The black screen of the BDSM social networking site pops up and I begin to navigate it. There are photos everywhere I look of lean women stretched out with rope and exposed genitals and latex clothes being worn from head to toe. I spend a half-hour familiarizing myself and decide to update our profile before doing much else. There are a ton of options to describe yourself. I pause a bunch to tab over to a new search page and read on words that aren't familiar.

I do some reading on the difference between Dominant and submissive versus Master and slave and am left with not much of a better understanding than when I started. Slave. I shiver at the thought and for the first time in a long time remember *The Sex Slave*.

I continue creating our online fetish persona. I don't want pictures of our faces posted but I want an avatar photo of something other than the default one. I pull out my posture collar and strap it on, feeling my body react to the pleasure of its tightness and familiarity, and use my phone to first snap and then upload a picture of the leather strap upon my neck, my almost-white hair framing it prettily, making a lovely contrast. I make it our profile picture and decide to leave my collar on for the rest of nap time. It feels so right there.

I narrow us down. I list us as married. Monogamous. Dominant and submissive. Heterosexual (I pause to run off and search of some of the other options that were listed; I honestly had no idea there were so many other sexual orientations). I know now and am glad for the education. I look at the suggested reasons for being here on the website. I click: Events. Friends. Mentoring. Education.

After filling out the profile I get lost in a sea of stories and images that are completely surreal to me. There is a whole world out there of "other" people. People like me. People like Leo. People like us. We aren't alone. We aren't unusual. We aren't freaks.

Thousands of people are listed in this very city. Men and women who understand this. I choke back surprised tears from the overwhelming community. A website full of people accepting this life. It's a safe haven.

I start to get nervous about the idea. Can we actually go out in public and meet these people? How do we talk to them? What do we say? Will they judge us? What if we aren't acting in proper "protocol?" Do we call every man "sir" and every woman "ma'am" just like in the rest of the world? I can't imagine how nervous I'd be.

I hear Emily awake and close the laptop, remove my collar, and try to shut down the questions racing through my brain.

***

"Vegas." Leo says with a certainty, fork paused midair holding a bite of my almost-famous baked ziti.

I wait for him to continue his thought. I've been texting him since nap, expressing my nerves about the idea of going out into the local

BDSM community. Emily is taking her pasta and smearing it into her high-chair table, turning it into mush.

I continue to eat the plate of home cooked comfort and Leo speaks between bites.

"So when we go to Vegas after Thanksgiving we can see if there is one of those 'munches' where kinky people eat dinner together or maybe even a local dungeon to check out. We can go together and nobody will know us and if we don't like it, we leave. Maybe then it'll be easier to go out here once we get back. What do ya think?"

I smile for the first time since nap, happy to have a resolution that puts me at ease, and raise my cold bottle of beer.

"To Vegas!" I cheer.

The Mister clinks his bottle to mine and gives a devious grin in agreement.

"To Vegas."

***

That night when the house goes quiet and we are alone as husband and wife, Leo dominates my senses. He blindfolds me, makes me listen to a strip of duct tape stretch out over my mouth, then puts earplugs in my ears. He binds me, removing any opportunity for me to move to touch him.

Leo Donnovan uses his darling wife's body as the body of a whore (his whore): spanking and pinching, biting hard until my muffled scream could almost break through, penetrating each hole at his desire. Inside this place of no senses, I live inside my own mind.

My mind brings me back for the second time today to the place where it all began.

I fantasize that I am a sex slave. Owned by a Master, used up, tied down, as bound in body and spirit as possible. I picture myself naked and exposed and vulnerable in a dungeon somewhere, my Dominant doing these things to me giving no regard for decency.

With no way of asking permission to orgasm and in the depths that is subspace I come. I lose count of the number of times. The first thing I realize after being untied and brought slowly back to reality is the hot, soaked sheet I am laying on. The second is the weight of my husband's strength embracing me.

I'm so safe. I'm home.

***

That's the thing about BDSM. It can become more than just foreplay to great sex. When the right people come together it becomes almost a spiritual experience. Two souls connecting, reading each other; a giving and taking that is at the same time entirely selfish and selfless.

I give my body over to my Dominant in the bedroom and in day to day life. In turn, he takes away all of my responsibility and all of the worries that accompany.

He fulfills his desires as a sadist and at the same time empties me out as the masochist I realize I may be.

He thinks of what is best for me and his household all the time first. He can only accomplish that because I think of him first. All the time. I hope it would go without saying that each of us put our child before anything in the world but I will add it in to avoid any confusion. Emily comes first in our life. Then Leo comes into consideration first for me and I come first for Leo.

I can best describe our power exchange, both in the sadomasochist play and in our Dominant/submissive dynamic as this:

Remember the trust building activity from vacation bible school or maybe a high school retreat? The one where two people stand lined up, one in front of the other. The person in front is instructed to stand straight and slowly lean backwards, letting themselves fall, trusting the person in back to catch them before falling on their butt.

This is the life we live in Total Power Exchange. Leo is in back, steady, waiting, certain, powerful, in control, ready to grab me and keep me from crashing. I am the one falling, giving complete blind trust over to somebody fallible, somebody who makes mistakes, and giving them the trust and responsibility that is my entire self.

We live mid-fall day in and day out, giving the other the trust and responsibility we each thrive under. I am constantly falling into his arms. He is constantly prepared to catch me. Each moment of my new life I feel able to let go of all constraints and be free.

But the whole while, try as you might to not doubt, you will still wonder what the pavement feels like if you are unceremoniously dropped.

I am falling backwards with entire trust into Leo Donnovan's arms. Could this possibly be the thing to move us forward? Or will it leave me hurting in a way I can't even imagine? I dunno. I just don't know.

Chapter Eleven

Sin City

Grandma Larchmont and I divide the Thanksgiving menu and she hosts the meal at her small condo in town. Turkey day is as simple as it gets. Leo watches football with my mom's current beau de jour. Mom and I trade places between the kitchen and tending to Emily and a good time is had by all. Now the dishes are all cleared and the bags loaded. I blubber the whole trade off of Emily to her grandmother who shoos me away as if she can't remember what it is like to leave a baby for the first time on a trip away.

Leo and I will be gone for four nights. We need it. I need it. I wipe my face dry, kiss Emily a dozen times, thank my mother a dozen times, and turn away.

Climbing into the car I wave good-bye to my girls until Leo drives out of sight. It brings us to the airport where we find a bar and promptly scour the internet to find a Vegas BDSM jaunt. I sip a chilled martini to try and calm my nerves.

"All I'm finding are swinger's clubs," Leo whispers to me, taking a sip of his coffee. He hands the tablet to me as an unspoken order: find something. After thoroughly searching I succeed. A small "alternative lifestyle club" off the beaten path. I mean, it's Las Vegas, right? I was bound to come up with some option.

"Look at this Mister. I found it." I nudge Leo.

He nudges back teasingly, "Whatcha got darlin?"

I hold up the screen for us, clicking on the "Dungeon Rules" tab, and read:

1. No cell phones or recording devices of any kind allowed on premise. There are lockers available for use. Please lock your cell phone up.

2. No touching of any person without their permission.

3. Do not touch property that doesn't belong to you, with the exception of what is provided by the proprietor.

4. "No" means "no."

5. "Yellow" and "red" are house safe words.

6. Dungeon Monitors or "DM's" are available at all times. Contact one if you need help or have concerns. They will be wearing DM armbands.

7. Do not interrupt another scene, including being too close to personal space or making loud noises nearby.

8. Condoms are required for any penetration and are available at every station.

9. Please clean up after yourself.

10. There is a zero tolerance policy for drinking or drugs. Play sober or go home.

"Holy shit. Leo. Can we really do this?" I ask with disbelief. My eyes are wide and jaw dropped, heart racing about the idea of going out into public and potentially having sex in front of others. I am petrified and turning tingly.

Leo reaches over and lifts my jaw gently closed, kissing me on the forehead. He moves back to bring our faces an inch apart, his hazel eyes sparkling at my blues.

"Hell yes, darling. We can. And we will."

***

We land on time and gather our carry-ons, calling to check on Mom and Emily (I can practically hear my mother rolling her eyes at me as she answers my myriad of questions about the day so far) and we go to wait for our bags to arrive at the baggage claim.

Leo stands behind me, his entire body pressed against mine, and the feeling of him against my rear mingles with the slight buzz from my earlier cocktails. It has me giddy to get started with the weekend of sin.

Looking for the suitcases, surrounded by those who just shared our flight, I feel my husband shift, dig in his carry on, and from behind me I feel my leather collar strap tight around my neck. I couldn't be more frozen in shock if he had pulled my skirt up for all to see.

From the back of my ear I hear quietly, "Calm yourself, Chloe. Nobody knows us here. You are my submissive and I will adorn you as I like. Unless I remove your collar for showering, this will remain on you until you come back to this airport. Do you understand my darlin?"

Looking around to the people surrounding us, all of them entirely ignoring us, I manage to speak into the air in front of me just loud enough for the Mister to hear.

"Yes."

"Good," he whispers. "But you're gonna pay for forgetting to call me 'Sir' as soon as we get to the hotel."

He's suddenly gone from behind me, leaving a cool absence against my skin, moving casually to get our luggage that I had all but forgotten. Feeling like I have a neon sign on my neck proclaiming "I am a kinky slut," I am escorted by my husband to the line of taxis waiting to direct us to the finest oversized hotel on the strip.

***

Check in is mortifying. Leo insists I stay by his side through the line, guaranteeing that I'm seen with my beautiful but conspicuous posture collar by all present. To the credit of the hotel concierge, he gives the collar a simple glance and just continues on with his business. I remind myself that not only were we not the only people in the world who lived the way we do, thinking to the thousands of profiles that existed in Vegas on our newfound social site, but that even those who didn't weren't necessarily "in the know" about what my collar means. I try my best to hold my spirit high (my head is already high, thanks to my collar ensuring my ideal posture) and remind myself that this could just be a fashion statement.

I smile at Leo as he stands with his ID and credit card at the counter. Looking handsome in a shirt and tie, refusing to sacrifice style for comfort on the day of travels, he gives me what I can only interpret as his "sadistic smile."

Shuddering at the thought of getting up to the room and the punishment that is hanging in the air between us, I do my best to keep my hand from reaching up to cover my collar. My loins get that heavy feeling of desire.

Before I can blink we are in the privacy of the suite. The curtains are immediately closed remotely by my Dominant, blocking out the view from the 22nd floor facing onto the hustling Vegas strip.

Setting the remote down he turns to me, hands in the pockets of his pricey dress slacks, he raises an eyebrow and speaks with the authority he now has over me.

"Strip. Now."

I do.

***

I stand nude, spine straight, hands behind my head for inspection. My toes curl into the plush carpet; such a contrast to the sand–lined tile at the beach house. I am below my pre-pregnancy weight thanks to the time I dedicate at the gym but my body is still different since childbirth. I am rounder and wider in the hips, my breasts softer than before and Leo tells me constantly how much he enjoys what he calls a "woman's body." My long white locks are twisted in a messy fishtail braid down my back. I feel sexy in my exposure; in the new body Leo and I have created together. I smile gaily at him, legs slightly apart, showing myself to him with no hesitation.

The circling begins. Looking me up and down. Likely deciding what price I should pay for forgetting to call him Sir at the airport. I am flushed all over. Excited for the play time. In a hotel. A Las Vegas hotel at that. No need for quiet. I can anticipate the quivering orgasm to come. I have never been disciplined by my Dominant and this heightens my excitement.

At last he speaks while continuing circling.

"Darling. You have two responses from here until further notice. I only want to hear from you either 'Yes, Sir' or 'Red.' Those are your only choices. Do you understand?"

"Yes Sir!" I say with a big grin, glad to know the answer and responding with a bit of smirk behind it.

Smack! His hand lands without warning across my bare ass. It stings and no lingering hand rubs it gently like during our usual play. Just the swat.

"Good," he says.

Smack! Again. Hard again, on the other cheek.

"Would you like another?" Leo asks.

"Yes, Sir." I respond more seriously this time, the bit of sass taken out of me.

Smaaack! Harder than maybe ever before, his hand lands on my ass cheek again. There is a gasp in my throat and I swallow it down.

"Another?" he asks.

"Yes, Sir," I say quietly.

Smaaack! The pain is intense now with nothing to soothe it after. He keeps asking me if I would like more and each time I have to make a decision. Either answer "Yes, Sir" and endure his lesson or utter my safe word and end it all. Each time I hear my roughening throat utter, "Yes, Sir." Each time my ass is set on fire.

In the beginning I count how many times I utter these two words with a corresponding spanking but eventually I stop. At some point the teardrops fall and through the crying I continue to make my request.

"Yes, Sir."

I feel like I will be saying, "Yes, Sir" in my unconscious dreams before he is finished with me. It starts to come out in a stream and hiccup in my voice, a slobbering, "Yessir (*smaaack*) yessir (*smaaack*) yessir (*smaaack*) yessir (*smaaack*)." I start to lose my balance and tumble after each strike. Eventually he ends it.

He pulls me close, whispering in my ear, my snot and mascara laced tears drench his shoulder.

"It's ok darlin. I am here. You're ok. I'm here. It's ok. You're ok. I'm here." Over and over again until my breathing resumes a semi-normal pace.

I survive my first true punishment. And damn. It's an effective lesson. I collapse at his feet, kneeling on the golden shag, moving from "Yes, Sir" to "I am sorry, Sir."

This is my lesson in punishment. It isn't fun. It's isn't sexy. It doesn't turn into a steamy sexual tryst; I was mistaken in thinking that. But. If done in a proper way for proper reasons that submissive is left with a gratitude towards her Dominant. With a lesson learned. She is glad for his leadership; happy to be molded. Comforted in knowing that he is indeed going to stay true to the promises he makes.

Because as I know all too well: a man who doesn't follow through on his promises is nothing but heartache.

***

Leo brings me to my feet and helps to lay me on the soft hotel bed blissfully belly down, my stinging behind gratefully up in the air. I hear him leave, shuffle through our luggage (for toiletries, maybe?) and start to draw the tub in a bathroom I have never stepped foot in.

After just enough time for me to almost fall asleep, emotionally and physically exhausted, he gathers me up and brings me to the warm bath to soak my body and mind. The bathroom lights stay off and my husband assists me getting into the bubbles. The vanilla scent fills my nostrils and before going under entirely I feel Leo remove my collar.

Glad he remembered because I had all but forgotten. The symbol of Leo's ownership is becoming increasingly natural across my throat.

"Mmmm... ahhhh..." is the closest thing to a coherent thought that I can voice. Leo sits beside me and I can't tell if he's there for the company or to make sure I don't fall asleep in the two feet of water.

"Close your eyes," he suggests to me softly and I do.

I feel a cold rag lay across my eyes swollen from crying and relax, truly let go, for the first time since leaving Emily behind with the only person I would trust to do so. It is as if time doesn't exist; responsibility doesn't matter.

The silence spills out between us but I know Leo is still there. I hear the water split itself and all of a sudden his hand is there. At my clit. I was expecting it earlier and instead I found only pain. Now I am expecting pain and instead I am feeling pleasure.

Rag still covering my tired eyes, my lower half responds and moves through the warm water towards him.

He asks into the unfamiliar room that fills with an echo, "Would you like me to enter you, my darling?"

In an instant, still on my lips, I respond in the newly cemented way: "Yes, Sir."

I have been trained.

In he goes, invading both holes with no further notice or questioning. His pointer finger into my pussy and his pinky in my "currently in training" ass starts the heat back up and in an instant I am begging for him.

"Please, Sir. Please use me." I moan. I mean it too. I don't care what he does to me; I am ready to accept it in. I just want to be used.

I feel something unfamiliar slide into my anus: a large gaping and then nothing. Another large gaping and then nothing. It continues. The anal beads, tethered together and filling my insides, totaling 7 in all. Each one fills me up more than before, collecting inside of me, into a place that was all but forbidden months ago. He is using one hand to stuff me up and the other is holding my hand, comforting me, letting me know he is there.

Filled up in back, the mister returns to my mound, this time staying on my clit, rubbing me in circles under the silky water. My punishment is almost forgotten with the exception of a still sore behind. I wonder if I will be bruised from his disciplining hand but I am distracted back to the circling bringing me to the peak of orgasm.

"Ok, Chloe. Part two of your lesson. The only things I want to hear are either 'Yes, Sir' or 'Red.' Same as before. Got it?"

Tears well up at the reminder of my mistake at the airport but I swallow it down easily at the presence of his working fingers, the pressure in my anus building.

"Yes, Sir." I respond and I hear a chuckle from the man above me.

"Good." Leo says. "Good girl."

The strokes continue on me in a rhythmic pattern, mounting, building, making my breath as heavy as the weight in my bum. Building to the satisfaction he asks in a teasing voice:

"Would you like to come?"

I whimper my request, "Yeeeessssiiiiiirrrrr..."

In which Leo Donnovan stops. The hand is removed, splashing out of the water and I am alone in the tub with painful butt cheeks and some sort of beads filling me up, body clenching, hips bucking up towards something that isn't there anymore.

I pull the washcloth off of my eyes and look at him, appalled. He is smiling wide; enjoying postponing my release. I smile back at him, cover my eyes with the washrag again, and relax back in the tub. I can win at this game. So it continues.

The mister brings me back to my climax, asking if I would like to come and like before my only answer is "Yes, Sir." Hand is removed and I regain my composure, breathing through the want.

And again.

And again.

At long last when the heat of my swollen insides is greater than the heat of my spanked behind he finally allows it to happen.

He tells me, "This time you may come. Are you ready, my love?"

Of course from my lips: "Yes Sir!"

He speeds up again on my clit, increasing the pace with just the right amount of friction and my release is building again for the umpteenth time. My rectum is filled with the round beads and every time I move they shift inside of me, moving, rolling, invading...

"Ahhh...ahhhh...!" I begin to holler and I hear the voice that matters say: "Come."

I do.

My insides quiver and shake, releasing the tension built up over the day. It is now that my husband reached down and removes the first bead from my derriere. He does slowly, never decreasing the friction on my front side but now also controlling my backside, dragging the ball that is trying to spread me at the exact same time that my body is clenching from the explosion.

It is painful and hot and repeating. The instant one bead is removed and my hole feels empty there is another one ramming its way out of me, pausing in the moment of being removed, halfway in and halfway out, making me convulse all over again. The orgasm continues for what seems like an eternity and when I settle I feel like I could instantly sleep.

Instead I lay in the getting-cool tub, twitching here and there from the remaining currents running through my body, and wait while Leo bathes me, just like that first night I went to subspace.

The mister helps me out of the bath and dries me off, wrapping me in a fluffy white bathrobe and he hands me a towel to deal with my hair. His arm around my waist he helps me towards bed but before I get in I pause and despite the soreness I drop to my knees.

I drop my forehead to his feet and just pause where I belong for a moment. Looking up to his eyes I apologize.

"Sir I'm really sorry I forgot to address you respectfully. I'll do my very best to not let it happen again."

He reaches down and lays a hand upon my head, absorbing my penitent gesture. Leo helps me up, kisses me gently, our tongues touching lightly. He hugs me tight and whispers close, "I forgive you. I'm sorry you had to be punished."

I choke up and choose to stay silent, nodding my understanding into the crook of his shoulder, filling my body up with our love.

✱✱✱

Dungeon night comes the second evening after a full day of relaxing, gambling, shopping, recovering. Leo has been distracted by his work which seems to follow him everywhere now. His phone constantly bleeps; there is always an email to send. I shake off my annoyance with that damn phone and do my best to prepare for what is to come.

Dressed first and waiting in the hallway area of our lush hotel room I pace in my new, black knee-high leather boots which bring me to the requisite ornate mirror hanging over the requisite mahogany office desk in the corner. I like what I see but I can hardly even register it as me.

Wearing a skin-tight dress made of a sturdy black, white and red plaid canvas, I fiddle with the zipper that runs the entire length of the front of the garment starting at the bottom and ending at my cleavage. Black ribbon X's crisscross down the sides of the dress from my hips to the hem, showing off my new curves in just the right way. The scoop neck renders this entirely too sleazy to consider this getup ever appropriate at home. At my neck is my black collar of leather and lace showing all in the dungeon that I am owned by somebody. That "somebody" is getting ready in the bathroom right now.

I touch up my red Marilyn lips and wonder how I am going to make out with Leo tonight without him being covered in it. My long platinum hair is falling in waves by my face and I see myself for the first time as a woman of Leo's creation. He has crafted me into the sexiest version of myself.

The bathroom door finally opens; there he is. Mr. Leo Donnovan. My Dominant. Looking like a million bucks.

His dark hair (with more strands of silver making an appearance each year) and goatee have been wet and combed neatly. Leo is in head to toe black: an expensive black dress shirt, close cut, showing off his trim body, black dress pants that I know will melt away to nothing if I go and touch him through the fabric, and black leather dress shoes. I am so busy noticing him I don't see him noticing me.

When I do I realize I am being eaten alive with his eyes. The sadist is largely present and I'd bet Leo is thinking of what he'll be doing to me later. I smile at him as he walks over to me and without an invitation, puts his hand under the short skirt of the dress I have on and lands on my bare, slick crotch.

Confirming I have nothing on but the dress, he whispers, "Fucking perfect."

He moves and gathers our coats. He helps me drape my new black corseted trench and ties my belt to keep the Vegas chill at bay.

"You ready?"

I answer with a smile and a, "Yes, Sir!"

"After you, my darling," he says with a motion towards the door and even though I am expecting it I still give a yelp when Leo swats my butt on the way out and into our adventure.

***

The glaring from strangers at us and my collar are more obvious tonight and I feel quite exposed by the time we head down the elevators and through the lobby doors to a waiting taxi. I do my best to gracefully slide in the cab door as Leo gives the driver the address off the strip.

The driver (Adam, according to the license in the front of the vehicle) gives us a strange look and asks in an indistinguishable accent: "You looking for da swinger's club? That's not one there, there are freaks coming in and out of there!" Adam waits unmoving.

The mister and his darling titter nervously and Leo (thankfully answering for us) insists that no, we are headed to *that* place. I slouch down in my seat until we arrive while my nerves have me shaking like live wire. I wish for a drink to bring the edge off but alas, the club and their no drinking policy.

After paying and peeling out of the cab, we stand for a moment, hand in hand, and take it all in. We've landed in front of a large grey industrial building that could have been located in any city in the United States. Unlike the mammoth hotels lining the strip, no neon signs or bright lights or fancy fountains lure us in. Only a white piece of plywood with two words in simple black paint let us know we have arrived: THE ROOMS

Earlier today Leo and I did as much recon on this place as possible, reading any available reviews, every word on the website, finding the group on the social networking site we joined. With no cameras or photos allowed though there is nothing we can do about trying to envision what we are walking into. I look to Leo standing next to me at the door. He is nervous too. Good. Nervous people stay aware.

"Can you stay by me please, Sir?" I ask quietly into the crisp air, no taxi or movement in sight, such a stark contrast to the city we know as "Vegas."

"Sure darlin. Let's go." Leo shoots me a charismatic smile erasing any evidence of his hesitation and pulls the handle of the heavy looking metal door. I have a momentary premonition of it not opening but indeed, the door swings wide and as The Rooms entry comes into view, I remind myself to keep my composure as the dungeon unfolds itself.

With perfect posture, I enter first.

***

It could be the lobby of any boutique hotel. An oriental rug covers the floor and the whole room has a red glow. To the left of the entrance is a doorway curtained off by heavy black fabric. Waiting to greet us are an entirely average looking man and woman with pleasant smiles. They break mid-conversation and the lady walks over.

"Welcome to The Rooms," she says. A maroon leather collar is across her throat, large silver O hanging off the front center. I relax, recognizing a symbol of her also being a submissive, and she comes towards me first offering to check our coats.

"You're new here."

We hear the observation from the man standing behind two glass cases filled with collars and Wartenberg wheels, lube and condoms and cock rings, even greeting cards bearing the image of a sensual dark haired pin-up, whip in hand.

"Well. Hello! I'm Master Vohn and this is my slave Kitty. We are the owners of this establishment. Welcome."

Leo reaches across the counter and shakes the large man's hand.

"Leo and Chloe." My mister responds in kind then asks, "How long have you owned this place?"

In that one question the two men launch into a dull conversation about business. There's a heavy looking door behind the counter and I wonder what will lie beyond.

I hear an "Excuse me" gently from behind and turn around to see Kitty holding out a water bottle. I accept the drink and return her smile. She is in her mid-forties, a buxom lady, more plainly put together than I look all painted up. She is prepossessing in her simplicity though and an air of confidence wafts off of her.

The slave is in a corset that accentuates her large shelf of a chest; on the bottom is a petticoat of a skirt reminiscent of the Wild West. I pick up on her genuinely good vibes and feel welcomed and comforted in her presence.

Cracking open the water and trying to hide my nerves I ask, "You're a slave? How is that different than being a submissive? If it's ok to ask... I am sorry if I am speaking out of place..." I flush red and hope I haven't offended her.

Kitty thankfully puts a hand up to stop my stammering.

"It's oh-kay, Chloe. Most of us in the community are always happy to talk about our lifestyle so long as the questions are posed politely. In the way Master Vohn and I see it, as a submissive, I continuously consented. Now as a slave I have consented to his will once and with finality to live under his guidance. I've completed his training, like service training and position training. We live together and work together; I am always at his beckon call, his servant. There are no more negotiations in our relationship. I am owned by him. A possession. But this is also only how we define it. Living Master and slave will look different to every M/s couple. Just like D/s looks different too. Does that make any sense?"

I nod, taking in the information and feeling a yearning building inside of me. What she just described is my actual fantasy. Not necessarily being chained to an unfamiliar dungeon and used by strange Masters. But to have one Master take all control. To be stripped of my options and allowed to live under his caring hand. I look to Leo, wondering if we could be that one day. Could I sign myself over forever?

Smiling wide across the room the mister says, "C'mon darlin. Vohn's giving us a tour."

I turn to say good-bye to Kitty but she is missing from the room, surely gone from one of the four doors in the foyer, only one of which I have been through. Leo and I sign the paperwork and show ID's, pay the door fee, and are briefed on the rules we've already read.

Master Vohn leads us behind the counter and pushes the solid door, hand ushering us in. The heavyset, gentle-faced stranger says ominously:

"Sir Leo, Chloe, welcome to The Rooms."

***

There's a gym locker lined hallway where we lock up our unnecessary stuff like my bag and our cell phones. The room is brightly lit and clean smelling and Master Vohn waits for us to finish before pulling back a heavy fabric divider. When we walk through at last we enter into the first real room of The Rooms.

It's a dimly lit social area and there are a few semi-nude to nude people mingling. On the left side of the room is a pool table and kitchenette. Vohn begins the tour.

"Ok. So. Anything in the kitchen is for your use and there are sodas, waters, and snacks available."

A cross-dresser in six inch heels and sequined cocktail dress is shooting pool with a short, bronze man. They halt the game as we enter, give a friendly smile, and return to their playing and chatter. Across the room are a large television and several pieces of standard living room furniture. Porn is playing, showing a tiny brunette with obvious fake tits sucking on a man who looks a little like a Ken doll.

The thought makes me giggle uncomfortably and the two Dominant men stare at me like they're waiting to be let in on the secret. I shake my head and drop my eyes, feeling like a complete goof, and I follow Vohn through the back of the first room, Leo behind me.

We go through a hallway and up a narrow set of dark winding stairs leading us to the second floor. All the while Vohn talks through his walking tour.

"Ok. So. You can have sex or play anywhere on this side of the first curtain by the lockers. Any form of sex is acceptable as long as it is consensual. Please, if it's on upholstered furniture use a towel to catch any fluids. Stacks of towels are everywhere. Many of the rooms have a bed, or chairs, or sex swings, and most of those can be cleaned. If you mess up the sheets, no biggie, just pull up a corner and that will notify the staff to clean the room. Each room has antibacterial wipes. Each room has condoms and lubricants too. Ok. So. Here is the first of the rooms."

But how can I notice anything with the show in this common area? A vivacious black woman is lying on her back on a leather ottoman in the middle of the open room. She is being fucked by two men, one penetrating her in the anus and the other plowing into her throat. Their moans and smell of strange sex fill the room and I am instantly horny. From being a voyeur, from the thought of having two men inside me, from her bravery.

Vohn escorts us in the first room. It's maybe 10'x10' and I will discover it's similar in size and makeup to about a dozen rooms all over the top floor.

Master Vohn, a man that must be on the plus side of 300 pounds with a reddish crew cut shining with sweat from the hike, continues.

"Ok. So. Each room has a different theme to fulfill whatever fantasy you can imagine. Each one has a window to the common room or hallway so people can see in. Each door has three options. One. Leave the door open and that's an invitation for others to enter. Not necessarily join, they still need permission to touch you guys or anything you have with you. But the opportunity for them to come closer and get permission is there. Two. There is a velvet rope that reaches across allowing people to peek in closer but stay outside. Three. A closed door means you are seeking privacy but the window's there so the DM's can keep an eye on things, keep everybody safe. Ok. So. This room is obviously the Egyptian Room."

The room is painted in pyramids by an average set designer and in the middle of the room is a "golden" throne fit for a king or queen. On a small shelf lining the back wall are two sizes of grape-leaf crowns, twisted and knotted. There are a bowl of condoms and several bottles of lube as well as a stack of clean white towels as promised. A gold platter next to the chair holds grapes and a large golden chalice awaits something cool to be poured into it. The wall holds several palm branches fit for paying homage to whoever sits being served.

Leo and I clutch sweaty hands, hot in the cramped room with the sizable proprietor and I feel moisture all over my body. My

Dominant is asking silently if I am doing well and I give him a big smile and a quick nod. He squeezes my hand and rubs his thumb against the back of it.

Master Vohn backs us out of the room and leads us around the back "L" of the open central area where the ebony woman is now flipped over on her knees, again taking the men from each end. Two men now sit on a couch masturbating in the most leisurely way, enjoying the real life porn.

I take a moment to pay close attention to the people and there is one thing everybody we have seen has in common: everybody is so normal. There are no models here, no body builders. I see stretch marks and scars, eyeglasses and crooked teeth. These could be nurses or cops or casino workers. Parents. Grandparents possibly, some of them. And they are all sexy. Sexy as hell. It's in the way they command their sexuality; own up to being who they are despite what is the norm in society. I see them as sexual inspiration; a nod to continue to embrace my own desires. An alluring welcome to the lifestyle.

Vohn speaks and pauses at each room we pass.

"Ok. So. Here is the western room."

Peering in to see hay bales and cowboy hats and the ceiling painted in a red hot sunset. In the middle of the room is a stockade!

"We opened this club about ten years ago and have done lots of work to appease both our swinging clients and our BDSM clients.

We do our best to accommodate any fantasy one may have, as you'll see here in the school room."

A young man with a camcorder is filming while a graying "teacher" bends a twenty-something year old woman in a plaid skirt over his knee and he spanks her bare bottom with a ruler. Each swat prompts a moan from her lips that sounds convincingly real.

I look at Leo and instead of watching the porn being filmed he's watching me. I near in closer to his body. Our tour guide moves along, going on and on about his business, showing us the medical room, stirrups and all, the space age room where black light and neon rules, the jungle room, and the rest of the themes. Some rooms are being occupied and some aren't.

Opposite a different set of stairs there is a door with no window. "Couple's Room" is on a simple sign.

Vohn pauses and explains, "Couples only room. The only people allowed in are couples who arrived together which would include you guys so feel free to check it out. There is a DM in there all the time and all sorts of furniture and toys. Peek in later."

He leads us down the other narrow, dark staircase and we walk into bright light. The light of the S&M dungeon.

***

This is what I have envisioned and it is as horrifyingly delightful as I had imagined. Men and women in collars; some leashed, some kneeling on the cold concrete floor. It's brighter here and for good reason. Some serious sadistic and masochistic play is going down. Nobody is having sex unlike upstairs even though Master Vohn indicated earlier it would be allowed.

Leo and I exchange intrigued expressions and Vohn leads us through the lower half of the building speaking quieter this time around. Gone is the techno music that blares through the upstairs of the building, now drowned out to only a dull thumping through the ceiling, and in its place are strikes of tools and gasps of pain and orders from Dominants.

I feel like I need to scream or pee or come. Something, anything, to let out the electricity running through me. Master Vohn library-whispers as he moves us through the bizarre new world.

"Ok. So. We have about a half dozen spanking benches, four St. Andrew's crosses, and two cages, one standing and one low to the ground. Over here is an A frame set up. Suspension rigs are in the back over there. Two tables for fire or wax play. Notify a DM if you will be doing any edge play in advance-"

"Um, excuse me Vohn, I mean... uh... Master Vohn-" I interrupt, embarrassed by what may seem as ill manners both in interrupting and not calling him "Master."

He stops me and interrupts me.

"Chloe, it's OK, I'm not your Master, you don't gotta call me that."

The sweaty man continues, "Just call me Vohn. You're pretty safe calling people by their first name or by the name they introduce themselves to you as. And you're... uh... kinda shaking." Raising his eyebrow to me, "Are you ok?"

I take a deep inhale like I practice in yoga and conjure up every bit of cool in my being. With so much newness and the sadistic vibes exuding from Leo behind me it is a hard task to relax at all.

I smile my best smile and respond, "I'm good. Thank you. Just taking it all in."

"Sooo... did you have a question?" Vohn asks expectantly.

"Oh, shit. Yeah." I plow forward, "What's 'edge play?'"

Vohn responds with an ease and patience that shows his passion. I can imagine anybody could tell how knowledgeable he is about the BDSM Lifestyle but it's also obvious that it isn't just knowledge; it's his life, his passion.

"Ok. So. Edge play is anything considered 'edgy' in the community. That will vary based on who you talk with but most people agree on things like gun or knife play, cutting or blood play, fire, sometimes wax, incest or age play. Consensual non-consent-"

I rush forward, interrupting again, "Consensual non-consent?"

"Rape fantasy, in a nutshell."

As soon as Vohn says the words my nipples form stiff peaks under the tight bodice of my dress. I'm instantly transported into my fantasy of the slave woman being used without regard. He continues talking to both Leo and me about it, furthering his answer, and the whole while I feel my pussy lips get slick. There's a strange feeling of excitement mixed with shame. I can't really want that, right? How awful.

Right?

Vohn's description: "It's a form of dominant play where the bottom consents to give up consent during play. You have to really know your partner you are playing with but you'd be surprised at the number of people, particularly woman, who fantasize about not just giving up control but having it completely ripped away from them."

Standing there with the fantasy of my mister ripping away all of my control without asking, the tour ends.

"Ok. So. This is it! Do you guys have any other questions?" Vohn says with a smile, his pause allowing the *swat! swat! swat! swat!* rhythm of something hitting somebody nearby followed by a man's voice, "Fuuuck! Stop pleeeeease!"

Vohn whispers to us, leaning closer, "'Yellow' and 'red' are safe words here. 'Stop' is not a safe word." He steps back and winks, waiting for any questions.

Out of my husband's mouth I hear, "Do you have any tools for sale?"

"Sure! Glad you guys are gonna stay and play awhile. I'll show you what we have Sir Leo." Vohn replies cheerfully.

Boy is he nice. Somehow nothing as scary as I'd imagined before arriving.

Leo looks me in my eyes and instructs, "I'll be right back darlin. Wait here."

Before I can squeak out a response the two Dominants turn together and walk towards where we began the tour, chatting quietly, leave me standing alone in a skintight dress, naked underneath, horny as hell, in a dungeon.

***

I'm afraid to move an inch. In part because Leo gave me the order and I don't want to disobey him. Not here, not with his tight collar around my neck. Also because I'm scared to death to talk to anybody. I stand statue still and watch a scene taking place nearby.

There is a tall, scrawny middle-aged man strapped to a St. Andrews cross which is basically an eight foot tall letter X made out of wood. His arms are bound with rope above him, and his ankles are tied to the bottom of the X. He is only wearing navy boxer briefs and a heavy chain collar. His backside is being flogged by an older woman, likely in her sixties.

It's entrancing to watch her flogger make what looks like the pattern of an infinity symbol across the man's back. There's another watcher: a collarless middle-aged woman stands silently directly across from me on the other side of the scene.

The submissive man's gasps make me gasp. I begin to breathe heavily and can see his pain (pleasure?) building. I am envious of him; being used, being dominated.

Just when I crane my neck to look for him, the mister appears. Over his shoulder is a new black and blue flogger similar to the one being used in the scene I am watching. He comes up next to me and I can't help but whisper my fear.

"Dammit, Leo. I can't believe you left me alone."

The relief of being safe floods over me. Leo smiles wide with his pink lips and his hazel eyes sparking with mischief, "You weren't alone, my darling wife. We had the DM over there," (he pauses to point to an incredibly built and incredibly dark man with a 'DM' armband waving a funny girlish wave at me) "keeping an eye on you. You're safe with me Chloe. Trust that."

In the flip of the wrist he reaches and unzips the top seven inches of my dress, spilling my breasts out for all to see. I gasp at the exposure and instinctively reach up to cover my chest. Leo quietly laughs that sadistic sounding laugh and pins my hands to my wide hips.

A man about our age passes by and glances our way, giving a casual, "Nice tits!" and an approving nod as if he was chatting about the weather.

My jaw drops, Leo laughs again and leans forward whispering into my ear, "My wife is the sexiest woman in this building. Maybe even in Vegas. Are you having a good time?"

His compliment makes me glow in pleasure.

"I'm having a great time, Sir." I answer and before I can calculate what he's doing, Leo reaches out, pinches my left nipple tight, and attaches a metal nipple clamp he must've just bought. The clamp feels like somebody is biting down with sharp teeth constantly on my breast.

Gasp. Again, jaw dropped, I watch Leo as he takes my other nipple and gives it the same treatment. Why does nipple pain feel like clitoral pleasure? Makes no sense. New clamps biting down as the fire roars in my body, Leo pulls me by my hands forward to hug me tight. In doing so the clamps press against me harder, more painfully, but then he kisses me deep and all thoughts of pain fade.

His taste is so familiar. It is the taste of the man that finally gets me. Our tongues meet and he presses tighter to me; I can feel him growing hard. I start to grind against him, aware that there are people, strangers, maybe that exotic looking DM, staring at us. I don't care. In fact, I want to be seen. Want to be desired. I imagine being the future fantasy of the people watching and when I moan inside of Leo's moving mouth it's from sheer stimulation, not for show.

He breaks away from the kiss (no red lipstick in sight on him) and faces me back towards the scene that seems to be wrapping up. Leo backs behind me and holds my body close to his, staff hardened from the kiss hitting my tailbone. His left arm wraps around my stomach and clutches me tight. My clamped breasts are out and on display, nipples pointed out painfully smashed and I do my best to channel the hurt into sexual excitement. *Does this make me a masochist?*

I am wondering this to myself when I feel Leo shift and take his hand under the short hemline of my dress and palm my entire region. His palm lays on my central opening, fingers on my clit, and rests his thumb in the crack of my ass. I immediately begin to grind against him and in my ear I hear: "Stop. Now." It takes me all of my willpower to do so.

The thin man gets untied limb by limb, the elder Domme taking time and care, whispering to him, stopping to massage each rope mark as they appear.

"Umph, damn Chloe, you are already so wet. Why?" Leo whispers in my back earlobe, holding me still, hand cupping my parts.

I respond in an instant, "You."

"Stop stop stop. Specifically, darlin. It isn't just me. No more fibbin'. What. Got. You. Wet?"

I gulp in air and spew out the answer feeling exposed in so many ways: "This. This Leo, everything down here. The dungeon. The slaves. Being watched. Being wanted. Being accepted."

"What about the consensual non-consent talk Chloe? I saw your reaction. Maybe nobody else would have noticed but nobody knows you like I do. What about that my wife?"

Leo's hands and words make me feel swollen and heavy with want. The man in the scene comes off the cross and surprises me by going over to the other female spectator where he drops to his knees in reverence; not to the Domme now tidying the rope into neat bundles.

The man's unexpected gesture of gratitude, of servitude, brings forth a tear to fall.

I answer honestly to Mr. Donnovan not because I have no other choice but because I want the kind of relationship where I can be free like that.

"Yes. That too. I want that. With you Sir."

He kisses me on top of my head in approval.

*** *

Leo guides us back upstairs to the couple's room. We arrive outside of the solid wooden door holding each other's hands; Leo opens the door. It smells like roses which smells like home.

We walk into the entry that is mostly pitch black. A muscular blonde man with a DM band strapped to his bicep is standing behind what looks like a restaurant hostess stand. The dungeon monitor clicks on a pen light creating a dim glow and with a deep voice asks, "Leo and Chloe, right? Vohn mentioned you may be stopping in."

Hand clenching mine Leo replies simply with, "Yessir."

The fair haired man replies, "Welcome to the Couple's Room. You are the only couple here now so feel free to check it out and get comfortable. Same rules as outside. Let me know if you have any questions and most of all, please, enjoy yourselves."

Moving forward we enter a large room to the left of the door, painted a deep hunter green including the ceiling, about three times the size of the other rooms we saw upstairs. There are shelves lining the back wall no doubt with both necessary supplies and "sensual" supplies. I see bundles of white nylon rope, shining bright in the room lit by gobs of candlelight. The walls are lined with various kinds of seating ranging from plush love seats to armless wooden chairs perfect for bending somebody over for spanking. There are vases of red roses on every surface that can hold them.

The star of the show however is the oversized bed filling the middle of the room.

The first thing I notice is the size. It's gigantic. It has to be larger than a king. *Do they have to make custom sheets*, I wonder, feeling my nipples throbbing in their clamps at the thought of what can happen in this bed. Next comes the appreciation for the workmanship in the custom piece of furniture. It is, quite literally, a bed made of branches. There are vines and twigs encircling each other on the four posts that rise up high on each corner. Along the top is a rectangle connecting the posts, again, made of varying size curling and twisting branches of tree.

It's something out of a fairy tale; an unexpected find in a forest where you will also find a prince to kiss you awake. I hear Leo from behind me ask, "You ready darlin? I don't know if I can wait any longer."

When I respond, "I'm ready," I feel him squeeze on my shoulder blades tensely causing my collar to tighten.

"I'm ready. Sir." I say with emphasis.

Already tingling everywhere Leo faces me and forces my chin up to look me in his light eyes.

"Yellow. Red. Do you understand?"

"Yes, Sir. Yellow. Red." It rolls off my tongue and sends sparks through my veins.

"Hold your breath." Mr. Donnovan instructs and I do so, raising an eyebrow regarding his strange order. Without hesitation he reaches across and releases the nipple clamps creating a searing needle-like fire through me. Despite held breath I can't help but scream in pain. He rubs my chest sending a soothing calmness through me. I look down as best as I can in my posture collar and see my gnarled nips standing straight up and more sensitive than ever before. Each brush makes me more turned on and I feel my pussy start throbbing.

"Hey. Darling." I hear and look up. I am again struck by the strangeness and familiarity of this man in front of me. Both flawed and still somehow everything I want to be around. Old us; new us.

Our eyes meet and he says simply: "I love you."

Before I can respond he pulls me close and hugs me tight. Tucking my head under his chin, feeling his chest move with breath, I match my breathing to his. Our first and possibly only public scene begins.

***

After a long embrace, feeling the comfort of him with every moment that passes, he leads me across the couple's room to the bed of branches. The genius part of this bed is the endless possibilities surrounding bondage. You can tie almost anything anywhere with any material. Leo sits me on the edge and tells me to relax (which is of course impossible). The bottom of my dress rides up and exposes my nudity and I have to force myself to stop from reaching to tug it down.

As he is at the shelves picking out needed items, allowing myself to feel risqué, I lift one knee up to the mattress and hike my dress even further, exposing my whole lower half. I reach a hand down, feeling the slick outside of my shaved body and use my fingers to peel back my lips, allowing my middle finger to rub lazily against my clitoris.

What I don't expect is that at the same time Leo is coming back to me, smiling at my play, another couple enters the room. They're a bit older than us, maybe in their early forties, but fit and nervous looking and holding hands like they are in love too. They stop at a loveseat directly across from the foot of the bed and just watch as I am frozen; hand on what was once a private area.

Leo fakes a cough, catching my attention, and directs, "Continue, darlin."

Well, shit. Now what? I thought I was an exhibitionist but now that the fantasy is put to reality I am freaking out. Leo walks over and puts a black silk scarf tight around my eyes and whispers in my darkness: "Continue. Now."

I manage better blinded. Left with my imagination and husband I can do it. I stick my middle finger deep. As it continues in and out of me I feel a tip of hard flesh at my closed lips and open wide to accept it in. I know it's 99 percent probably Mr. Donnovan but the knowledge that it could be some other stranger's cock fuels my masturbation. I wrap my tongue around the shaft and roll it around, my finger still fucking myself faster and faster. I suck at a steady rhythm, feeling like I am putting on a show, wanting to do the very best I can.

The dick is removed and a hand grabs my wrist near my vag and straightens out my sopping wet digits into a straight point. My wrist is bent and all four of my fingers and my thumb are forcibly implanted up to my top knuckle near my palm. Holy shit. I gasp in the shock but can barely make a sound as my throat fills with man again, sending me choking on his size.

Hand planted I fist myself, trying to open myself up and fill that deep ache, cock gagging me while I build to my peak. I hear a moan coming from a strange voice elsewhere in the room and their excitement brings me to the edge. In the instant I hear my mister above me order, "Come!" I begin squirting. It gushes forth and he fills my mouth simultaneously. I shake all over and before I know what is happening, my mouth is emptied, hand removed, and my behind is lifted and shoved back onto the bed. Still blind and dripping down my crack, I feel Leo's mouth on my cunt, lapping me up, nursing on my swollen clit, his goatee scratching my sensitive bits. I begin laughing and it quickly turns into moaning. I wonder if the couple is still watching and the thought brings out another wave of orgasm, bucking my hips up to meet Leo's mouth. He sucks my clit, pulling it out with the suction, and I am in heaven.

The weight comes off me and I'm alone. In this moment, I don't care where he is off to. I am wholly content and relaxed. Until I feel the sting of what must be Leo's newly purchased flogger across my thighs.

"Get up." He orders sternly.

I move to do so, swatted leg hot, feeling uncertainty from the change of pace and lack of visuals.

I stumble to the edge of the bed of branches and stand on the floor with my calves still touching the bed frame.

"Undress."

Shaky hands find the zipper. The unfamiliarity of the new clothes and my nerves make undressing a task and I pinch the skin on my stomach.

"Owww!" I whine, hating myself for sounding like a crybaby. It brings tears in my eyes behind the silk and I wonder when the roller coaster of emotions will end. For a moment I wish to open my eyes and be safely back in the little queen bed in our tiny lofted beach house, smelling the two dozen roses Leo gifted this week instead. Right now all I smell is my own sex and my husband's sweat and domination. The roses have taken a backseat.

I toss the swatch of plaid fabric that makes up my dress to a random side of a random area in a room which may or may not contain other people watching my naked body stand on display less than a year after giving birth.

Leo commands, "Kneel."

I do. I am living in a version of *The Sex Slave* for the first time ever. My body belongs to him to control as he will see fit. In this moment of all moments I realize: I've forgiven him.

I'll be damned.

This is Leo, the real him, the one who I married, the one who I fell in love with. The one who turned his car around and came back to find me after our first date. The one who is saving me from a lifetime of being somebody I am not.

I don't know what the future holds but I'm certain that I've forgiven his past mistake. A weight lifts from me. Inhaling deeply, giant sunshine crosses my face and tears of happiness sob out.

Leo, perplexed, "Are you OK?"

The laughter comes deep from my lungs, head back to the sky. I have never felt as free as I do under Leo's command right now. I am naked in body. In life. In spirit. Risking getting reprimanded I pull off my mask. I am there on my knees, covered only in my womanly juices and his collar upon my neck, looking to my husband's familiar face. He has the black and blue flogger in his hand. Smiling wide and true I tell him, speaking in a tone that surely indicates how shocked I am by the revelation:

"I forgive you. I forgive you, Leo. I love you and I *forgive* you."

He's so caught off guard that he is rendered motionless. His shirt is off now and he is standing in his dark slacks looking as if he is playing the childhood game of "Red Light, Green Light" and somebody has called red light on him. The only thing moving are the tails of the flogger in his right hand, swaying from the air moving around us. After a full minute of us in this silent staring he drops the flogger.

He joins me on his knees. Taking my cheeks into the palms of his hands, my imperfect, newly-forgiven husband brings our noses to almost touching and begs with a doubt in his voice: "Say it again, Chlo."

I smile wide, tears streaming, feeling perfectly honest in the statement, I repeat, "I forgive you, Sir."

He puts his head down to my bare chest, clutching me tight around my midsection, pulling me into him, and I feel the silent splash of teardrops against my naked body.

The tears do not belong to me.

After somewhere between five and fifty minutes of us in a kneeling embrace Leo lifts me into the bed made entirely of twisting branches and makes love to me. No tools required.

***

The flight transporting us back to reality is bittersweet. Looking out the window from my seat on a crowded plane taking us home I can't help but feel torn. I cannot wait to see Emily. It is as if I have left a piece of my heart on the Gulf. But I needed this time away to appreciate how much I do miss my girl when we're apart.

Sometimes in the thick of mommy-hood, I've felt each day draining me a little of my woman-hood. The part of me that loves to read casually. The part of me that uses the bathroom alone. Going to the movies by myself on a rainy weekday afternoon, filling up on popcorn and watching whatever happens to be playing, carrying a small clutch instead of a diaper bag, drinking without fear of a hangover. It's good to be reminded of that part of me still existing. I am more than just a woman driving a still new smelling minivan and listening to nursery rhymes instead of hip-hop music for fear of my child hearing the vulgarity.

I head home as a whole person, filled up with myself again. A woman that I am proud of being. I have entirely shed my old skin this weekend. I am the phoenix rising from the ashes, finally finished being torched. Now I am flying high, adorned.

I, Chloe Donnovan, am a submissive. My husband, Leo Donnovan, is my loving Dominant. This isn't role playing for us; not anymore. This isn't bedroom games or kinky fuckery. This is us.

Asking me to turn off my submission now would feel like asking me to make my eyes stop being blue. This is just who I am: proud, serving, excelling at being the woman behind the man, a natural born follower, a partner to my head of household. I am me and that is gonna have to be OK.

I feel Leo's thumb rub against the back of my hand he is holding and I look to him, smiling softly as he kisses my forehead.

My best friend Leo Donnovan. He looks young, traveling in atypically laid back attire. It makes him look even younger than he did when I met him years ago. A black and white baseball cap perches on his head covering up uncombed hair and his plain tee and plaid shorts combo makes him look like a college skater boy. It's endearing to see him this way and makes me feel better about the casual cotton maxi dress I have on. I've added a light sweater to cover my shoulders and upper arms for traveling before leaving the hotel room because even though it's winter in heated places like Vegas and Florida a chill can still come about.

It's a good thing too. My body is covered in marks. The rest of our weekend of debauchery is a blur. After recovering much of the day following our visit to The Rooms we meet up with Master Vohn and slave Kitty at a little local dive off the strip for dinner. The two are fascinating to spend time with and answer a million and one questions we ask about BDSM. They encourage us to find our local munch and begin meeting people. We say our good-byes and promise to keep in touch online.

Afterwards we head back to the plush hotel room and Leo wrecks my body again, making good use of his new implements of pain and we fuck until the sun comes up. We sleep until the sun is setting on our final evening in Sin City, awakening feeling disoriented from mixing up our nights and days so much since arriving, and order a half dozen room service items.

We eat dinner (breakfast?) in the hotel room while chatting, joking, gossiping about our experience.

At some point Leo asks out of the blue:

"Chloe, we're staying together right?"

Even though I want to answer affirmatively, to erase his fears, to assure him that with all the work he has done to prove himself both heartbroken over his mistake and worthy of a second chance I will likely be staying married to him, I can't say it. Something stops me from doing so.

Does my forgiving him mean my trusting him again? Forever? Forgiveness is about the past and trust is about the future. I need more time. I have another three months of living D/s with Mr. Leo Donnovan; living as his wife, his homemaker, his whore. I am going to live it out before making a final decision. I promised myself I would and the woman I am now holds true to a promise to herself.

I only muster, "I dunno Leo."

I turn from his face, shielding myself from his shock.

So as I fly home with soft clothes gently hiding my skin covered in bruises from the falls of the flogger, bite marks rich and red, hickeys from the sucking until I screamed for it to stop, I reflect on that choice. I close my eyes to the clouds pushing me closer to real life that feels more like a fantasy life every day and all I envision behind my eyelids is Leo throughout every step in Vegas, phone in his hand, furiously texting and stepping away to make private calls.

Every time I had asked about it he simply said, "Business."

It's just business.

It's just business.

Chapter Twelve

The Decision Looms

L ife goes on in our "new normal." Our first Christmas with a child is magical. The air is dry and crisp, the beach empty. I make Leo's favorite breakfast and we spend the day relaxing as a family: watching holiday movies, napping, loving.

A week later Leo and I cuddle underneath a blanket on the back porch to watch the city commissioned New Year's Eve fireworks shoot off boats on the water. We clink champagne glasses and share a toast and a kiss. All I can do is smile inside at what a great new year this is going to be. After the grand finale Leo tugs me by my collar indoors where he pulls out his newest tool, a small singletail whip. On the first night of a new year I lay in bed and the sting of the whip bites into my skin turning me into a pooling mess of sexual submissive.

I'm so glad to be out of the year that the "mistake" happened. The relief is overwhelming and most of the time I've never been happier. Even though life appears completely average from the outside our household has gone through a metamorphosis. Leo and I talk constantly. About everything. Nothing is off limits now. It's only important that I am honest and forthright; there are no right or wrong answers. After forgiving him for his past mistake Leo has been lighter, freer, living with pep in his step. He seems to dress and bounce out the door for work excited to be going there and comes home as soon as able (which is sometimes late as well). I mean, people in his industry work whenever the clients are available, right?

In the evenings we get together and live in what seems like, honestly, happily ever after. I have almost no cares in the world. Parenting becomes fun as my child is becoming less of a helpless newborn and more of a toddler. She is truly the light of our lives.

I love getting fit, training my body, and my yoga practice is progressing. I'm considering running in a local 5K coming up and a magnet holds the flyer for the race on the fridge near my daily schedule.

We've ventured into the local BDSM community three times since returning to Florida from Vegas. There is nothing similar to The Rooms here (not surprisingly) but there are a wide array of groups that meet. The first munch we attended was awkward walking in the door and of course we were nervous as hell about the possibility of seeing Leo's coworkers or my mommy friends sitting at the long banquet table inside the private room of a local Mexican joint. But if somebody we know is there too, then hey, they're there too! What could they possibly have to say about our presence?

My hand shook lightly in Leo's palm as we walked into our first munch together and we were greeted by some of the kindest, most easygoing, slice-of-life folk I've ever met. You don't really know who does what or if the man or woman leads the dynamic or whatever so you just talk politely to each other. Within ten minutes I realized that my nervousness was unnecessary.

There is a relief in talking to other real world kinky people. It's not just that they don't judge you for how you choose to live; it's the speed at which you can have a conversation. They understand phrases like D/s or 24/7 TPE. The Lifestyle community really does have their own language and even if you don't understand something you can always ask anybody around and they'll answer it honestly and to the best of their ability. I left that first munch abuzz with acceptance and new knowledge: that the word "leather" means more than a kind of fabric, the best online corset store, whispers of local underground play parties, and the screen names of a dozen delightful local people who understand what it is that we do.

Now we regularly check in on the events board for our city and attend what we can when we can wrangle a grandma for a babysitter. Valentine's Day is about a week away and then it's just a hop, skip, and a jump until our date on the beach to determine the future of our marriage.

I'm going to stay. I'm going to make it work. Re-sign our D/s contract. Maybe try and negotiate the whole "can never masturbate" clause because I miss being able to touch myself and maybe other minor contract changes. But despite the pain of the past I want to stay married to my Dominant husband. I wanna live like this *forever*.

***

Valentine's Day. The day of romance and love. I should be over the moon but I haven't been feeling right the past few days. A funk? A mood? It happens sometimes even when everything seems to be sailing along on calm seas. It's a feeling I can't quite put my finger on; an itch that can't be scratched.

Leo has given me instructions for the evening. I am to drop Emily off with Mom and then go home to get ready. He wants me in red. It isn't uncommon nowadays for the mister to dress me to his liking but while I have always found it endearing today it rubs me wrong. Red on Valentine's Day. How cliché.

I wrap up the antique car book I bought as a gift and when the two dozen red roses get delivered to the beach house I dutifully place the flowers in water like I have done so many times before and send a thank you text to my husband. I take a deep smell, remembering the red roses of the Couple's Room. I kiss Emily, grab her overnight bag, and head for Grandma Larchmont's house.

Once back alone I work hard to shake my blues while getting ready. I try to convince myself that I am just struggling with the one year anniversary of Leo's affair. When I received the list of messages they shared back and forth I looked for certain dates and lo and behold, there they were. They chatted on New Year's. On Leo's birthday in January. Last Valentine's Day they talked back and forth all day, saying God knows what while I prepared for the arrival of a child. How disgusting.

Even though I have crossed the bridge, the pain still rises up. Not as often as before but sometimes. I pick up my cell to call Leo at the office and see if he can talk through this with me. Voice mail. I dial up DeLuca to ask for her advice. Voice mail. *Sigh.*

I proceed to "red" myself. Red lips. Red nails. Red pumps. Red full length cocktail dress, brand new for the occasion. I look myself over in the tiny bathroom mirror where I have watched myself transform from frumpy postpartum schlump to svelte trophy wife. For the first time, with brilliantly light locks in giant curls and smoky eyes looking at my perfumed body, I don't really know if I do recognize myself. I've changed so much. I hope it's for the better.

"Get it together, Chloe." I say out loud into the bathroom and from behind me I hear in a deep voice:

"Get what together?"

I jump, heart beating out of my chest in fear and spin around to see my husband. If he looked young on the plane home from Vegas, he looks much older by the same scale. In a navy blue suit and a white, perfectly starched shirt and red tie I am seeing the husband as how he will look in his forties; he is debonair but unpretentious.

Leo's face moves from smiling in approval of my look to worry about my startled reaction.

He moves closer to me, kissing me on the forehead and asks, "Chloe? Darling? Are you ok? Didn't you hear me come in?"

Gathering myself into his chest, careful not to fuss my newly applied makeup, I shake my head.

He grips me close and asks, "What do you need to get together?"

Here's my chance. This is the moment to open my mouth, to spill my anger and concerns, express my hurt that last year at this time he was romantically involved with another woman, to spew vile words and hatred for the shitty past situation. To say anything other than what I actually do say, lying to my husband for the first time in as long as I can remember.

"Nothing. I'm OK." I plaster a fake smile with an effort to make it appear real and continue, "Let's go. Happy Valentine's Day, Sir."

I breeze past him as fast as my heels can take me. He follows but I can tell by the shift in his attitude he knows I just lied to him.

***

At the expensive and apparently quite popular Italian restaurant we've never been to before Leo and I loosen up a little bit in the dark, oversized booth over a glass of champagne. Red and pink balloons cover the entire ceiling and the darkened lights and smattering of candles give each table a bit of privacy. It's romantic. Almost too much. Part of me wishes we had stayed in and had a kinky kind of night, something that involved leather and rope instead of lasagna and a dining room full of strangers.

I'm on a second glass of champagne when I ask Leo if he wants to exchange gifts but he insists not yet. Instead, ten minutes after arriving he excuses himself to the bathroom. I turn around to see smiling couples sharing food on forks or holding hands across the table while being served coffee and I can't help but wonder who else may be a little bit "alternative."

Leo comes back after quite a bit and immediately hands me the silver and black box from his side of the table. I hand him the wrapped book (already disappointed that I hadn't thought of something better) and after pausing to let Leo order our meals we unwrap our Valentine's Day gifts.

I blush all over after opening my box and look across to him in wonder. This makes my gift look boring as hell.

Leo is smiling devilishly and asks, "Do you know what it is?"

"A vibrator, right?" I whisper, leaning forward, dropping the box into my lap covered in a white linen napkin to protect my new red dress. I smile wide at his nodding. Peeking at it in my lap again I reach in and touch the "device." It's small, about three inches long and half that in diameter shaped like a pill capsule. All of a sudden without my pushing or moving anything the bullet starts to whir softly.

I can't help but yelp and pull my hand back away from it, narrowing my smiling eyes at Leo. Taking a drink of his water to stifle his laughter his other hand stays in his suit pants pocket. It's wireless. A wireless vibrator. Finally we found a sex toy that he can really be in control over.

"Miss?" I hear beside me and I slam the cover down on the gift box and swing my head to the end of the booth where the stout waiter in a restaurant tux is holding up a bottle of champagne.

My Dominant saves me from my blustering and blushing by answering on my behalf, "Thank you sir, she'll have another."

While my glass is filled and a plate with a simple caprese salad is dropped off by the food runner I watch the mister across from me with his sadistic "I've got plans for you wife" look on his face. It probably looks innocent enough to anybody around us but I know better. I can predict it coming. Once alone:

"Go to the bathroom Chloe. Put it in. Deep. Leave your panties on over."

I ask him with a perfectly groomed raised eyebrow, "Is requesting for this to wait until later an option Sir?"

Leo answers, "You can ask all you want."

"Leo, may I please use this later?" I request in the sweetest voice I can conjure.

I feel the box begin to lightly buzz in my lap.

"OK OK OK. I'm going. Knock it off." I say winking, setting the napkin on the table and sliding out of the booth.

I take the box with me and head to the ladies room. Every stall but one is full. Go figure. I go into the empty one (in the middle, of course) and pull my black satin underwear down, feeling incredibly grateful that I had chosen a sexy pair of vintage-style briefs, giving me a little more hold for what I am about to do.

I sit and relieve my bladder entirely and once wiped I do as instructed. I take a manicured hand and silently spit into the cup of my fingers. I rub my folds open and almost instantly I am turned on. Now I am being used the way I was hoping to be used this Valentine's Day.

My heart is thudding in fear waiting for somebody to peek over or under the stall and catch me in the act despite knowing that is a ridiculous notion. I insert one finger and use it to loosen myself up a bit. I take the new toy out of the box and it's obvious that Leo removed it from the original packaging and cleaned it in preparation for his plan tonight. As I slip the cold toy in my hole I do it while lightly smiling and shaking my head. *What did I get myself into?*

The bullet settles into me and before wrapping up and calling it done I remember Leo's instructions to plant it "deep." I use the finger again to push it up deeper, the looped "rescue string" still coming out of me but less of it now. I lead the loop up toward my clit for safe keeping and pull my tight panties up, cinching the vibrator in place. I stand up, getting tissue and cleaning off my hand as best as possible for now and flush. Bringing the empty box with me I open the stall and head to wash my hands. I make it all of two steps before I stop in my tracks.

Holy. Crap. I'm in a ritzy restaurant, dressed like a knockout, and I have something penetrating me. The plastic string is tugging at my clit with every step I take. I am not even to the sink yet, the thing isn't even turned on, and my nipples have hardened to a peak and my panties are starting to dampen. Fuck you, Leo Donnovan. Fuck you.

I make my way over to the sink to soap and wash my hands with my head down the whole time. Another lady is washing up too and I am not prepared to meet eyes or make casual conversation. I hightail it out the door and back to the tall booth to give Leo a gentle nudge, admonishing his evil tendencies, knowing he'd hoped I would be just as aroused and uncomfortable as I am right now. Always pushing me and my limits. I turn into my bench and... nothing.

Leo's gone.

***

I sit down and gasp at the unusual added weight inside of my lady bits. The string is digging into my clit and there is no ladylike way to make that adjustment. I cover my lap in my napkin again, down some water, go through my clutch and freshen my lipstick, pop a mint, and after all of that begin to tap my fingers, frustrated.

I check my phone. Nothing. A minute goes by, then five.

Finally Leo comes back, stopping on my side to kiss me on the forehead, sliding his phone into his pocket.

"Sorry darlin. Urgent call, business deal." He slides in his side and when he sees me with my mouth agape staring at him he asks, "What?"

"What? *What?* You had to take a business call this late on Valentine's night when I was in the middle of doing *that?* You left me." I finish with a voice that took off as pissed and landed more hurt than anything.

Leo's looking at me apologetically and responds, "Yes, darling. I had to take the call. You know that's part of the work I do."

"But Leo, shit Sir, it's been, like, I dunno… a lot lately." I try not to sound like I am accusing him but I'm also hoping for a response that will satisfy me.

"Is this what you lied to me about earlier? Is this what you wanted to ask me but didn't?" he counters back to me, not answering my question at all.

"Yes. Sir." I spit back.

My eyes are welling up with tears and I hate this. I hate that this is a concern. When will it disappear entirely? When will I stop doubting? When will the trust come back? Maybe never. I feel foolish, a dolled up average homemaker parading around as a sex goddess, sitting in a crowded room with something inside of me, tears in my eyes, and a husband I can't trust. *Sniffle.*

"Well, mister? Nothing to say?" I demand again.

"No. Darling. Nothing other than I'm not ever going to hurt you again. I love you. Only you. But I have to work. I have to answer my phone when it rings. Can we go back to a nice dinner now please?" Leo's eyes are clear with seemingly honest intentions. I want to believe. Sensing my hesitation, Leo pulls out his phone and sets it in the middle of the table.

I've stopped checking; I want to so badly now. But I have to move forward. We have to. Sniffling back my tears I give him a silent shake of the head. He reaches his hand to me across the table; the moment my palm lands in his my insides start to buzz.

It startles me at first, sure, but it's softer than I'd thought it would be. It's completely silent, sound drown out from the vibrator's depth and the chatter of the surrounding room. The back hits right into my g-spot and the vibration follows out of me, along the thick rescue string, setting my clit to buzzing.

"Ahhh!" I squeak out quietly, looking at him over our clasped hand meeting in the center of the table, before settling into a quiet, "Ahhhmmmmm."

Just like whenever Leo and I play the rest of the world begins to disappear which is chancy since we are indeed in a public place. Sitting at the dinner table, red tablecloth helping to hide my squirming bottom, Leo sends me on the ride of a lifetime during the remainder of the meal. He is the director of a symphony with the remote being his baton. The remote can apparently change and adjust speed and pulsing sensations and he does so with a mastery that impresses me.

I adjust to the speed of the first initial setting and Leo brings me to the second, breaking hands with me to arrange our meals in front of each of us, keeping his left hand in his pocket on the remote and his right both eating his entree and feeding me mine.

Second speed works me deep at a continuous pace while Leo eats, not pretending to make conversation, just watching me, analyzing. I almost peak right there in the booth but he stops it before I get there.

Smiling at me, he reaches across to my plate and breaks off a piece of my dinner and brings it to my mouth. I chew and wiggle in the seat hoping for it to come back on but no dice. He takes a bite and then feeds me another. Repeat.

My lower half is finally cooling down and it is only then that it starts again. I feel him pass up the first two speeds and go straight to the third for the first time.

I gasp, he smiles, and we sit across from each other, mentally connected by our energy. He is playing me perfectly in the way one can do when they know somebody incredibly well. Our plates disappear as I am reaching the point of orgasm again. The string creates a soaked ridge between my sensitive parts and my wet underwear and it takes every bit of control to not grind my hips.

I hear a low "Mmmmm" building in my throat and then the bullet turns off. Damn him. The final course arrives and as soon as I am composed Leo starts his final "course." The vibrator goes to a pulsating beat, cycling through the three speeds with a brief pause in between and a lingering final speed. It runs through every inch of my body and I feel like somebody could cut the connection between us with a knife. Nobody else exists. Nobody else matters.

Buzzz. Buzzz! Buzzzzzzzzzzzz!!! Pause.

Again.

Buzzz. Buzzz! Buzzzzzzzzzz!!! Pause.

Again.

I am there again. I am going to come. In my fancy red dress. In the middle of a crowded restaurant. It's gonna happen. I open my eyes wider to Leo indicating where I am heading, asking for permission without speaking a word, moving my hips the tiniest centimeter back and forth over the strand rubbing my vibrating clit and then it is gone.

Leo turns off the toy, motions to our server passing by, and hands him a credit card from his wallet. Dinner is done.

I, sadly, am not.

***

We burst out the door and I can feel now when I walk how embarrassingly wet my underside is. I have entirely soaked through my panties. Have I soaked through my dress? Or left a dampness behind in the private, high backed booth? I don't really care though; we are still connected and I feel like I am vibrating with my Dominant's presence.

I need him so badly. Into the dark crisp night we walk away from the parking lot where his car sits. I want to ask where we are going but I realize I don't care about that either and shut my mouth. Each step makes it harder to stay properly non-orgasmic and I turn the corner to the back of the restaurant with him, his hand around my waist and directing me forward as fast as he can.

The back of the brick stand-alone building is lined with a wooded area which is not uncommon on the Gulf Coast. Where we live is basically a city dropped into the Everglades and there are marshy areas lined with tall palms and cypress everywhere. Leo, still directing me, pays no attention to the change from pavement to grass and brings us thirty feet into the darkness. At this point I don't give a shit about anything. I am nothing but a sexual submissive; I am doing what I have been trained to do over the past months. What I have wanted to do over the past fifteen years.

Leo stops at a wide tree and spins me, pressing my back against the hard rough bark. It takes the wind out of me and in an instant his mouth devours mine, his hardness pressing into me, using his hands to grope me.

He removes his mouth from mine and brings it to my neck and collarbone, sucking and licking. Biting. The dim lights illuminating the service entrance to the restaurant give a glow to us in the wooded area. I feel his hand go up my dress and feel my crotch. Leo stops and looks at me, narrowing his eyes, and asks menacingly, "Did you already come?"

"N-n-no- fuck no, Sir. No." I answer quickly, wanting him to come back and kiss me with those wide lips again.

Faster than I can think he instead starts to tie me up, spinning me the other direction to face the tree and stretching my arms around the rough trunk. I can almost touch my hands together but not quite and I wonder if my new dress will be ruined.

I hear Leo growl to me, "Stay."

He paces around to the other side of the tree, pulls off the once Christmas-card-worthy red tie, and binds my hands. I begin to ache from the position almost immediately. My cheek is resting on the tree, already getting rubbed raw, facing the restaurants glow in the dark of the night.

He circles back, bends over to the dirt, picking up the heavy coffee table book I gave him earlier. I see him in the corner of my vision wind up and swing it hard, paddling my bottom. It thuds against me and I give a groan of familiar pleasure.

He takes a moment to pick up the hem of my dress and tuck it into the top of my high-waisted undies, revealing my behind to the marsh full of who-knows-what. I instinctively struggle against the ties but only result in scraping my delicate skin. Whimpering, I feel the vibrator start inside of me, full speed ahead.

Slam! The book lands against the fatty part of my butt, pushing my whole lower half forward into the tree and I stumble to stay upright. I do my best to recover and stand there, ass to the wind, heels sinking into the marshland, and vibrating on the inside as Leo continues spanking me with the hard backed book. I feel myself easily now accepting the pain and turning it into pleasure; slipping into subspace.

I barely register the book hitting the ground and a familiar sound I hear at the end of every work day: Leo slipping his belt out of the loops of his pants.

This time when my butt is swatted the stinging pain reaches my throat and I have to swallow down a scream, afraid of who may hear us leaving the restaurant. The leather is used to strike my thighs and calves, my back, my butt, carefully avoiding things like my spine and kidneys like he'd learned. I take it and take some more; and take it again and again and again. It feels horrible and primal and right. I am floating. I am free.

Leo comes close to my body from behind. His touch electrifies me. I have been on the verge of orgasm for so long now and am getting exhausted from holding it back, from choking it down. I close my eyes and rest my forehead on the tree, a shitty substitute for a pillow.

In my right ear, I hear an unmistakable metal click. Leo just opened his knife, a three inch single blade pocketknife that he carries everywhere he goes. The sound makes my heart speed up excitedly.

Leo breathes in my ear, "Don't. Move."

I learn in that very first instant the thrill of knife play. I have never encountered anything better able to make my body submit. Fast. As the sharp edge touches my jugular I am terrified to move a single millimeter anywhere on my body. I focus all my mental energy on keeping my physical body still, willing my planted heels to stay steady, and I feel my husband's hot breath at my neck and his cock on my tailbone, pushing painfully into my worked body, hard as a steel rod.

"You didn't come, did you darlin?" He asks me quietly, our heaving chests matching inhales and exhales, both of us high on adrenalin. I start to instinctively shake my head no and feel the slightest nick in my neck from the blade. Tears spill down. I want to pause and think about how frequently I cry when playing like this and analyze this strange physical reaction to such sexy, wanted acts but I force my mind to stay in the moment, trembling to think about what would happen if I'm distracted.

"No." I squeak out instead, sniffling, throat full of emotion and pussy still vibrating into the night.

"That's a good job my love. Good job." Leo murmurs.

He kisses the back of my tussled hair and removes the knife. I feel him kneel down behind me and take the knife to slice my underwear apart; it's so close to the most delicate parts of me. Once I'm fully exposed the tool clacks shut and Leo's palm grabs my sex.

"You've earned this. Come."

My orgasm gushes out of me onto his hand, shifting the bullet around inside of me and spilling the come down my thighs and calves. I inhale and feel it trickle out; the relief overwhelming.

Leo creates friction with his hand and my clit and it keeps the juices flowing out of me. He unzips his pants behind me and releases the beast and with swift motion fills my pussy up further, his dick pushing the vibrator still deeper. He pounds into me, giving us both the connection we have been seeking, tearing my dress to shreds on the bark and biting the back of my shoulder blade while coming into my darkness.

This. This is our day of romance.

***

I'm back at the beach house, having been carefully untied and left resting on the ground while Leo brought the car around to gather his delightfully torn apart wife. Soaking and freezing, shaking like a leaf, feeling entirely ruined in the best of ways, Leo loaded me up and brought me home. I feel so used and it feels so satisfying.

He helps me to the toilet, starts the shower, and then kneels in front of my mangled body, meeting my eyes to his.

"I love you, Chlo," he mutters in sincerity, pulling a stray twig out of my hair and tossing it in the trash.

"I love you too, Leo." I respond and after a moment, feeling the steam start to rise out of the shower I ask him, "Did you like your book?"

He laughs a deep belly laugh and I join him.

He kisses me and orders me to get myself clean. Glad to be alone for a minute I hobble into the shower with my thoughts going back to where they drifted earlier in the night.

God, I cry so much now. I mean I have always been an emotional gal but sheesh. When we play, when we have sex sometimes, when he is dominating me. Why the constant tears?

I pour coconut shampoo into my hands and suds up, thinking about the crying issue. I conclude it's about release. Emotional release and physical release manifested through tears.

When I truly, one hundred percent, submit my mental and physical will to another person that has earned that trust despite imperfections it's just plain overwhelming. Leo and I live this D/s lifestyle all day, every day. And while I thoroughly enjoy the way our D/s dynamic is growing, a lot of it involves some pretty mundane stuff. Who cooks and who pays the bills is not always a sexy matter though I do appreciate knowing what to expect in the functioning of the household.

Play? Like tonight? Sexual power exchange brought to life? That is the physical submission he and I have each been waiting for ever since the last time we engaged in that way. He is finally in control the way wanted by each of us. My body and mind physically let go and become his tool. His submissive. Dare I say his wife enslaved.

The tears that spill over are a result of that sweet void that comes from letting go; from the freedom that lives only there. I cry as thanks and relief unspoken. They aren't tears of sadness, or intense pain, or a desire to not be doing what is happening. My crying is not a sign of weakness. It's a sign that I am free.

I hop out of the shower feeling the high still and quickly throw on a towel, eager to share this thinking with my mister. I swing the door open and through the shifting, swirling steam I see Leo sitting under the covers in bed, the glow of his phone illuminating his face and he is writing speedily. He simultaneously looks up and shuts the phone off, asking casually, "Hey darlin. How was the shower?"

Making a snap decision that I can't explain I plaster a smile upon my face and change intended direction.

"Good. Ummm, can you get me the peroxide and bandages? I am pretty banged up."

"Sure. Anything else?" he asks, setting his phone upside down on the nightstand next to him.

"Nope! Thanks Sir!" I reply with my heart stammering inside of me and head back into the still steamy bathroom where the fake smile instantly switches off.

***

I sleep an aching, troubled sleep and wake up pre-dawn. I look to Leo and see him next to me in the moonlight. My heart feels torn into a thousand pieces.

"Trust me, Chloe," he had demanded going into this and I promised I would. I could do that, right? What has been wrong with me lately? Is it the feeling that something is again "off" with Leo and his behavior? Am I just being overly critical? What if he never really changed but just got better at hiding things from me; a criminal busted now more adept at performing the crime? These are the questions that keep me up at night and consume my happiness.

I need to talk to him. That's the cure and I know it. Express my concerns. Set up an appointment with myself, Leo, and DeLuca, go sit on her little couch together, address the issue with honesty and give Leo a voice. That's the solution.

Knowing there is no way I am headed back to sleep my feet hit the hard floor and I throw on a long sweater over my softest cotton nightgown that I used last night to cover my sore body. I head out to the beach, inhaling the cleansing salt air and listening to the waves coming and going. My decision is coming up. My day in the sand, the one when I will stand up and tell Leo that I recommit to our marriage permanently; that he did everything right, that I believe he won't hurt me again.

Turning right each step I take in the opposite direction of the beach house wakes my body up a little more (man, I wish I had stopped to brew some coffee first) and my mind can't help but roll over our history; snippets of what makes "us" worth saving.

Leo Donnovan. Chloe Larchmont. Bringing a levity to what were entirely responsible lives, making each other want and learn, fucking in the dark nights and in the light of day without abandon. Furniture shopping with Leo for his then-bachelor pad, teasing him at his desire for the so obvious choice of dark leather everywhere, calling him a "walking prediction," cuddling on the couches in the brightly lit showroom, never letting go of clasped hands.

Countless hours spending time as he watches some sports programming on the television while I fold clean laundry and put it away neatly, getting a lift from the domestic duty.

Prepping me for the first time on the back of his motorcycle, buckling a spare helmet from his garage onto me, a younger Mr. Donnovan looks in from his full face helmet with eyes sparkling and voice excited:

"Your body is going to want to do its own thing Chloe and that's gonna get us in trouble. You need to let me be in control. When I lean into a curve, you lean with me. If you try and compensate and lean the opposite way you'll just throw us off balance. You have to let go and just trust me."

I did so. I clutched his midsection and rode under the bright stars of the Arizona night, winding through the golden mountains, and I relinquished control to Leo. I let go and he led me safely. His body moved with precision underneath my arms and the wind blew by and world disappeared around me. I began learning submission on the back of a bike.

Now submission everywhere. Heart full of him, mind full of us, I turn around to return to the beach house watching the sunrise on the horizon. I know that everybody says the Gulf Coast of Florida is better for sunsets but the world has given me the gift of a dazzling sunrise and it brightens my heart with each step.

I walk up the stairs to the perched sandy abode and let myself into the kitchen. The smell of coffee hits my nose and I dive into a cup as quickly as possible hoping to heat up my body from the chill of February on the beach.

I hear the shower running. *Leo must be getting ready for an early morning work day*, I think, and head in to greet him and let him know I have arrived back safe. I notice his coffee cup sitting on the nightstand next to his phone that is still plugged in and facing upside down.

I feel like I am walking against a tide pushing me away from heading over to his side of the bed. I push on anyway. Every cell is telling me to stop, to trust, to not pry. Heart pounding, cold sweat takes over my body and I set my coffee next to his. I pause and listen to the shower, my mind screaming, *Stop Chloe. Put. The. Phone. Down.*

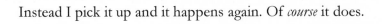

Instead I pick it up and it happens again. Of *course* it does.

Chapter Thirteen

Hold On, Pain Ends

After sliding the phone awake I see a missed call and a new voice mail waiting. From six thirty in the morning. Hearing the shower still running I dial one and listen, the woman's voice cracking my heart in two the instant I hear it.

"Leo. It's Ann. I know, I know, don't call when you're with your wife. But this is urgent and you have got to sneak away to call me back as soon as possible. Call me ba-"

I hang up, not needing to hear anymore.

I am stronger this time around. Smarter. I replace the phone, go to cook breakfast, and with no tears in my eyes fake my way through the morning, formulating the plan. I help Leo out the door while the anger boils in my veins and as soon as I am alone I call Grandma Larchmont.

"Ma is there any way you can keep Em until two? I need to handle some business this morning." I ask over the phone doing my best to hide the sickness in my voice. I don't do a very good job.

"What's wrong Chloe?" she demands, loud enough that I move the phone from my ear. Sigh.

"I just need to handle some things. I will talk to you about it later. Can you or no?" I ask with no fight in my voice.

Pause.

"OK. Two. Come here for lunch," my mother agrees, thinking she can cure any ailment with a home cooked meal. The thought of food makes my stomach churn sick. I fight it down, already creating the to-do list in my mind. Hanging up I set to work.

I pile items by the front door. Pack and play and sheet set. Bottles and baby feeding accoutrements. Most of Emily's clothes. My clothes. Important documents from the tiny den area, birth certificates, my family photo albums. My laptop. I'll certainly need that to look for a job. I go through the beach house methodically and fairly. I even take the time to clean the kitchen from breakfast and throw the wet clothes in the dryer. *My last act of domestic service.*

My phone bleeps twice while I am busy untangling our lives. The first is a return call from Ruth DeLuca.

"Mrs. Donnovan, hi, I missed a call from you yesterday, how can I help you?" the polite woman asks.

Not missing a beat I reply with certainty, "Hi Ruth, I just wanted to let you know that we won't be needing your services anymore and to ask you to cancel our next appointment."

"Is everything OK, dear?" she inquires gently.

I do my best to reassure her that Leo and I are great and simply feel as if we have gotten to where we need to be. I roll my eyes as I say it. I don't want to disappoint the woman who worked so hard on salvaging our broken marriage. This isn't her fault. That lies with one person.

Hanging up and getting back to loading up my minivan, making sure everything is left in order for Leo and that I have taken everything I could possibly need during the separation I hear a second bleep. Leo. A text:

Last night was incredible. You are incredible.

I again roll my eyes at my phone. To keep him from becoming suspicious I text back right away:

You're pretty incredible too. Have a great day.

Send.

Have a great day cause your night's gonna be pretty rough, I think angrily and on the heels I wonder if this Ann will be sleeping in my little side of the bed in the beach house tonight, come over to comfort my husband. And she knew he was married just like the woman in Atlanta.

I shake my head and continue to work; getting myself free of his grip. I can do this, I tell myself. And I know that I can.

Deciding to leave Mr. Donnovan a note, I grab the daily schedule that I need no more off of the fridge and flip it over on the kitchen counter. I use the pen that I used to dash out my weekly grocery list to scrawl out a different kind of note. I jot quickly and without much thought. I have business to handle. It reads:

I know about Ann. I won't do this again. Please don't call me. I'll make arrangements with my mom for you to spend time with Emily.

I head out the door to leave, stopping in the doorway and pausing there, feeling something nagging.

Heading back to the nightstand on my side of the bedroom where I will never sleep again I grab my leather posture collar and our D/s contract that we signed almost six months ago. I return to the note on the kitchen counter. I scrawl a large black "X" through each page of the contract. I know there's no legal bind to this document but I want to break the emotional one. I write VOID in bold letters over my signature at the end of the lengthy document.

I can't believe I forgave him. My heart feels like it is physically breaking and I force the pain back. I am so much better at managing pain this time. He's trained me well.

Focus Chloe. I slide the voided contract under my note and with pen still in hand, pausing again, I then add to the bottom of the note:

Fool me once, shame on you. Fool me twice...

I place the so-beautiful collar that I've grown accustomed to wearing on top and wonder wistfully if I will ever wear one again. Next to my collar I place my wedding band. He broke it all.

After packing up the van and locking up the house I drive straight off the beach and into the urban downtown area and head directly to the bank; to a lock box belonging to only me.

I remove the $20,000 cash that was my first anniversary gift and shove it in the zippered purse that I brought for this precise reason, leaving the metal door of the safe deposit box hanging open, now emptied.

Entirely composed and moving on autopilot I continue down my mental list and leave to find a weekly rental suitable for myself and my child. Business as usual. No time to hurt. No chance to feel. Just keep moving.

By the time I hit Mom's condo at 2 in the afternoon as promised I have a new place to live about a half hour up the coast, light groceries in the fridge, everything unpacked, clothes hung and in drawers, my daughters makeshift crib built in the single bedroom next to my new bed.

I will never put myself out there like this again. What a fool. Blinded by love. Driven by lust. Never again. I am smarter than this.

Never. Again.

***

It's about six in the afternoon and us girls are getting settled into the fully furnished condo that I was able to rent cash when the first call comes in. I send my cheating husband to voice mail.

Ringing again. Voice mail again.

I stare at my phone in my hand and can easily guess what's coming next.

Bam. Text:

Call me right now.

The order enrages me. Who does he think he is? He isn't my Dominant anymore, telling me what to do, snapping his fingers, making demands.

I think, *he can just call this Ann*, as I pull the battery from my phone. I scoop up my girl and sing a familiar nursery rhyme, dancing with her in the kitchen. I force a smile upon my face and keep it there through her dinner and bath routine. By the time I lay her at the bottom of her playpen at bedtime the exhaustion is making my head and body throb.

I go into the strange bathroom and find my way around, allowing myself to just stand under a stream of hot water in the shower, trying to heal myself, to wash away the day. The disappointment is sickening though. I told my mom I left Leo when I picked up Emily. She cried. I didn't (and still haven't) and kept it as simple as possible.

We have irreconcilable differences; I don't want to talk about it. I am fine, Emily is fine, I need Mom to be a liaison for a bit while I put custody and papers in place for the legal separation and inevitable divorce. My mother looks older for the first time I can remember in many years. I've been so involved in trying to repair my marriage since moving here she and I haven't spent much time together. It makes me feel guilty and surprised at myself. Maybe I should have been more balanced. Well from now on it should be easier.

I think "easier" and my heart hurts. Why should it be easier now that I am divorcing?

Because I have been expecting this all along. Was I ever prepared to trust Leo fully again? Was that ever even possible? I've been waiting for the bubble to burst ever since we moved here, thinking that no way things could improve, that it was impossible to move on from where we were. Like fate fulfilling the prophecy here we are at the end again.

The hot shower soothes my body and I keep an ear open for sounds from my girl, starting to mentally make a plan for the next day and next few months.

I need to let Leo see our daughter and I need to start looking for a job as soon as possible. I need new interview clothes and my mind turns over the possibilities for childcare for the first time ever. I haven't worked in a year and a half. Would it be hard to do again? Should I try and find something on the weekends and see if Mom could help me with Emily? Should I start looking into daycare tomorrow? Ugh.

For a moment my heart pines to have the life back that I thought I had two days ago. But I will never sacrifice my dignity to get it.

I force myself to get clean before my water runs entirely cold and once stepping out I look into the bathroom mirror naked. Wow. What a transformation I have made in the last year. I remember finding out about the Atlanta mess and seeing myself through watery eyes not recognizing my image. It's a feeling of déjà vu; eerily familiar but so different somehow. Where last year I had short unkempt hair that I barely took the time to blow dry now I have long locks that shine white. What were gnawed up fingernails then are now perfectly manicured natural nails, painted stop sign red for the holiday yesterday. God was that just yesterday?

Of course the biggest difference is my body. Not even just the absence of being uncomfortably pregnant. As I stand naked in front the mirror I pay attention to myself for the first time since last night; covering myself in long sleeves and full length yoga pants for the move today, relieved for the chill in the air as an excuse.

I am scraped all over, rubbed raw from the tryst in the wooded area. I have heavy bruises on my bottom and thighs and a smattering of inch wide rectangular black and blue spots, the obvious marks of Leo's belt. The small red nick that stings my neck is almost invisible unless you look closely. My breasts are angry and red, painful to even put on a sports bra from being fucked against the tree. I am torn up.

I remember last year, the first half of the déjà vu, and how much I hated looking myself in the eyes in that mirror because even though I had just learned my husband was living a lie, I was too. I had lied to him and every other person I've dated besides him and even myself since high school. I've known for so long who I wanted to be, what I wanted out of life, and I was too scared to say anything.

At least now when my marriage is dying for the second and final time I look at my tattered and lean, imperfect body and I fucking *love* myself. I was wrong last night to have questioned if the stunning lady in red could possibly be me. That was me and this naked, used up submissive is me too.

I absolutely love who I am. I asked for this. Of sound, clear, healthy mind I wanted this. I begged for this and fantasized this to life. That doesn't make me strange or a whore or any less of a lady. It's just a part of me. Not all that I am, no, but it's ingrained in my blood; unable to be turned off. I want to serve. I will never allow myself to be denied that or ashamed of it again. I fought to be this. I fought and I won.

I look across the bathroom counter and make a split decision, doing something I haven't done since living alone post-break-up in my post-college apartment. I grab the bar of soap from the sink still new and just unwrapped a few hours prior. Looking at my naked body I lean forward over the counter and stand on my toes using the soap to draw on the mirror.

At first it is a huge lopsided heart surrounding my body. I stand back satisfied and smile for the first real time that day. I'm going to be OK. I have myself, the real me, and the real me can do anything.

I start to step away and at the last minute dash with the soap again inside of the heart, scrawling:

Hold

On,

Pain

Ends.

Hope.

***

I crawl into the unfamiliar bed naked and quiet and put the battery back in my phone for the first time since disarming it earlier. The familiar jingle rings out making my stomach feel sick in anticipation. Should I listen to his voice mails and read his messages or not?

I go to the messages first and entirely delete the twelve waiting texts from "The Mister" without even opening the thread. I want to hear his voice. I call the mail box and it says I have six new messages waiting. It plays the oldest first, the first one from when he discovered me gone. Heart hammering, I press one to play and there is the voice of the man I once called Sir. He sounds frustrated. Not upset, not apologetic, but pissed. Asshole.

"Chloe. Call me back; this is a huge mistake you're making. Ann-"

I hit end. I can't do it. Not yet. Hearing her name in his voice is like a knife to my heart. I go back into the voice mails and delete all the messages without listening to them, hitting 7 as fast as I can, arms held out far from hearing distance.

I draft him a text:

Emily and I are safe. You can pick her up Friday at 7 at Mom's. Please don't contact me. In case of emergency, contact my mother and she will contact me.

I read it three times over and hit send. I instantly go into my call settings and block Leo's number. I know it can't stay this way forever. I know we will have two decades of co-parenting to sort out. But not now. I can't yet. As tired as I am I lay in the silence unable to fall asleep, hating myself for wondering what Leo Donnovan is doing at this moment in time. I expect the tears to finally come.

None do.

***

I walk a lot the first few weeks. Meditate a lot. Spend a lot of time with my mother. What I don't do is talk to Leo Donnovan. I wonder wistfully if he is even making the attempt anymore. Does he miss me at all? Is the beach house a mess? Has he hired a maid? God forbid has this Ann come over and started folding his plaid boxers and white undershirts?

I replay the message constantly in my mind: "…don't call when you're with your wife…"

I focus on restarting my life as a single mother of a young child and I have still yet to shed a single tear. Maybe I have cried all I can over this man. Maybe they've all been used up.

Free of my schedule as a wife and submissive I've created a new schedule in my head, refusing to crawl up into a ball and die. That's not who I am now.

I spend the first few days finding a great day care for Emily. My mother has reluctantly helped trade off custody so I don't have to see Leo quite yet. I can't; I'm afraid of how I will react if I do. I am devastated by the idea of hearing whatever his excuse is for what happened.

When the first weekend comes up I bring Emily to Mom's with a weekend bag packed after she arrived home from work feeling relieved that Emily has her familiar crib to go back to. When I hand my daughter over my chest empties, my heart detaching and following my girl.

I spend the entire weekend in comfy clothes creating a résumé (it's been years since I've needed one) and applying for local jobs. Any time I turn on music or the television I see something that reminds me of him so I sit and work in silence and focus on what I need to do. Job. Permanent place to live. Lawyer up. Custody. Divorce.

Every time I see my mom she tries to talk about the separation, not caring that it hurts me to hear. As a grandmother, she wants the reasoning for us breaking up her granddaughter's family unit. No matter how she approaches it I keep mum. I am embarrassed and ashamed; all familiar feelings to me from last year. I have every reason to leave, the easiest excuse in the book to give, but something keeps me from spilling the story. So instead she dotes upon Emily, allowing me free time to process the emotions and establish a new way of life. One without Leo.

I miss my husband. No doubt. Who we were as D/s certainly but also him in general. Our friendship. The person who never judged me. God how we laughed. How we loved.

The new routine is simple. Get up in the morning, let Emily watch her favorite cartoon and snack on cereal; I get myself showered and ready for the day. Get her ready, take her to the new day care, and go back to my condo. I pick up, make a fresh pot of coffee, pull out my laptop, and "go to work."

Check the web for new job postings, apply for a few, catch up on news, narrow down the search for an annual rental, looking for something close enough to Mom and Leo's for convenience. One time I search for "divorce attorney." I stare at the search results that come back and immediately hit the tiny red X in the corner, tucking it back away.

Early in the afternoon I get Emily and do something fun with her and every other night I drop her off at my mom's for Leo to pick her up for the evening. When Leo has Emily I go to a local park or a nearby beach and spend a few hours sitting in silence staring at nothing. I review every decision I have ever made in my marriage. Play it out over and over again remembering every detail from courtship on. Sometimes I get lucky and can silence my brain for a few moments.

It's been a month. The hardest and most lonely month of my life.

***

It's a Monday morning and while it kills me to bring my girl to daycare after just getting her back into my arms I drive her there at nine and head back to my routine. I start the coffee and as I'm waiting for it to finish brewing I hear an unexpected knock at the door for the first time since moving. My heart pounds. Who even knows I live here? Is it Leo? Did Mom cave in to his charm? Did he serve me with papers from an attorney? Is he ready to start the divorce?

I walk slowly to the door and look out the peephole. Grinning, I open the door and take the cheese strudel from my mother's hands. I greet her with a hug and ask:

"Ma! What a surprise! What are you doing here?"

She answers instantly, prim lips pressed together, "I want to talk to you about Leo."

I set the pastry down on the kitchen counter and turn her well-dressed small frame around to guide her back outside. Determined woman that she is (and always has been) she acts like dead weight in my arms and we both laugh at each other acting foolish on a sunny spring morning.

"Ma, I don't wanna hear it." I insist, straightening us both out.

This time she looks at me seriously and replies, "Chloe, I don't really care. You still want my help in this mess you are going to hear me out. Now get me some coffee and a piece of that," she points to her pastry, "and join me on the balcony."

Dressed in a perfectly pressed pantsuit looking like the dictionary picture of "sophisticated woman" my mother heads to the glass slider.

Rolling my eyes at her order-making I get two plates of strudel and two cups of coffee and settle into the fresh air beside her. I take a moment to wonder when the summer rains are supposed to begin again and realize that we moved here about a full year ago.

A horror creeps into my brain and after hearing Mom tell me the date when I ask it's confirmed. Today is one year exactly. *The* day. One year ago Leo and I sat in the sand together and shook hands on giving it until exactly today.

Oh well. Guess I don't need to make that trip. My heart breaks a little at the thought. So much good. But oh so much pain.

I can see my mother watching me, waiting for me to start talking and I sit quietly, my mid-morning snack untouched. Five minutes into the silence Victoria Larchmont reaches across the space and does something she hasn't done since I was a child. She holds my hand.

"Chloe. I know I wasn't always available to you when you were a child. An only child raised by a single mom sometimes gets lonely and even though I saw that in you, I was helpless to change that. I had to work. It wasn't an option. There were bills to pay, college tuition to save for, and while child support helped it didn't pay for me to stay home and raise you up like you do now with Emily. Or did. Whatever. I would give anything to go back in time and try to make things work with your father. I don't know. Sought counseling, made more compromises, whatever. For the chance to stay home and watch you grow up day in and day out.

"Don't get me wrong, dear; it wasn't that I was doing anything to harm you. You thrived, always. I worked while another child's mom was a chaperone at the field trip. I hired a tutor instead of helping you with homework. I missed out. But it was necessary and I did my best to be a good example of a career woman to you instead, to show you what it looks like to be an independent woman.

"Now I see you here with your own little family and you all looked so happy. If you want to give up the ability to stay home with your daughter that is your choice. But I want you to think about it very hard. Because you will only have one chance to make this very permanent decision. One."

I rip my hand away from hers. I can't believe what I am hearing.

"This is about *Emily?* This is about your granddaughter?" My anger escalates my voice. I remind myself to be cool, that she didn't make this problem. I continue doing my best to keep an even temper.

"That's bullshit Ma. What about me? I'm your daughter. What about my best interest? What about my happiness?"

Pursing her lips again and sighing heavily she continues her speech she has obviously driven over to deliver:

"I *am* thinking of your best interest. I am *always* thinking of your best interest, that's what mothers do. And that is why I want you to see things from further away before making a decision. You have tunnel vision on this, Chloe. I want you to think about your impact on the entire family. To consider fixing this."

"Leo cheated on me Ma. In Atlanta. That's why I'm here, why we moved here. He had an emotional affair with a coworker while I was pregnant." I spew the truth with a hammering heart, relieved and horrified to have it exposed. What I am not expecting is her response.

"I know. Leo told me," comes from my mother's pained face.

I stammer out, "Whhhat? Wh-when?"

She is calm while I begin to shake. "Yesterday. I spent the day with Leo and Emmie. He asked me over for lunch and I agreed. I stayed for coffee while she napped and he told me. He told me everything."

Then it hits me; now as my anger bubbles over it is directed at the right person.

"If you know all of this, you know he cheated on your daughter, how dare you tell me I should be talking about reconciling? What the fuck, Ma?"

The conservative, Catholic woman who raised me up reels a little at the "f-word" like I knew she would. When she responds it's a bit tenser; more agitated.

"I never said to go running into his arms and be blind to his faults. Don't put words in my mouth. And don't you dare curse at me again. But I want to tell you something Chloe. You were always such a happy girl. You marched to the beat of your own drum and it left me in awe because I don't have a bit of that in me.

"But sometime after high school I saw your passion dull. I didn't know what to make of it. You were still healthy and functioning as a reasonable adult should but you were muted somehow. Always going with the flow. Agreeable, when the daughter I knew was always pushing buttons.

"Until you met Leo. Until I saw you around him. Until I saw the way he looked at you while you were turned away. It's as if he switched your light bulb back on and it has only gotten brighter and brighter. You practically glow when you're around him. So don't for a second think this is about Emmie. This is about my girl, the girl who was glowing until a month ago."

I choke back the lump in my throat. "Ma? Did he tell you about Ann?" I ask weakly, feeling defeated.

She pushes her lips together wide and I watch her tear up.

"Yes. He did. *You* need to talk to him about Ann."

"No way. Nuh-uh. Never."

I stand up clanking the porcelain plates and cups into a stack ready to be done with the conversation.

Mom follows me as I move to the kitchen and hurls across the room, "You have to Chloe. Or I am done getting involved. No more hand-offs. You can arrange for Emily with him yourself."

I turn to her and can only beg a wounded, "How could you?"

Looking at me with red rimmed eyes she answers: "Honey, sometimes parenting is hard. Even when your children grow up. All I ask is that you meet him and let him explain. He took today off work and asked me to give you an address and have you meet him this afternoon. If you do this I will support whatever decision you make. But I can't participate like this anymore. Not after hearing him yesterday. He's heartbroken, Chloe."

The last sentiment makes my heart stand still. I take the sheet of paper she's offering and expect to see the name of the beach where we were supposed to meet today scrawled. Instead there is an address I don't recognize.

"Where is this?" I hold up the sheet in inquiry.

"I don't know." She says, looking to the left like she always does when she isn't telling the whole truth.

I pull out my phone and load it into GPS. Forty-two minutes.

"Ma you promise if I do this then you let the issue go? I'm a grown woman, after all."

"Yes. You better get going." Ma makes her promise trying and failing to hide her grin.

I look at the clock and ask, "What about Emily?"

"I'll get her and take her to my place for dinner."

I groan inwardly about what I am about to do but this is part of being a grown-up with a child. I am going to have to see him at some point. Might as well bite the bullet.

I go to the bathroom and freshen up, telling myself I don't really care about how I look but dotting on some makeup and brushing my hair anyway. I start to leave and turn around to give my mother a tight, two-armed hug. She tenses at first like she always does and then gives in and wraps her arms around me.

I whisper, "I love you Mom."

She whispers back, "Just listen to him dear."

Chapter Fourteen

Trust

The entire drive I shake like a leaf. It's a throbbing shake; an all body muscle spasm that quakes and then stops for several moments, quakes again, stops. I hear blood rushing in my head trying to drown out all that I heard from my mother this morning.

The drive seems to take forever but is over all too soon. Entirely confused by the surrounding area my navigation leads me off the interstate that lines the coast and into a suburban neighborhood. There are large yards everywhere, fishing boats in half the driveways, elderly folk cleaning their driveway with a hose. I take lefts and rights until I'm lost.

I see my destination approaching on the phone and look up to see a house with the correct address. It looks like a transplant from the northern states: two stories with a white wraparound porch lining the entire building. The home is painted the color of seagulls, the beachiest version of grey I have ever seen, and bright white accents are everywhere. Off of the front is an American flag moving lazily in the spring breeze and I notice a white rose bush in full bloom.

It's a stunning home situated on what looks to be quite a bit of land. But so what.

I park at the bottom of the long driveway that could fit a dozen cars (but hosts only one other than mine right now) in case I have the address wrong. I take out my piece of paper to compare with my phone. Here it is. This address. In Leo's handwriting. Bizarre. Entirely confused I try to decide what next. Should I knock? Call Leo? Call Mom? Leave?

My eyes notice the sleek, expensive SUV parked twenty yards in front of my van. I see a Florida vanity plate and read, feeling sickness gathering in my throat:

ANNAR 52

It's her house. Leo brought me to meet his mistress. I break out into an immediate cold sweat and put my hand on the knob to switch to reverse and- *oh my God I see the front door opening-* I slam my foot on the gas and back out and take one last miserable glance at the home...

Screeeech! I slam on the brakes.

Running down the sidewalk towards me is a woman my mother's age if not a little older. She has graying hair tucked in a librarian style bun and there is a pen stuck through the fat middle of it. In one hand she has a clipboard and the other she is using to balance herself on sensible black pumps as she runs towards me, doing her best in the suit she is wearing.

I watch curiously as if I walked in on the middle of a movie; confused by the plot. I shift into drive and prepare myself to get away as the harried looking woman arrives at my window and makes a motion like she is rolling an old-fashioned car window crank. I push the AUTO button to send my window down.

The highly-thin, strange looking woman, knobby and awkward, puts her hand on a hip like she is working out a stitch and breathes for a second. She moves the clipboard to the crook of her left arm, waves a hand as if to fan herself, and extends a handshake.

"Mrs. Donnovan? Hi... it's sooo nice to meet you... finally!"

I turn to ice. This is indeed the voice of the one and only "Ann." I hear the same tone that I heard on my husband's voice mail.

I handshake quickly so the stranger will remove her hand from my window. With a dropped jaw I listen to her ramble while still catching her breath:

"I am so excited... to be doing this today... phew... I can't even tell you! Really... this has been the highlight of my year... this is something special. I hope you are happy with his choice, really."

I finally cut off her hitching voice and interrupt, "Excuse me, who are you?"

"Oh, right... my goodness, I am so sorry... I guess I just got caught up in the excitement! I am Ann Armeda and I work at the brokerage with Leo."

She titters excitedly and pulls a business card off the clipboard and hands it to me.

Sure enough. Ann Armeda. Realtor.

She continues prattling.

"Leo and I partnered up about six months ago when he said that your family was looking for something permanent at the end of a rental period. He said he wanted to do all of the hard work in looking at homes, appraisals, bidding, that y'all have a small child and you wouldn't want to be toting the baby all over the place. Sooo I offered to help him with the leg work – he's always so busy, I don't have a clue how he manages it all- so that I could help make this a special surprise for his little family. Chloe Donnovan, welcome to your…" Ann plants on a forced smile and throws her hands up like an aging award presenter on a daytime game show.

"…brand new house!"

I am actually living in the twilight zone. No. Really.

I maneuver my van haphazardly into the grass on the side of the road with no warning to Ms. Armeda who backs up, looking confused.

I look at the business card. The woman. The house. Her car which I can now see is emblazoned with an oversized magnet on the side telling people to call her for all their real estate needs! Back to the woman. The card.

I look at the house and it looks like what Leo and I would have chosen for our dream home. I throw the shifter into park, open the door with keys still in the ignition, and stumble out. My entire body feels numb. The realization of the situation overtakes me and I bend at the waist and vomit up my morning coffee.

***

Ten minutes later after cleaning myself up and apologizing to Ann for my reaction I'm entering the door to Leo's home. What would have been our home. It is perfect.

I get a clearer picture of the reality of the past few months thanks to Ann's non-stop chatter and excitement. Leo had been charged with making all decisions and taken it upon himself to find a new home for his darling wife and child. I think the words "his darling wife" and my heart feels like it is frozen in ice.

His darling no longer.

He apparently spent lunches and made detours during his days at work to view homes for us. I interrupt my realtor-turned-tour-guide leading me through the home and ask, "When did he close? There's stuff everywhere."

"A couple weeks into February. It was a real struggle, the sellers almost backed out last minute. The rest of the time has been spent getting you guys set up. He hired a decorator. What do you think?"

Of course. Valentine's Day. That's why she needed to talk to him so urgently.

"I love it." I muster before clamming up again.

I am surrounded by my family embodied. We are everywhere the eye looks, a little piece of each of us, a home that has been crafted from love. Leo has entirely outfitted the kitchen and I glimpse into the cabinets to see new plates and dishes, never used pots and pans. How does he know what a cook needs? As I touch the retro-homemaker apron hanging on a hook near the refrigerator tears well up for the first time since the marsh behind the restaurant on Valentine's Day. I fucked it up. I didn't trust him and I've probably lost him.

"Let me show you the kids rooms upstairs," the realtor says in a tone that is quieter than I've heard, maybe sensing my emotions.

I swallow the pain down and follow, touching the dark wooden banister that matches all of the floors I have seen thus far.

"Leo says you have a daughter, she's one right?"

I confirm her guess and look as she opens the white door at the top of the stairs.

It's a princess room, a nod to our little princess, pink everywhere. There's a crib on the back wall and a white noise machine plugged in on a nearby dresser. He's thought of everything.

Backing out, Ann goes down the hall to another closed door.

I walk into the middle of an almost-empty room painted a pale yellow containing only a nursery style glider and a bookshelf containing children's books. Ms. Armeda's words are my best dream and worst nightmare all at once:

"Leo said there may be more little Donnovans running around in the near future so he wanted to keep this mostly empty."

She smiles at me wide, unknowing that it would never happen. I feel faint.

Nothing could have prepared me for her leading me downstairs and through the back of the house to the master suite. French doors separate in front of me and she walks away, giving me space to take it all in.

I am transported back to the Gulf of Mexico. The room has an indigo ombré paint that emulates the sun setting on the water. I can't count how many times I have seen this exact color in the last year. It continues onto the ceiling which is smattered in tiny silver dots making it look like the starlit sky on the edge of the world where the land and water meet.

The wood floor has a plush, sand colored rug underfoot and the windows have soft flowing white sheers just waiting to blow in a breeze. But all of this beauty is secondary.

Taking up the majority of the master bedroom intended for the mister and his darling is a bed of branches just like the one we made love on during our trip to Vegas. The twigs and twisting branches are painted bright white to look more like it belongs on an abandoned beach instead of in a forest. The huge mattress is covered in a white comforter that would be impossible to keep clean with a child. This is supposed to be our haven; our retreat from the rest of the world. I think of being bound to that bed by my husband for decades to come.

I've seen enough. I turn away from the bedroom and find the realtor looking out of one of the many sets of French doors at the back of the home staring at a glistening pool, baby fence tall and locked.

"Where's Leo? Is he coming here?"

"Well, no. He asked me to give you the keys and only said that you'd know where he was." The woman raises an eyebrow at me in confusion as if to ask why I don't know where my own husband is. I ignore the look and head for the front door.

"I gotta go." I shout behind me and shuffle the woman out of Leo's home. I lock up, take one last look at the house, and head to the beach.

***

It takes me an hour to get there. I wonder the whole time if there is any real chance that Leo will be waiting for me. Forgive me. I stop at a drugstore on the way unwrap a new toothbrush, freshening up before driving to meet him.

I can't believe he bought a house. An exquisite new house, big enough to grow into but small enough to not be ostentatious. It was his gift to me. I know it as surely as I know my own name. Intended for today; a permanent gesture of his dedication to our family.

He talked about maybe having another child together. A sibling for our daughter. If I had only asked him about the voice mail. Trusted him. The entire year he had been an open book, never making me dig or snoop to catch him doing anything wrong.

Gah, why hadn't I asked?

Leo Donnovan paid his dues and is continuously doing so. We had been at our lowest low, seemingly impossibly down, and we bounced back. Made things not just right but even better than before.

I gather out of the driver seat of my van and walk out into the sandy public parking lot and head to the beach access. I go directly to the spot where we sat one year ago, almost to the minute, and cross over the dune to the water.

Leo isn't anywhere in sight. Of course he's not.

I wonder what will become of the Donnovan house. Will he put it back on the market? Live there alone, sharing custody, bringing Emily to her adorable little princess room every other weekend? I move with sadness aching through me to the edge of where the dry sand meets the wet and plop my butt down, grateful for my long bohemian skirt and close knit tank because the wind is picking up more and more by the moment and it looks like a storm is headed my way.

I take a moment to pull my wildly whipping hair into a long braid and think to my message on the mirror at the condo from that first awful night. Hold on, pain ends. *Pssh*. What do I know about pain?

I took my husband's wife and daughter away from him as a knee-jerk reaction, one that could have been prevented by a number of different decisions of mine. I should have talked to him. Alone or with our counselor. I am confident in hindsight that Leo would have walked a mile to put me at ease.

That's the problem with marriages and all relationships maybe. Things always seem so black and white in hindsight but what good does that do? There is no manual for a marriage; no way to guarantee success. But if there were a script to follow it would be incredibly short: Communicate.

Communication is not just about talking. It's about listening. Really hearing each other; seeing each other. Compromising. Knowing that you won't always hear things that you like and that you will have to say things that may hurt your partner. But if you have a mutual respect and only say things out of truth and the hope that it will make the relationship stronger then those hard conversations are worth it. Every time.

I lay defeated in the sand. I have about twenty minutes left before getting soaked by my calculation. I pull out my phone and look for any missed calls. Nothing. Maybe I misinterpreted his message delivered by Ann. Maybe he's at the beach house. Maybe he's changed his mind and saw me here and decided he couldn't forgi-

"Hey!"

I hear the familiar shout and all of a sudden he is walking towards me. Mr. Leo Donnovan looks better than I even remember, wearing light khaki slacks and a long sleeved shirt that is blowing like a sail in the great wind, giving me glimpses from here on the ground of his flat stomach, lighter skin than mine because he spends his days in the office and until recently I spent mine on the beach. He arrives as I stumble to my feet clumsily, his eyes staring right into me with a hint of steel cold grey, the angry sky and angry mood reflecting in them.

***

I start talking first as I adjust myself, "Leo, I'm so sorr-"

"Stop." He holds up his hand.

I notice he still has his wedding band on; the one that I placed on him a year and a half ago in the Vegas sun promising my commitment to him.

"You do realize this isn't where we are supposed to meet, right?"

Huh? I look around in confusion, "I have no idea what you're talking about Leo."

I notice how weary he looks. The man grimaces and nods his head as if this is exactly what he expects to hear. He points over my shoulders.

"See that big fishing pier out there? Last year we were about a mile north of it. You are sitting..."

I flush all over, "South. Oh my God. I don't know how I got it wron-"

Interrupted again.

"It's just you, Chloe, it's just who you are. Throwing caution to the wind. Jumping first and only then looking. So involved with what is going on in your world everything on the outside takes a backseat. Do you know how tiring that can be sometimes? How fucking exhausting that can be? Let me ask you a question. Had you even *once* thought of the fact that our lease was coming up on the beach rental? Wondered where we were going to live? Where your child would be sleeping at night?"

I hadn't. It didn't even cross my mind once. I was living in a world of yoga and beach; vacations and gifts and kinky sex. The life of a carefree submissive. My wildest fantasy. But what I had forgotten about was that while I was busy skipping around in a frilly apron, Leo was doing the hard work, carrying me and my obligations. I had all but given up on paying attention to our bank account being certain that if I swiped my debit card money would be there. I pay attention to my hair and nails. Leo pays attention to life insurance policies and healthcare renewals and apparently our lease ending. He has shouldered the burden with only one request: trust.

I see now why the trust is so important. I think back to my feeling like I was living in the trust fall exercise, falling back into Leo's arms, knowing that he would be there to catch me. I wonder what a different experience that exercise would be if the catcher knew the catchee didn't trust them to be caught. Constant doubt. Cringing; waiting for the fall. No matter how many times he caught me and set me gently upon my feet the next time I doubted again. I'd be exhausted too.

"No. I hadn't thought of it."

Despite the opportunity to scold me his only response is another question straight from my stream of thought.

"Do you have any idea how difficult it is to lead a household built on doubt? I don't blame you for my mistake in Atlanta. Would never. It's a burden I will bear for the rest of my life. But at some point darlin the doubt has got to end. And I don't know if you will ever be able to stop doubting."

"I can!" I burst in with emphatic conviction. The first raindrop hits my nose and I hear thunder roll. The beach-goers quickly head to the parking lots, oblivious to our entire world being decided. "I will Leo, I do already. I am so sorry. Please-"

"I don't know if I believe it. It seems so easy to say Chloe. But how am I supposed to really believe that the next time a woman calls my phone you won't split again? That you won't take my family away from me? This is a nightmare. My very worst nightmare." Leo's voice cracks with pain.

Try as I might to simply lay down I can't help but bristle up over his participation in the whole thing.

"It's not that easy, Leo. You cheated. When I was pregnant. It's pretty much the shittiest thing I can imagine doing to another person. And this whole issue could have been avoided had you included me in this house thing. You could have told me about it. Not hidden the calls."

"But my phone will always ring!" Leo shouts. I can see fury boiling inside of him as he is struggling to keep it under control. He's pissed. And now it's sprinkling on us.

"My phone will always have strangers call! I will get texts from men and women that you don't know every day. Every day! I can't do what I do to support us, to keep you home and comfortable, if I can't work. You said you'd trust me. You failed. You made a mistake Chloe, a big one like I did, and now we need to decide how to move forward. If we can trust again. If we can fix *this* mistake."

"I know we can Sir..."

My voice drops off at the title but I force myself to continue, to try and make him believe in me. Believe in us.

***

"I know we can Leo because I learned something about trust since being gone. I dunno if I could have learned it any other way but I finally understand!

"'Trust' is just as much about me trusting in myself as much as it is about trusting you. I don't *need* to be your wife or your submissive. I've proven to myself that if something bad were to happen I'd make it. I know that now. That's really the trust I was missing. Trusting that I am a strong enough woman to handle whatever life throws at me.

"And isn't this a better way? Instead of feeling dependent on you I just wanna be with you. I want to be your wife! I want to be your submissive! I miss my ring Sir. I miss my collar."

I choke out the last admissions with a sob. The tears missing from the past month finally come and empty out. He stares at me pitifully crying in the rain. Studies me. Gauges my words.

Leo, not short for anything fancy, just my Leo, slowly reaches into the pocket of his now thoroughly soaked pants and I watch the raindrops fall off his eyelashes. He pulls out my wedding ring and holds it across to me in silence.

Instead of taking it from him I hold out my left hand; he slips it on me like he did the day we became man and wife.

Leo shouts over the din of the increasing downpour, "What did you think of the house?"

Without hesitation I shout back, "I love it!"

Just as quickly he responds, "I love *you*."

We move forward timidly and kiss in the rain until our mouths feel familiar again; until the sky entirely opens up. I let out a squeal as Leo grabs my hand and we run together to the parking lot, where I will let him lead me home.

Epilogue

I've just been captured and devoured in our private yard surrounding the grey two story home by Mr. Leo Donnovan. My Dominant. My husband.

He's now relaxing in our oversized bed-of-branches eating the reheated pasta dinner that could almost be called breakfast at this point, watching a sports recap quietly, decompressing after such an intense night of play.

I step out of the shower in the connected master bathroom and steam envelops everything. Enjoying this quiet time to myself I sit nude and damp on a towel covering my makeup chair in front of the bathroom vanity. Wiping the makeup mirror I stare at myself magnified 5 times. More than I'd ever dreamt possible I am completely content with who I see. The contentedness has nothing to do with my physical features.

I'm seeing a woman who wakes up every morning unapologetically herself. A woman who continues to grow and learn. A woman who is in a happy, loving marriage. Raising a happy, loving family.

A woman who trusts her husband.

A woman who trusts herself.

I am Chloe Donnovan and I am a submissive. I am my husband's sexual submissive and service submissive. We are in the midst of our second six month D/s contract and I have yet to be able to negotiate my way into getting my right to orgasm back. *Maybe next time we re-sign,* I think wistfully. I'm already practicing my speech.

My Dominant controls my nights and my days, my goals and my fantasies, my clothes and my attitude, my every move. This power he has taken frees me to be me. The woman I see magnified in the mirror chased the life of her dreams and won.

I am the Mister's Darling.

Suddenly exhausted from the takedown and the adrenalin I put on only a light spritz of Romance to wear to bed and join Mr. Donnovan under the covers.

Without saying a word my husband turns off the television and pulls me into him so close that it would feel suffocating if it weren't so comforting.

I try to catch a few moments of shut eye before the alarm goes off and I have to pick up our girl from Grandma's house but my mind wanders. I turn over ideas about what to get Leo for our second wedding anniversary coming up soon.

Cotton. The traditional gift for the second year is cotton of all things. How could I ever top my paper gift?

I smile at the memory, drifting off to sleep with a pleasantly aching body, peace in my heart, my faithful partner by my side, and the comforting knowledge that tomorrow I will get to wake up and simply be me. The *real* me.

Flaws and all.

###

Acknowledgements

How can I possibly begin to say thank you to all of those who have supported me in this venture? This storytelling- my personal story telling- came out of catharsis; the need to cut it out of my soul and tuck it away and revisit it when I want instead of the past always floating around at the edge of my thoughts.

But I never would have even considered the thought if it hadn't been for my biggest supporters. As a girl who constantly tells people, "Look, I am not a writer, make no mistake, I am simply a submissive telling her path," thank you to every single person who responded, "Shut the fuck up." I love you all. You believe in me when I don't believe in myself. I am my most beautiful when I see myself through your eyes.

Thank you to my local kink community, who are some of the most amazingly brave and authentic people I have ever encountered. You teach me and open your arms to me and accept me for who I am. If it weren't for your kindness and inclusion, the Mister and I may have had a very different path along the way.

Thank you to all of my family. You support me and my wildly ways and never once have demanded I bring my head out of the clouds where I float. I told you I had written a book and not one of you laughed at the notion. I will never forget that.

Thank you to my dearest friends. I always heard that it would be desperately hard to make friends as an adult; how blessedly wrong that was for me. Without your encouragement, my story would still be locked up tight and weighing me down. Your friendship helps free me. The real me.

Finally, to the Mister. My husband. My Sir. This story told is your path too. It's one filled with tears and memories and moments of extreme personal struggle and growth. Thank you for allowing me to tell our tale, for your unending support, for helping me to be perfectly imperfectly me. Without you, Sir, there is no tale to tell. Without you, Sir, my life would be dull. You are my laughter, my success, my everything I hope to be, and everything I want to love.

I have seen the very best of you and I have seen the very worst of you.

I'll take both.

Kind Regards,

Mrs. Darling

About the Author

Mrs. Darling is a whimsical woman living in a Modern Day 1950's M/s Household. She and her husband run a traditional household together and practice full time power exchange in their marriage. In addition to hobbies like cooking and baking, crafting and sewing, and all things home related, Mrs. Darling writes non-fiction about BDSM and her life lived as a submissive. She is active in her local kink community and enjoys volunteerism.

If you would like to read more about the 1950's Household, you can find Mrs. Darling's essay on the subject in the book "Paradigms of Power: Styles of Master/slave Relationships" by Raven Kaldera, available in ebook or print.

Connect with Mrs. Darling

Feel free connect with Mrs. Darling to follow her path in submission:

Email: Mrs_Darling@outlook.com

Website: MrsDarling.org / DarlingDiscovered.com

Facebook: Misses Darling

Fetlife: MrsDarling

Instagram: 1950s_mrsdarling

Twitter: 1950sMrsDarling